VIPER

NEW YORK TIMES BESTSELLING AUTHOR

MARATA EROS

VIPER

Book 8: Road Kill MC Series

New York Times BESTSELLING AUTHOR

MARATA EROS

ISBN-10: 1717709737

ISBN: 978-1717709738

All Rights Reserved.

www.tamararoseblodgett.com

Cover art by *Willsin Rowe*

Editing suggestions provided by *Red Adept Editing*

Music that inspired me during the writing of Viper:

Slipknot

Duality

Bad Wolves

Zombie

DEDICATION:

Delores O'Riordan

You made the art of my words more beautiful with your music.
Your absence from this world is a robbery.

Chapter 1

Viper

"I say kill the bitch," Storm announces, reclining his big frame in the chair, balancing on the back legs.

Looking out over the brothers, I see everyone is in attendance, except Trainer. His old lady's poppin' out a kid, so he gets a pass.

A frustrated sigh slips out of me before I can rein it in.

Sometimes, a man is just a glorified babysitter, and this is one of those times. At the end of the day, I feel like I'm wrangling a posse of cats.

"Can't kill a chick—that's just wrong," Wring states, and I watch Storm figuring he's got the balls to stare him down.

Interesting. Storm patched in recently, and he's still gauging his weight within the hierarchy of the club. But Wring is an ex-Navy SEAL. He's quiet with his menace—like all of us ex-soldiers are. I was special forces too. Never revealed my ex-Navy SEAL status.

Didn't want to.

Kept shit to myself. Better that way. Gives the guys less to think about if they don't know. If there's information about me from before I was the president of Road Kill MC, that only makes my job harder.

I dragged myself through the knothole of the Gulf War. Spent two tours there. The brothers of the Road Kill know *those* deets. Only Noose knows the shit I won't talk about.

Sometimes I catch the big bastard eyeing me up. Coming up with mental checks and balances. Or coming up with diddly squat.

Who the fuck knows? He's not exactly a transparent guy. I stifle a snort. That's a no-shitter.

But now we got a *situation*. First, it was the fucking gangs, then it was mafia bullshit. Now we got a sex-trafficking ring jonesing in on our region.

Not gonna happen on my watch. We don't like scum infiltrating our pond. Pissing where we live.

Right before Krista, Trainer's new wife, went on maternity leave from the school where she teaches, she became aware that her school was a target for these sick fucks. Actually, the club had found a reference to the trafficking with photographic proof— thanks to Noose's keen instincts—that there were certain "children of interest" at Krista's school.

Whole thing makes me want to hurl chunks. That there's fucking pervs out there that'd cause harm to the defenseless? Can't wrap my brain around that shit.

I take a deep inhale then let it out slowly, rhythmically tapping my fingers on our old carved wooden table where we meet for church.

"None of us like the idea of killing a woman," I state.

Sounds of affirmation make their way around the table from the fourteen brothers.

9

As quiet as a tomb, Storm continues to silently challenge me with his glare. His dark strawberry-blond hair is shoved into a buff-colored hair tie at his nape, and a deep-red beard groomed into a perfect rectangle covers his square jaw. He's brutally fashioned, like a lot of the men who find themselves within the embrace of the MC. His nose's been busted a couple of times, the bridge jogging about a third of the length down his beak.

He's loud-mouthed and inconsiderate.

Storm's also proven himself to be an asset. His skills and quick thinking have saved the day in dicey situations. He's either brave or stupid—I'm not sure which—but his loyalty isn't in question.

That's key in the Road Kill MC. Without loyalty, a man will never be a brother.

Storm shakes his head. A strand of some of the kinkiest hair I've ever laid eyes on shakes loose, dipping in front of a pair of bright hazel eyes. "We got *proof* of the bitch's involvement—she lures these little kids, and then—*boom*—she gives them to these fuckers." He whips his arms out, narrowly missing Rider, who's seated to his right.

Rider leans away, giving him what I affectionately refer to as the "half-eye."

Noose stands, catching Storm's attention with a chin hike, and snorts. "Never pictured you to off the ladies, Storm." His dark-gold eyebrows rise slowly. One is bisected by an ugly scar he got courtesy of a torture session a couple years back.

Storm makes a cutting gesture across his throat with his palm. "If someone's that brand of shitbird—chick *or* dude—they deserve to stop breathing." His hands slap down on his denim-clad thighs, the front legs of the chair tapping hard on the poured concrete floor. "If this twat is handing over the kiddos to freaks, let's take her out. Now."

"You're a bossy fucker," Wring comments casually from his usual corner, grooming his nails with a switchblade.

"Someone's going to lose an eye," I remark dryly, attempting to diffuse the overflowing testosterone.

Wring gives a low snicker. "Shit, I haven't heard that in a century."

"Hello!" Storm scowls at us.

I lift my chin and say in a low voice, "I'll do it."

Every brother leans toward me, and the surprise I read in some of their expressions sets off my irritation. "I'm in shape, and I ain't fifty *yet*." I stare every one of them down.

Snare leans forward. "You don't *need* to, Viper. We got enough brothers to do the dirty work."

I feel my eyes harden as I take in the group of tough men. "This is a woman and a premeditated clean-up. Feels wrong, even though we know she's aiding something foul as fuck," I say, clipping the last word off at the end like an amputation.

Noose takes my comment as his cue to debrief the men. "And she ain't no troll, fellas."

"Fuck," Wring mutters. "Was hoping she was hiding under a bridge or something."

Killing's always ugly, just feels worse to take out something beautiful. "Still female. Still feels wrong." My stare shifts to Noose in a subtle signal to move forward with what he has. "Spread 'em."

Noose smirks then draws out black-and-white glossies from a large manila envelope, tossing them out on the table like playing cards.

They spin then finally settle in a haphazard display across the polished wooden surface.

Every man leans forward.

The woman's a real looker. Don't have coloring to go by. Hell, her hair could be any color of brown.

Those eyes could be any color.

But that gaze holds me.

And any military man would be the first to say they've got a sense of scale for a person's size. This broad doesn't know her picture's being taken; that much is obvious. And the stuff that surrounds her gives me a clue to her size—small.

My dread deepens.

In the picture that's come to rest in front of me, she's standing by a park bench, handing off a kid around maybe six years old, though I'm no fucking judge. Never had any kids of my own.

I clench my teeth. Her face is angled up at the man. His profile is obscured. Shadows from the low branches of trees hanging overhead stripe his face in a million shades of gray in the broken, dim light.

But not her—oh no. The sun lights her face just perfectly. Every curve of cheekbone, soft triangle of chin, and lips so kissable it's a slice of tangible despair as I gaze at her face, knowing we've got to eventually end her.

Maybe not as fast as we'd like, either. We'll need answers first. My eyes run over the photo for a third time. Not gonna like what I got to do to get them, either.

I cup my chin and briefly close my eyes, accepting the rawness of the upcoming task.

"God, I don't know, Vipe?" Snare pushes a photo away with a finger like the image burns. "Don't think I could do her."

I open my eyes and take in Snare's clear distaste at the possibility of killing a female.

Noose taps the image closest to him once, and after a lengthy pause says, "I could."

"Me too," Storm replies instantly, raising his upper lip in sneer.

"I will, even if I can't." My voice is soft, my intent hard as I survey them all. "She's obviously gorgeous, and damn good at looking harmless."

Maybe in some ways, she is.

"I hear a *but.*" Wring hikes his platinum eyebrows, stopping his ceaseless self-groom with the knife.

I nod in his direction. "We can't let tits and ass with a pretty face rob our focus from cleaning the scum that's infiltrating our pond." I give a single rap of my knuckles on the table. It's loud in the well of their contemplative silence.

Lariat speaks for the first time, his dark eyes cutting through us. "If anybody's assuming our territory is fair game, we'll be on their radar if we start letting shit slide. Kent is *our* territory—and greater Auburn, Federal Way—hell, I'm gonna toss in Seattle too." His deep chuckle is possessive, and certain.

I hold back a grin.

"Gettin' greedy," Snare comments in a sing-song voice, his dark blue eyes twinkling.

"Fuck it," Lariat says, black eyebrows low above eyes so dark a brown, they damn near swallow the pupil.

"That's my line," Noose quips.

Lariat gives him a long-suffering glance. "Why the fuck not?" He laces his fingers, resting his hands on the table and hiking his shoulders.

"Why indeed," Snare agrees.

"Anyway," I hold up my hand, palm out, "I'm not going to ask any of my brothers to do something I wouldn't do myself." I level my stare on the ex-SEALs first then let my gaze sweep the rest of the men.

"Why?" Wring asks, voice thick with suspicion.

I chuckle at his caution. "Too easy. If I start passing on any fucking detail that makes me squirm—or I start wanting to grow a vagina—I've lost my respect, and I don't deserve to be Prez of the Road Kill MC." I point at each one of them—fourteen today. "Not you guys' respect, but mine. For myself." I park my thumb in the center of my pecs, damn glad I have the *cajones* to make my little pronouncement. A couple of years ago, I was getting soft. After a few dicey events, I got a wake-up call. I couldn't be committing violence if I couldn't make the cut—no pun intended.

Ever since, I've been working out hard, watching carbs, and hitting the weights. It sucks to have hard liquor instead of my favorite beer, but hey—having the beginnings of a six-pack on my gut is reward enough for not getting to pull down a brewsky.

Now I can actually *do* some dirty work.

And it doesn't get filthier than killing a beautiful woman—or any woman.

I've killed females before. In war. When I had no choice. While following orders. Didn't like it, though. Not one tiny bit. I know Noose, Wring, and Lariat have done shit for our country they're not proud of. Serving and pride in being an American don't always mix. Sometimes bad deeds are necessary.

Nobody asks if a man's up to murder when he joins the service. However, murder finds a man if it means to.

But we can't let Arlington's packaging dissuade us from the greater goal of keeping our turf *ours*—and keeping the bad shit out. We're not going to tolerate gangs, *especially* kiddie pervs.

"We respected ya, Viper—even when you had a beer gut," Storm says.

"Thanks a lot." I nod slowly at him. Then just as slowly, I raise my right hand. My middle finger sprouts like a chubby.

Frowning, Storm huffs. "Just callin' it like it is."

"Y'know, if you hadn't just gotten patched in—your ass would be kicked right now?" Snare comments in a voice as dry as the Sahara Desert.

Storm nods happily. "Oh yeah. Feels good to shoot my mouth off without getting punched for it."

With my hand still raised and finger extended, I straighten my elbow, hiking the entire thing. "Don't push it." I let my arm drop back to the table with a thunk.

Storm snorts, leaning back in his chair again. "Besides Trainer, I've done the most crap detail of anyone here. I can finally speak!"

We stare at each other.

"You look decent now, Viper. Don't tell me you're getting to be all needy and shit?" Storm smirks. "All sensitive about your looks?"

"All right," Wring says, and causally slaps the back of Storm's head with his palm.

He's closer than I am. *Convenient.* A grin forms on my face.

Storm's head lurches forward, nearly coming into contact with the table. "Fuck!" His head whips to Wring, his slitted gaze shooting daggers. "I hate those goddamned brain dusters."

Wring meets the unspoken challenge, his light, azure eyes narrowing like glacial razors. "Learning when to shut up is a talent. Something for you to think about honing."

"I thought once I patched in, my brand of honesty was gonna be appreciated." He shrugs.

"You're fucking honest, all right," Noose comments, carefully plucking each glossy from the table and reinserting the pictures into the manila envelope one by one.

"You let Trainer get away with saying *anything*," Storm rants.

"Trainer's a special case. And he learns pretty damn well," I emphasize, remembering how Krista patiently taught him to read, plowing through a learning disability and a seriously fucked-up childhood.

"He's not a dick," Lariat adds in a mild voice.

Storm narrows his eyes at Lariat. "Favoritism."

Everyone groans.

"Why'd we patch him in?" Snare's lips twist as he smirks, the motion making the small knot of scar tissue across his upper lip flatten.

"Masochists, all," Lariat says.

Storm grins. "See, you fuckers like a little check and balance." He gives a decisive nod. "Along comes, Storm and—*boom*—ya got all the balance you can stand."

"Funny… I don't feel very balanced," Wring gives him a speculative look.

"'Cause, dude, you're kinda psycho." Eyebrows hiked, he spreads his arms and juts out his chin.

Lariat and Noose join Wring in staring at Storm.

"I know you guys are badass SEALs. Fuck—*duh*. But I gotta be able to say what's here." He touches his chest lightly. "And not be afraid to get whacked like a junkyard dog."

I keep forgetting Storm is the youngest of all the brothers. At twenty-three, he's virtually a baby. "No whacking Storm," I say in a light voice.

My ex-SEALs smirk.

"No whacking Storm," Noose repeats, clearly holding back laughter.

Lariat and Wring repeat the decree.

Finally, Snare says it last. Though he's not a former military man, he's tight with those who are.

Storm's face washes to smug. Ignoring the sarcasm, he switches topics and goes right for the jugular. "I want to be with you when you do her, Viper."

Not who I was thinking of taking with me… *but* his comment about me favoring Trainer hangs between us, and I want to make the situation fair. "How about you and…" I give Noose a look, and that's enough for him to know I'm looping him.

His smoky eyes glitter back like sun on dirty glass. "Ya sure you wanna do the killing, Vipe?" Noose asks in a quiet voice. "It won't cost me what it'll cost you. The tab might be higher for others."

Noose is a family man. Rose just had twins not too long ago, a couple of years after Arianna. However, he casually tosses around killing a woman because she means harm to our community. Serious fucking harm.

Essentially, harm to those he holds dear.

Maybe Noose is harder *because* he's got kids. Could be that being a dad, thinking about how it could be *his* kids in jeopardy, provides him all the motivation in the world.

I don't need to have kids to want to protect the innocent. I don't like what this woman is doing, just on principle.

Looking in those pale-gray eyes, I *know* he'll do it, shelving the cost for later reflection.

Or possibly, no reflection at all.

"I'll do it." I turn my head in Storm's direction. "You come, but I'm in charge of this little operation. We do it fast, nab her for questioning—that's the only agenda short term. Mine."

"Damn," Storm says with soft disappointment.

I feel my left eyebrow lift. "What do you have against women?"

Storm's eyes darken, like the clouds that gave him his name. "What *don't* I have?"

Noose and I exchange a glance. Storm doesn't know it, but he almost didn't get patched in. Lots of sweet butts won't be with his brand. His idea of sex is rough. Hard.

The type some women can't live through.

I never get in the way of three things: if it ain't with an animal, it's with someone of age, and it's consensual, then it's okay by me. Even though it's just barely, he stays within my moral parameters, so I can't penalize him.

"Maybe not the best job for you with the hate you got for bitches," Rider, another brother, says.

Storm nods. "But I can enjoy the show."

Jesus.

Noose's eyes widen slightly at that.

And Storm called Wring a psycho? *Maybe it's all about perspective.*

Noose begins talking in a flat voice. "Bitch's name is Candice Arlington. Born 1981, five feet two, buck ten. Educated. Speaks four languages. No husband or kids. There's some blank spots here that I couldn't break through to grab additional intel. Don't like the holes in her timeline. At. All."

"She's no spring chicken," Snare comments thoughtfully. "Candi-baby doesn't look thirty-anything." He frowns, clearly remembering the photos we saw earlier.

True. I whistle. "What the hell is *this* woman doing running kids?" Something doesn't add up. The situation seems too pristine—too *good*, for lack of a better term.

Noose slowly shakes his head. "Clean as a damn whistle. Can't find shit on Arlington."

"But pictures don't lie," Snare adds, voice dripping with disdain, jerking his jaw toward the folder Noose has in his loose grasp.

It's not brain surgery to add up all the thoughts at the table. We all saw the concrete proof of her handing off a kid. A picture *is* worth a thousand words.

Noose holds up the folder with the photos inside, tapping the corner against the table. "We know she's bad. Up to her ears in it. Everybody remember Allen Fitzgerald?" Noose pauses for affect.

Every brother pulls a face of clear disgust with the memory of that evil rich bastard.

"That fucker who was Krista Glass's half-brother—had an order in for a ten-year-old girl." His eyes are heated smoke as he stares through us. "And Ms. Arlington was gonna deliver. We found a huge deposit in her account, matching the same figure as a withdrawal from his."

"That is sick as *fuck*. Allen was gonna force Krista to marry him *and* have child pussy on the side? Dis-gust-*ing*." Storm sneers.

"I'm really holding back about now," Wring comments in false serenity, eyes intent on grooming his nails by blade.

"Maybe less honesty," Lariat says to Storm in a drawling deep bass voice.

"Right, sorry," Storms says then opens his mouth *again*, no sense of self-preservation in sight. "For the record, nobody should ever touch a kid. They die just for *thinking* about it hard enough." His eyes darken to stoked embers inside his resolute face.

"I think you just like the dying part for Candice Arlington." Snare's lips twist, puckering the scar running over his cupid's bow.

"You're right," Storm replies instantly. "When it comes to kids getting abused, I'm *all* about the killing."

I sense history there, but I'm not digging too deep on that one. Those hidden gems of misery have a way of rising without excavation, becoming unearthed in their own time and due diligence.

Wring begins to whistle tunelessly as he cleans his nails a second time with the switchblade. I've noticed that's his habit when there's tension.

Like now.

"Okay, we're set," I say, simultaneously closing the discussion and church. "I'll think about a date and have church once it's done."

The men are quiet. Only loaded silence.

We made a decision, but I'll be damned if it sits well with me—or the brothers.

Chapter 2

Candice

"You know I can't meet with you. It's gotta be one of Mover's men. A Chaos Rider," he adds unnecessarily.

"I hate them all," I say softly and mean it.

I wish I'd never been tapped to do this job.

But it's what I do. As a linguist, and with my background, I had what the Bureau needed.

And I'm an undercover fed with unique skills.

As I recite that in my mind, it all sounds *so* impressive. But the reality is different. I have what they need because of what I don't have. A life. A husband. Kids. I'm just a shell of a human being. A vehicle for their justice. A weapon to be used against crime.

Hell, I don't even stay in the same state, nomadic by occupation. How long can one person be untainted by taking down sex trafficking rings?

The answer: *Not long.*

I've been doing take downs for five years, and I said this would be my last one. I promised myself.

As I break away from my conversation with Puck, I look down at the solemn eyes of the seven-year-old boy clutching my hand as we hurry toward the meeting point.

I gently squeeze his hand.

"Am I gonna be okay, Miss Candi?"

Closing my eyes briefly, I struggle with a quick prayer that never feels answered. When I open them, Calem's anticipation for my reply has wilted a little.

He's familiar with me. After all, I've been posing as the art docent at Calem's elementary school for the last year.

I slow, smoothing light-brown hair back from his brow. The chunk of hair immediately tries to return to its former position directly in front of his eyes. Doe eyes in a deep chocolate color stare back at me as if I'm all-knowing. *As if.*

"Yes," I answer.

"What?" Puck says, irritated by our lapse in conversation.

I'm careful not to use Puck's name. He's all the family I have. "I need to go."

After a heartbeat's pause, he delays our inevitable goodbye with, "Funny how we both got into law enforcement."

Not funny at all. Desperate. Reactive. In no way, shape, or form was it *funny*.

"Yeah," I answer softly anyway. Puck can revisit our childhood nightmares, but I won't by choice.

Especially not in the middle of a handoff, either, where everyone I come into contact with believes me to be a mule or a high-level former cherry too old to be wanted. Too used.

Though they still do. Men do still want me. Because of my small build, people often mistake me for younger. I'm almost thirty-seven years old, with a pert face that some might think is pretty. But I think of myself as cute, and that's a generous self-assessment.

What's important to me runs to the purely practical. *Can I take care of this child long enough to get him to Puck and the temporary witness protection program?*

I'm trained to be able to, but every time I execute a successful drop-off and hand over a child, I can't sleep or eat until I get the confirmation from Puck. I need to know that the perv took the bait and came to collect, then instead of getting his sick rocks off, he got locked up for his efforts.

One down. A million to go. I sigh. But just one man stands behind this nest of snakes. And Puck and I want him. Badly.

"Candi?" Puck says intensely into the cell.

"I'm here."

After a beat of silence, Puck says, "Don't freak me out like that."

"No worries. Just thinking."

I can almost feel his relief over the cell. "Don't think to hard, baby sister."

"No." My voice betrays where my thoughts just were, though, and my brother knows them. Intimately.

After all, we share a lot of the same memories.

"There's just a few more kids. We're circling this drain, Candi—I promise. We'll find who's responsible."

"I know." Sudden tears threaten to fall, and my vision blurs. I stop walking through the park for a moment, desperately collecting the shreds of my psyche that threaten to blow away in the light breath of an early autumn. I tilt my head back, staring into a sky that is such a deep blue, it shouldn't be daytime. In Indian summer, though, it is. Calem's small warm palm is tucked inside my larger one.

Solid and real. Terrible. I can't let him go.

I must.

I don't know why this particular child is so difficult.

"It'll be okay, sis."

I lower my chin and nod, though I know he can't see me. "Yep." My inhale is shaky. The glue that makes me *me* is brittle, coming apart at the edges.

Maybe I'll just dry up and blow away?

"Call me from the new burner."

"Yes," I manage to answer.

I end the call and hunt down a trash can.

"Hang on a second, Calem." Dropping his hand for a moment, I take apart my cell phone, extract the SIM card, and throw the cell in the trash.

Still holding the dime-sized SIM, I gently tug on Calem as I seek out another can.

A dented blue trash receptacle with a domed top presents itself as I round the bend of the snaking asphalt that winds through the park. I chose Gasworks Park, dead center inside a former industrial area of Seattle, on purpose. I am not as noticeable here. I could look like any other mom of this age category taking her son for a walk.

Grimly swallowing some emotion I won't name, I drop the SIM in the trash, and from there, I move swiftly toward the rendezvous point.

"Miss Candi?"

"Hmm?" I give a vague reply as my eyes drink in the park, assessing threats and the target simultaneously.

There.

A tall, threatening figure sits on a park bench, long legs thrust out in front of him. Brilliant late-day sunlight whitewashes his hair, bleeding through the tightly bound strands and turning them the color of wheat dust. An MC cut decorates his broad chest.

My heart rate speeds.

The bigger they are, the harder they fall, I automatically recite.

"I don't want to go."

I hear this a lot. I answer as I'm trained to. But not without compassion.

I slow and sink to my haunches, automatically smoothing my shortish skirt underneath my legs.

I wear low heels with specialized cushion and firmness—sort of James Bond shoes, but for a girl. If I tap the heel a certain way, a two-inch spike will shoot out the back of the stacked platform from the widest part to be used in a reverse attack.

Roundhouse kicks have so much more force with a blade attached to a shoe.

I know this from experience.

Deliberately calming my breathing, I stare into Calem's large brown eyes. "I promise you that this scary guy will take you to my brother, who kinda looks scary too. Then the bad man will come, thinking he can take you."

His dark eyes widen, too much of the whites showing.

I hate the handoffs. First the MC criminal liaison then the one who is even worse.

I tap his slightly upturned nose. "But then my brother will meet you later." I still don't use Puck's name. I don't say my brother will collar that fucker and save Calem.

Solemnly, Calem nods, his heart in his eyes. His trust.

Emotion seizes my eyeballs, holding them prisoner, burning them with tears I can't shed. Won't. "How many times have I told you this?" I ask, holding my eyes wide open so the tears don't fall.

Calem holds up three fingers.

I feel my right eyebrow pop, and I shake off the edges of despair.

He shifts his weight. "Maybe like four."

I'm quiet for a few seconds.

Finally Calem admits, "Yeah, you've told me lots'a times."

I smooth his hair that's fallen forward a second time.

 "And you stay quiet until you see my brother. I need you to be brave for me, Calem." I wait then add, "How will you know it's him?"

He smiles the truly open smile only children seem to have, and I get a sudden pang for not having any of my own then ruthlessly shove the emotion aside.

It's not for lack of want. It's because I'm saving everyone else's kids instead of having a family of my own.

"He's gonna have a hockey stick on his arm."

I give a smile. "With a…?"

"Puck!" He jumps up and down, quickly forgetting his anxiety in the excitement of secrets shared.

I put my finger against my lips in the universal "be quiet" gesture, and his smile fades. "That's right, Calem."

He whispers, "And he kinda looks like you, Miss Candi."

I nod. Hard to miss Puck's and my unusual auburn hair color. Sometimes people think my hair is dark brown, but it's a very dark red, almost like mahogany. Even I concede the contrast of my hair against my light-golden eyes with the vaguest hint of green is unusual.

Looking nondescript is an advantage for undercover work; having memorable coloring is not.

Standing, I take his hand again, and we walk toward the figure flopped on the bench.

I resist the sudden urge to wipe my damp hands on my skirt.

Jesus, how I hate the bikers.

Up close, the guy looks like military somehow, and I can't shake that first impression.

I'm meant to be observant. I didn't climb the Bureau ladder of success, bypassing males inside the male-dominated FBI, without being aware and discerning.

He withdraws the sunglasses, and eyes like hardened flint meet mine. I've never seen such an unusual iris color. It's like captured smoke within the whites of his eyes.

Right now, they storm as they rake my figure.

This scrutiny—I'm accustomed to. Bikers are all the same. Their eyes always start at my feet and work up.

This one's a little different, though. He begins at my eyes, and that unnerving gaze slowly drifts down my body. It's not lecherous but studious.

Instantly, I don't like his brand of attention. Not sure why. Just a feeling. I trust my instincts. Lots of women don't. Trusting mine has kept me alive.

Deep down in my brain, my mind is already solving this problem with the handoff.

That's when I notice his patch.

Road Kill MC.

Not Chaos.

I have time to think, *Why would I have a rival club doing the handoff?* Then something is flying toward my face.

I sink to nearly my heels. Habit. Instinct.

Thank God my skirt's not so tight that the clothing constrains my movement.

Calem squeals in fright, and I jerk him around, flat-palming him onto the lawn and out of my reach—and the biker's.

I barely note he's tumbled on his rear before the man rises from his seemingly casual perch on the bench. He feints a punch, and I see his hand isn't in a fist. He's gripping a knotted rope in a confident grasp. The rope's stout and short.

Deadly.

Thrusting my palms behind me, I plant them on the asphalt path, bringing my foot forward.

No time to tap a heel and sprout a blade. I do an old-fashioned knee strike instead.

He goes down as anticipated.

Calem is screaming at my right.

Abort, I think when someone locks on to my long hair.

I clamp down on the pain as he drags me toward him.

Flipping me over on top of him, he thinks to subdue me. The fat abrasive rope length stands between us— promising unrequited violence .

A hard headbutt later, I'm smoothly rolling off him and landing ungracefully on my ass, flashing my panties to the world.

Two more bikers are striding fast toward us.

Shit.

I stagger to a standing position, seeing double for a moment as I haul Calem off the grass and reach inside my purse with my free hand.

Even after what I did to the big guy, he's rising like a determined zombie from the ground, an ugly lump beginning to rise on his forehead.

I'm sure I have a matching one. Headbutting an assailant guarantees practically knocking yourself out in the process.

By feel, I clutch my mace inside my purse and jerk it from the special pocket.

I open my mouth and scream in a ringing voice, "Fire!"

Heads swivel in our direction. People who didn't notice Calem screaming and a woman sparring with a man finally turn to find a huge guy looming before me, mace in my hand, and a young child with me as two huge bikers approach. I'm sure the visual is eye-catching.

I stay out of easy-striking distance, eyeballing the biker's dangling rope. "Back up." My voice is calm, confident my alert of "fire" will bring the bystanders I need. The ploy is hugely successful for a small female with a child to protect and only her wits to do it with. It's a proven fact people respond more quickly to a scream of "fire" rather than "help." Not everyone wants to help. But they sure like to *see*.

I rapidly consider my options.

On my own, I can do a flat-out sprint for three-quarters mile. Most people, men and women, would be hard-pressed to catch me. *Can't escape with a kid, though.*

My eyes quickly assess the two approaching bikers. One of them has crazy-kinky hair that's a reddish-gold and a deep fire-engine red beard. He has my murder in his eyes.

Lunatic.

The other man is quiet. Like cool water seeping steadily to my position. Maybe ten years older than me, he has a solid build of five feet eleven or so. He's also determined. *Hard.*

I need to get the fuck out of here. I back away and let the advancing bystanders take care of this shitstorm that's brewing.

A crowd gathers, facilitating my cause, and Calem is mercifully full of tears instead of words. A hysterical kid would be more damage than even I can contain.

"I don't know what they want," I say in a clear tearful voice, eyes shifting to the MC trio. I just remember my dad coming to my bedroom, and it's all the memories I need to produce the hot flood of tears.

Works beautifully, every time.

"Me and my baby," I say, piling on the common endearment for authenticity, "we were just playing in the park and these men—"

All eyes go to them.

"Threatened us," I say on a slightly wet-sounding endnote. My words are saturated by tears as I meld into the crowd.

They part like the Red Sea, allowing the innocent through while their critical gaze goes back to the bikers.

Exactly where I want the focus.

Perfect. My eyes dry, and the warm breeze of a dying summer steals the wetness on my cheeks.

One pair of pale blue eyes never leave me, though.

I turn, feeling that gaze burning into my back as I weave between benches, water fountains, and eventually, to my car.

That look held so many things—too many to decipher—but one part was pretty clear for interpretation: *I'll be seeing you.*

I had no trouble discerning *that* unspoken promise. And Candice Arlington fears no one.

But maybe I've met the first man to scare me since… my own father.

Chapter 3

Viper

I keep my shit under wraps—barely. Noose convinced me he would be great as the stand-in. Since I'm a behind-the-scenes-guy, I agreed.

I didn't trust Storm not to beat the fuck out of Arlington.

As it turns out, that didn't matter much.

She took down Noose like felling a mighty tree.

But the day sure didn't begin like that.

"Got her." Noose passes binoculars to me.

I press the bar against my forehead, and though I need readers like some old fucker at night, I see pretty well during the day.

My eyes take in the park, and I know when I've made her.

God, she's a tiny thing.

Guilt swamps me, followed closely by my old friend, anger.

All it takes is the vision of that innocent little boy clinging trustingly to her hand, and my mind hardens right up.

I had a wife. I've been with a lot of women.

Loved my wife's guts. Passed the time fucking other females after she was gone. But my heart remains under lock and key. I never told anyone, but losing Colleen about killed me, just as sure as a gunshot to the chest.

I brace my mind against the memories that flood me. I won't accept them. Not now. I try never to think about Colleen. Never visit her grave. Might just lay there and starve to death if I do.

I manage. Mostly.

Tramping down on my emotional shit that came from nowhere, I take in the woman.

Got that she's thirty-seven, on paper. She looks about twenty-nine in person.

I zoom in with the binoculars, taking in her face close-up, as close as the magnification will allow.

Nope. I squint. The eyes are the right age. Hard. Jaded. *Sad.*

I yank my head back then look again. Holy fuck, of course she's sad. Trafficking little kids has got to take its toll, even for a miserable broad like her.

My eyes sweep her form. *Goddamn do I not want to hurt a female.* My attention shifts to the boy looking up at her like she's the end-all, do-all.

Steel fills me. *Got to.*

I hand the binoculars back to Noose.

"It's her," Storm says, being quiet for once. "I'd know that face anywhere."

Noose looks at the two of us. "We grab the bitch then drop off the kid at the police station."

I nod. The boy'll be safe. Arlington won't be.

My mind's already sifting through what we'll have to do to make her talk.

Road Kill MC has a spot for torture, like a lot of clubs have, with a concrete floor and a drain in the center.

I close my eyes against the images.

Storm probably has the same set of visuals running through his brain, but his eyes are open, feasting on Arlington.

She's on a last-name-only basis. I'm already distancing myself from my future actions. Most willingly.

"I'll give the signal when I'm ready," Noose says, opening the door of our club POS truck. I close my door. It's primer gray, but the rest of the truck is dull red with a chaser of rust like lace at all the edges.

I start walking.

We know Arlington's on the other side of the knoll at the top of the hill.

Noose jogs to where the meeting point will be and tosses himself on the bench mere seconds before Arlington walks up the steepish incline.

I know when she spots him.

She hesitates, as if glaringly unsure.

Come on… come on.

After a few seconds, Arlington keeps walking.

Good.

The kid must say something because she sinks to her haunches, tucking her skirt behind her knees in a ladylike gesture that makes my jaw clench.

Ladylike, my ass.

More like lady pimp.

My lips lift in a disdainful sneer, and Storm echoes my thoughts.

"Pretending snatch," he grits.

I turn to him in profile. "Lots of hate," I say, though he's not wrong.

"Fuck yes," he grates out.

Might have to flesh out what the hell's made Storm so rage-filled toward the fairer sex. Better to know what kind of brothers I've got, like identifying the arrows in my quiver. Don't want to shoot blind.

Seeing the loathing in Storm's eyes as he watches Arlington, I realize that having knowledge might be better sooner than later.

I give a slight shake of my head. Shouldn't have brought Storm. Too volatile.

Too late now, ya dumb fuck.

With sour resignation, I turn back to Arlington. She exchanges a few words with the boy as she squats before him.

The boy says something then jumps up and down excitedly, screaming a word I can't quite make out.

Storm does, though. His deep-red brows draw together. "Puck?"

I shake my head, not making any surface connection, though some niggling memory bites at the edges of my mind.

Then she's standing, and our attention is where it should be—on the mark.

Noose isn't worried about his plan. He'll sideswipe Arlington in the temple, exerting just the right amount of force. Then it's lights out for the lady flesh-trafficking enabler.

When I asked if he could kill Arlington by hitting her too hard, a slow, shit-eating grin spread across his hard face, obscured by his incessant smoke ring fixation.

"Nope, Vipe. *This*, I got. I could do it to a baby and not hurt 'im."

I frown, giving him the look the comment deserved, then whip my finger toward the knotted end that's half the size of my closed fist. "You're talking about hitting a baby with that?" As I think of Noose's infant twins, my frown turns into a disbelieving scowl.

Noose rolls his eyes, waving away the rings, breaking them into uncoiled smoke.

"Fuck no, you're so fucking literal. I'm just sayin'—I got that much *finesse*. Don't worry. I won't kill the bitch. That negates getting the info, eh?"

I nod. *Sure does.*

When Noose extracts the rope, I hold my breath. Right then, I realize, belatedly, I don't want to kill Candice Arlington. It's in that crystalizing moment before violence, I commit to the atrocity of torture to save kids, but I'm not sure I have the balls to finish her.

I fight not to look at Storm.

He could finish her. But he would do it for the wrong reasons. Reasons I don't yet understand the motivation for.

Remembering our earlier conversation, I watch the reality unwind before me like a bad movie.

Noose is like a cat, leaning forward and swinging the end of the rope like an extension of his own arm.

But it doesn't land.

Arlington's already dropped low, shoving the boy onto the grass on his butt.

She sort of throws herself backward, flattening her palms against the pathway like she's ready to play Twister. Bringing her foot up, Arlington turns it sideways at the last moment, plowing her instep into Noose's knee.

He howls then goes down.

"Fuck me running." Storm's voice is breathy with surprise as he begins to rise.

I stand from where we've been sitting in plain sight of the park bench where everything just went pear shaped.

"Plan B," I announce.

Storm's brows come together. "What's that?"

"I'll make it up as I go along." I toss over my shoulder, but I'm already striding toward them.

Storm doesn't have any problem catching up. Young and tall, he matches my stride as we nearly jog to where Candice Arlington puts the moves on Noose.

We lurch to a halt when she yells, "Fire!" her feminine voice ringing like birdsong.

Holy *shit*. My head whips around, and everyone who hadn't noticed the mess going down does now.

People start milling toward Arlington. A couple of industrious-looking guys are jogging.

Fuck.

We stop with only feet separating us as she cries for all she's worth, having extracted a can of mace like a magician pulling a rabbit out of a hat.

Christ on a crutch. Could this get any worse?

It does.

Noose finally stands and limps toward her. *Persistent fucker*, I think with an almost fatherly pride then squelch it.

First things first—we got to survive this bit of chaos.

Candice Arlington is much more than she seems.

She says all the words right, relentlessly backing away and through the gathering crowd.

I watch her escape—with the boy.

My eyes mark her, willing her to turn and see the silent message I'm sending:

I'm coming for you.

Arlington doesn't hesitate when she interprets my clear, unspoken message. She spins in the opposite direction, her spine stiffening as she hurries away with the boy as though she still feels the weight of my gaze burning at her.

Through her.

"That is beyond fucked up," Storm comments unnecessarily.

I give him a look, telling him to shut up.

Noose pants through his mouth. "Fucking dislocated. That bitch knew *exactly* what she was doing."

"I like that she subdued you," Storm says, continuing his unhelpful and suicidal commentary.

"Shut. The. Absolute. *Fuck.* Up," Noose grits.

Finally, merciful silence fills the truck as I race to the club in the hopes Doc can patch him up.

"That was sheer buffoonery," I say, almost to myself. "With a healthy dose of arrogance." We fucked up, no doubt. And we made ourselves and the club in the process. Every advantage of time and surprise is gone.

Noose shakes his head. "Remember all those holes in her timeline I was jawin' about earlier?" he says through clenched teeth, holding on to his messed-up knee like a lifeline.

"Yup," I say, tramping the accelerator.

"Found out what one of them is."

Storm folds his arms across his chest. He's prison-yard strong, muscles on top of muscles. But he works his legs too, an unusual feature in men who lift for size. They get so set on looking huge on top, they miss the legs. Storm doesn't, so he's just that massive.

"What?" he asks, still surly from being shut down.

"She's got martial arts training. Instinctive. Shouldn't have known what the knotted rope meant. Did." Noose's jaw's clamped tight. He doesn't open his mouth but continues talking through his teeth. "Somehow, Arlington knows weapons, and not just the obvious shit."

Not just another pretty face.

"Who could know you'd tag her ass with a rope? I mean, hell"—Storm reties his hair, more for something to do with his fingers than actual need— "I'd think you might strangle me." He grunts. "But I'd never see a rope as a bludgeoning tool."

Knot training was just beginning as my tour ended in the '90s. I know knives and hand-to-hand combat. Hell, guns are like second nature. But rope manipulation escapes me. Came too late to that game. Now there're entire units in the Navy trained with just that, while knives are left to other SEAL units. The whole tamale is precisely specialized these days.

"She'll see us coming a mile away. Gave up the club. Gave up everything. Arlington is cautious and dangerous. Fuck," Noose seethes.

"We'll have to make a play for her tonight," Storm announces.

"Agreed."

That's if we're not already blown, and she's told the powers that be… everything.

"Grab her at her place, then she'll sing."

I glance at Storm, then Noose and I exchange a glance. His expression clearly tells me Storm shouldn't be seeing to any of this.

I hear that—I got him.

Noose is too solid to question my authority in front of Storm. He'll let me do my own thinking, and I love the man for it.

Noose may be rough, but he's smart and a great male to have at my back.

We pull up to the club after what seems like years to get there. I shut off the truck and hop out. As Storm puts Noose's arm around his neck, and I jog around the truck and scoot in underneath the arm on the other side. Noose is tall, has me by four inches plus, but Storm is nearly as tall as Noose, and between us, we half drag him inside.

We walk into the club, and Crystal is the first one to spot us. *Of course.* I bite back a groan and keep moving.

She makes a wide berth around Storm and beelines it for Noose. She's had a wet clit for him since day one.

It's a miracle Rose hasn't killed her. She doesn't have to worry, though. Noose has had more pussy than a man can plow, and he's only got eyes for Rose.

But Crystal's a determined sweet butt—I'll give her that.

"Ooh, baby, what happened?" She oozes her false charm.

Noose's pale irises flick to her then away. "Beat it," he says without rancor.

She pouts, not really put off. Crystal's received harsher words than those. She mostly ignores him and trots after us as we make our way to Doc's room.

He's got the double golden arches on the door. At least, that's what they appear to be. A red rectangle is dead center on the solid steel, with two, golden arches spread in the middle.

Upon closer inspection, the "arches" that parody the famous burger chain are actually the silhouetted legs of a woman wearing high heels.

Underneath the "legs," in small lettering the caption reads *Lovin' It.*

Doc's got a sense of humor.

He's probably browsing porn on the internet as we get ready to blast in there.

Old perv. I chuckle to myself and hit the lever with one hand, opening the door.

There's Doc, nose to the computer screen. His head pops up, and two eyes, slightly buggy from the magnification of his specs, regard us without surprise.

His gaze scans Noose hanging between us, and he issues a close-mouthed *harrumph* as he stands.

Noose gives a small flutter of fingers and promptly passes out.

Marvelous.

Chapter 4

Candice

I attempt to flatten my heart rate, going into auto-Zen mode, deep breathing, the whole routine.

My palms are sweaty on the steering wheel, dampening the faux leather cover wrap the car came with.

"Miss Candi?" Calem sniffs, and I fight to keep my eyes on the road.

"Yes, Calem."

"Was that man the bad man?"

Hell yes. "Yes," I say automatically. He was *definitely* bad. Ex-SEALs, expert-knotter bad.

There's no way that I'd ever escape him again. I'm a trained expert in hand-to-hand combat and two forms of martial arts, and most weaponry is practically an extension of the part of my body that wields it.

I give a soft snort. Never had a way with ropes and knots, though.

I knew it was coming into vogue as an assassination technique, though I always felt it was messy and a handy way to leave DNA behind.

Knives, on the other hand, are nice and quiet. Gloves mean there's no easy way to trace to the assailant.

I blink long and hard, squeezing my eyes shut as long as I dare. Thinking about weaponry is a safe distraction from what's just happened. I needed it.

The simple thoughts regurgitating inside my mind calms me.

When my breathing is finally under control, I say, "He was the wrong bad man."

My periphery catches sight of Calem turning his head, studying me in profile as I steadfastly maintain my speed. I'm not worried about being found quickly. I changed my license plates ten minutes ago. I have an entire billfold of plates inside the trunk. Thank God Calem is a cooperative boy and didn't melt down into a puddle of incoherent babble and delay our escape at Gasworks Park.

"I didn't know there were *wrong* bad men, Miss Candi."

Put like that, my remark is nonsensical. I try to think of an explanation that makes sense to a seven-year-old.

Squinting, I'm happy to note that I'm going in the opposite direction of the commuters, leaving Seattle at a time when people are returning from the suburb communities of Redmond, Kent, and Bellevue.

Taking a deep breath, I explain a little further. "I think *that* bad man was an enemy of another club."

"Club?"

I give his little face a swift glance, see the pucker between his brows, and sigh.

"Remember when I said there are guys who like to ride bikes and not live by the law?"

"Uh-huh," he admits cautiously.

"Well, there are different kinds of clubs."

I pass Sea-Tac Airport to the west of I-5. Using the middle lane and hanging on to the double-nickel speed limit, I watch for the 167 cut-off coming up after the hill and around the curve of multi-lane I-5.

"What kind was he?" Calem asks.

"He's with Road Kill MC."

"Like dead animals?"

I bark a laugh. *Out of the mouths of babes.* "No, honey, actually, I think their club stands more for the amount of road they can travel on with their bikes. Distance." I'm well-versed on all the clubs of the region. The rival MCs, both Chaos and Road Kill, have bad blood that goes back a long way.

As far as the feds are concerned, Road Kill MC always comes up clean. We're very sure they're running guns, but we've not been able to prove it.

That's not the case with Chaos, though. Right now, our man on the inside is playing president of Chaos. His road name is Mover. Some say he's playing dirty.

Meanwhile, my brother's playing at being a rider.

Trouble is, we think the prez has gone rogue.

Puck hasn't, though, even after years of being deep undercover. He doesn't like that trafficking underage flesh is now resurfacing after female trafficking had been successfully shut down just a year or so ago.

Every minute they know about each other's roles within Chaos MC, the room for error grows.

It's not a matter of *if* Puck will be revealed as an undercover cop, but *when* Mover will give Puck up.

I can't let that happen. But Puck's as stubborn as I am. He won't quit until the last perv is marked and imprisoned.

This was the last of them associated with this ring. Puck's right. We're circling the ring leader like sharks scenting blood.

Puck and I would retire together. He's not getting any younger. And though he calls me "baby sister," that's a misnomer. We're Irish twins, just a year apart.

"Do you think they kill animals on the road?" Calem asks, breaking into my thoughts while still sounding uncertain about what "Road Kill" means in the context of bikers.

I shake my head, slapping my blinker down with my index finger. The red light is glaring as it pulses inside the tight quarters of my compact car. Smoothly blending with merging traffic, I take I-405 heading east. Southcenter Mall looms to my right as I monitor cars, slowing my Scion. "No, I think those guys are all about riding their bikes." I risk a glance at his face. "Hey."

"Yeah?" Calem answers quietly, shifting his rear on the passenger seat.

Shouldn't be in the front where the air bag is, I think guiltily. *Damn.*

"You did well back there, honey."

His little fingers curl around the front of the seat, and he leans toward the console that separates our seats. "I was scared. He was gonna beat you up with a rope."

True. The sad part is that incident is not the worst Calem's seen in his young life.

Calem is an orphan.

His mom was a crack whore, his daddy a pimp. He was an easy trafficking mark. He'd caught a streak of luck for a time because the mother had a younger sister who wasn't a user, whore, or otherwise a dysfunctional mess.

Madison took him in, where they lived in a great school district in Kent, and enrolled him at Martin Sortun. The aunt probably sacrificed a lot of social life for little Calem. Madison won't have to worry about that anymore, though.

Because she's dead.

She was a millennial. Rode her bike to work every day. Then one morning, she shot out between two buses.

The third one couldn't stop in time and sent Madison's body flying twenty feet. I saw the photos of her body lying on smooth black asphalt like a broken doll. With Calem's aunt dead, his one hope gone, he was immediately tagged as a candidate for perv central. Little kids with no mommy or daddy are automatic picks.

Some people might say I'm unnecessarily thorough— detached even.

Why would I *need* to know about Road Kill MC, when Chaos Riders is the intermediary in the trafficking?

Because knowing what seemed unimportant has saved my ass more times than I can count. Like today. What if I'd been unaware about the clubs? I was suspicious from second one because I saw the rival's name on his cut.

What happened to the biker from Chaos I was supposed to meet?

I wonder.

"Miss Candi?" he asks in a quiet voice, startling me from my deep thoughts just before I miss the cut-off to the armpit cities of Kent and Renton.

Tapping the indicator again, I sweep right, finally on 167 then say softly,

"He didn't beat me up with a rope, though, did he?"

A genuine grin spreads his cheeks, revealing two missing front teeth. "Nope. You kicked his ass!" Calem covers his mouth with a hand, eyes wide.

"I'll let that swear word go this time, Calem," I say in mock reprimand.

The kid's been through too much for me to correct him. Besides, my adrenaline-soaked system has about had it.

I've never done this before—brought a kid home.

Never had to. Self-chastisement creeps in.

Slowly, so slowly, I reach my free hand across the center console and flip my hand over, palm up.

He slips his hand into mine, and I dare to hope that we'll still get Calem to safety. That I'll figure out why the wrong club was there. That I'll connect with my brother and make sure he's okay.

Fear thrills through me.

Puck believes the handoff happened. He's going to end up at the wrong place at the wrong time.

There's no way he can know things went crazy. Without letting go of Calem's hand, I accelerate— tempting fate—to get home and find out if my brother just landed in a trap.

Puck

Candi should've phoned by now.

I can set my watch by my sister. She's always been the more responsible one between the two of us.

Even when she couldn't afford to be.

I steel myself against the bad memories of our childhood, which threaten to rise like a toxic oil slick in my mind.

Usually, I'm fucking better than this.

But hearing that vacant tone in her voice over the cell dredged up all the shit.

All the shit we swore we'd never talk about.

I look down at the bobbing bleached-blonde head of the sweet butt who's going over my cock with smooth pulls and swallows. She works my tool like a champ.

Just can't stay hard, though.

Cocks aren't good actors. If I'm thinking deeply fucked-up things, that takes the *hard* out of the *on*.

I'd hoped letting Kristie suck me off would take the edge off the feeling I've got. The feeling that bad shit's going to go down.

But even though I have a great view of her tight ass and she's got a mouth with suction like a Hoover, I can't make it happen.

I'm worried about my sister. The handoff.

The kid—as always.

Candi and I are *this close* to realizing our dream of leaving the life and getting out from under the fucking hamster wheel that's deep undercover law enforcement.

God damn.

To complicate our lives further, I told Candi my suspicions about Mover. He's dirty. He's feeb, and I'm a cop. The two don't mix.

No one does the shit he does, even deep undercover, and continue to uphold the law. I feel like I'm waiting for him to drop the hammer. On me.

On Candi.

She's the first female FBI spearheading the takedown of a child sex trafficking for an entire region.

Kristie stops sucking with a release and smacking pop of lips.

My prick falls over on my bare thigh like a dead flesh tree.

Resting back on her bare heels, she huffs.

"What the fuck is this?" she sweeps her palm toward my uninspired junk.

Yeah. Well, see, here's the thing: my sister and I are essentially cops protecting kids against sexual predators.

And you're fucking all the snakes in the nest, sister.

Yup, that's probably most of it. Instead, I say with halting authenticity, "Don't know. Sometimes I'm not in the mood."

"Since when?" Kristie pouts her full lips. That mouth's been on more cocks than I can shake a stick at.

My eyes run over her body, and there's plenty to see, since the "dress" she's wearing is like a strategically placed Band-Aid of sheer pale-blue material, currently hiked up to her waist.

She leans back all the way. Stretching out her legs in front of her, Kristie plants her palms on the floor of the room I keep here at the club, opening her legs and giving me the full pantyless show.

Long hair that's been dyed blonde so many times, it's more like straw sweeps the floor as she arches, the pink folds of her pussy spreading to reveal her wet center.

Not all chicks get turned on sucking a man off. Kristie does.

God, she's hot. No doubt.

Right now, I'm just too in my brain to think about sex.

And that's saying something.

I'm known for having an on-command boner. I can get it up twice an hour. And at straight up thirty-eight, that's bragging rights.

That's when my sister isn't doing a handoff or when I've heard from her at the time I anticipate.

Ignoring the view, I stand, stuffing my uncooperative limp dick inside my pants with a hike, and zip up.

"Ahh," Kristie whines.

I roll my eyes. "Nothin' personal."

Or maybe it's *all* personal. I feel the scowl form. "I gotta move." My tone says, *"Don't fuck with me on this."*

Kristie's not a smart girl.

"But I was hoping we'd fuck," she whines and stands in full view of the club hall beyond my open door, not bothering to pull down the skirt, baring her slit and landing strip of dark hair that proves her not-natural-blonde status to all comers.

A brother walks by, takes a look at her parts on display, and cracks up.

Kristie flips him off.

"Been there, *done* that!" He laughs, hiking his pants, and saunters off.

"Fucker," she mutters.

I can't stand it. Normally, I try to stay in character, but sometimes, like now, my soul gets in the fucking way of my Academy Award performance.

"Straighten your skirt, Kristie."

"Fine." With an exaggerated sigh, she jerks down the hem of the skin-tight scrap of shimmering material, and it just skims the bottom of her ass cheeks. Her chipped screaming-scarlet nail polish contrasts with the blue fabric.

I'm suddenly weary. Tired of the charade of being a rider. Tired of three years on the detail.

First, we got rid of Ned, the fucking female flesh trader. Then we found out that the tide had turned to kids instead of women.

I was so pleased that somehow, Allen Fitzgerald's house "accidentally" burned down. Still, the evidence of his interest in prepubescent females had been duly noted, leading us to the new ring Candi and I were now unofficially working together. But only we know that. Because she's more than a sister. She's my best friend, someone who survived our childhood by my side. We don't keep secrets.

Couldn't. Not if we wanted to live.

When the similarities of the cases we were each working collided, we knew that we were actually playing against each other. So now we work together.

A handful of people within the Road Kill MC know who I really am, but they won't give me up, unlike the one man who could do serious damage. I suspect he has passed to the other side already.

Mover. Road name only. I still don't know his real name.

Kristie runs her fingers down my bare arm, jutting a hip out. "When do you wanna hook up again?"

I don't jerk my arm away, but now the lips she just had on my cock seem filthy instead of hot.

This entire job is souring.

I need to get out and take Candi with me. There's never a chance of us finding anybody to spend our lives with and having a normal existence if we can't get off this never-ending Ferris wheel of the horror of humanity.

I drop my arm, and the gesture causes Kristie to release her grip.

"I don't know. Got shit to do. We'll hook up again when we do."

Anger washes over her features, showing the mean streak that hovers right underneath the surface of so many of the washed-up sweet butts. They want to be property, but the reality is, when every rider has ridden them, nobody really wants to make them permanent. They never see it, though. And… the cycle continues. It's sad.

It's reality.

"All the bitches say you're all stallion in the sack. What sack? You can't even get it up."

Words fill my mouth. Every one of them is unkind, biting, honest, and superior.

I don't need this shit.

But looking into her hurt, overly made-up face, I can't bring myself to add another wound to the many that others have already put there before me.

I'll just be less for saying all the shitty things I want to.

And I've always wanted to be more. So instead of responding, I turn in the opposite direction. Brushing by her through my open doorway, I walk out of the club, heading for the trunk at the back of my fat boy.

I'll call Candi's landline, let it ring once, then hang up. She'll know it's me. She has a Vonage line, so she can take the same number anywhere in the world and the number presents as though she's in the same US residence regardless of location.

She should be home now.

We haven't seen each other in three years. Can't risk showing up.

I promised her that I'd never come to her house or do anything else that would compromise her cover.

I don't break promises. Especially to her.

After extracting my cell, I tap out the number from memory, knowing she's already dumped the burner we spoke on earlier.

It rings once.

I tap *End Call.* Then I wait.

Ten minutes tick by as I look out over the deep woods guarding the Chaos Riders' clubhouse.

A vein in my forehead begins to throb, keeping rhythm to my thudding heartbeats.

I slip the cell back into my trunk, lock it up, then hop on my ride. I'm about to break a promise to my sister for the first time in my life.

Chapter 5

Viper

"How long?" I ask Doc. He holds up two fingers.

"Two mofo *months*?" Noose says, incredulous. Stubborn fucker is grinding his teeth through the pain.

Sure enough, he's got a dislocated kneecap. Must hurt like hell. Probably hurts his pride more.

"I can't ride?" he nearly yells.

"What about fucking?" Storm asks, one eyebrow rising to his hairline.

I swipe a palm over my face, tired to the bone.

"Don't worry about my cock or me sticking it in Rose. Got it?" Noose's glare is mercury fire on Storm, who's not known to be the sharpest tool in the shed when it comes to delicate deliveries.

He's more the hammer-between-the-eyes type.

Storm rolls his large shoulders into a shrug. "Just saying…"

"Don't," Noose seethes from between his teeth.

Where's Wring when we need him? He usually moderates all this bullshit.

"Okay, okay—I think whether Noose can fuck or not is the least of the worries on this one, Storm."

"Don't think he'll need additional surgery, but he'll have to do physical therapy. And it was not easy getting this thing straightened out. Had to call in a favor. I'm just a general. Like Angel's eyeball? Had to call in a favor on *that* one too. Specialist job."

I'd been there. Her mom, Beth, needed some work too. What a disaster that was.

Kinda like this is shaping up to be.

"Yeah, what Vipe said." Noose glares at Storm.

I pierce Noose with my eyes, letting him know in no uncertain terms that Storm isn't the one to be blaming. "Listen, things went south fast on this."

"No shit." Storm snorts. "Lots of civvie eyes on the whole thing."

"Took us an hour to extract ourselves, all the time Noose is dying."

Noose's brows drop low over his eyes. "I was not dying."

"You weren't feeling that great," I clarify.

Noose is silent.

I briskly change subjects. "I'm going to go after Arlington. Storm will help. I'll think about taking a third brother."

"Wring," Noose says instantly. "He'll do best with a woman."

What he means is he'll flinch less.

"Snare isn't going to be okay with it. Protected sissy too much." Noose chuckles.

Storm whistles. "Better not let him hear you call her that."

Noose grimaces as he tries to lift his leg with both hands, adjusting his position on the hospital bed we have stowed in the closet of Doc's office.

He waves a palm at the comment like he's getting rid of a bad smell. "Fuck it. It's funny, and it ain't never gonna be *not* funny." Noose smirks and begins slapping the front of his cut, clearly searching for his hardtop box of smokes.

"This is our infirmary," I remind him in my blandest voice.

"Fucking kill me now if I can't, by Christ, have some nicotine."

"Pussy," I say, as calm as a windless day.

Noose rolls his eyes. Discovering a semi-crushed pack, he manages to pluck an unbroken cig out and lights it up, cupping his hand around the tip of the cigarette. The end flares then dies to a simmering orange-red coal.

"Who is this little girl that took out Noose the Moose's knee?" Doc asks quietly.

"A woman that's gonna talk then die," Storm says.

"Oh," Doc says, rocking back on his heels. "I'm not for all females, but I don't like murdering them. I *am* a doctor—was."

We don't talk about his use of past tense.

I focus instead on Storm spewing our plans in front of somebody not directly involved.

Doc's a retired brother. Can't ride that well. Even a trike isn't a solution. But he's part of the club. Saved a ton of lives. That's what counts—loyalty.

Sometimes service to the club comes in different flavors.

I clap Doc on the back. "This particular female deals in kiddie peddling."

Doc's features arrange themselves into lines of disgust. His lip lifts, the bridge of his nose scrunching into a ripple of flesh. "That's fucking disgusting." He shakes his head. "Guess the broad deserves what's coming." He sounds resigned.

"Definitely." Storm chops the word off like he's got an ax.

Doc's exhale is slow and thoughtful as he looks at Noose's injured leg. "This kind of damage I've seen some in my time."

One of Noose's smoke rings floats between Doc and me. With an irritated swipe, my hand breaks the perfect circle, sending the cloud of smoke floating to the ceiling.

"Done by who?" I ask, trying to gain a better sense of what kind of woman we're dealing with.

"Assassins, pros, martial arts folks. Military." His eyes shift to Noose then me.

Noose and I look at each other through the haze of his smoke. But he's got his fix, and he's stopped bitching. Thank God.

"Okay so the woman gives kids to the creeps to abuse," Storm says. "She's obviously not defenseless." Storm zeros in on Noose. "And no offense, Noose, but she handed you your big ass."

Noose's eyes hood. "I'm gonna kill him."

"Not yet," I say.

"Anyways," Storm continues, "they probably gave her training and shit. Just in case a deal goes bad. Enough for her to get outta a tight spot."

"She didn't engage me," Noose says with slow consideration. "Arlington defended then took off. She's smart as fuck."

Yes, she is.

Candice Arlington used the element of surprise well. But no matter how well she was trained, if a man matched her skills and outweighed her, she would be out of her league. Essentially, she'd get her ass kicked.

"So we bring in Wring. We have an inkling of what skills Arlington's got. Can't surprise us a second time." I raise an eyebrow. "Is it fair to say her skills extend to weaponry?" I ask Noose.

He grunts. "Yeah, fucking affirmative on that, Vince."

Noose will sometimes slip and say my real name. He knows more about me than I do. Keeps it all to himself too. Really appreciate his radio silence. He knows about Colleen. How she died. What she looked like. A lot of the brothers patched in after she passed. Noose hasn't said a word about my old lady to anyone.

Never could knock her up. Sudden grief seizes me like a tackle from a linebacker. Unexpected and fucking unwelcome.

Would have been a bit of joy in my fucked-up life if I could still have a part of her on this earth. But all I got is memories.

The details of her face are soft in my mind. Not sharp like they used to be.

Despair doesn't rule me, but I find it gives me orders when I least expect it.

I don't follow those commands. Wouldn't be standing here if I'd listened to the small voice nagging at me to end my shit after Colleen left me.

Forcing my head back in the game, I answer, "Then we have to assume she can handle guns, knives—"

"She's got the hand-to-hand down pretty slick," Storm says.

Noose's brow ridge dumps over eyes gone pewter with irritation. "You're not gonna let that go, are ya?" He shoots smoke in Storm's direction.

"Probably not," Storm admits. "Perfect blackmail potential."

"Dick."

Storm grins.

"Boys," I warn. Unbelievable that I might have ever been that young. That brash. That dumb.

Probably was, though.

I give Doc my attention. "So he stays here overnight."

Doc nods. "Yeah, this is drive-by medicine at its finest. My buddy came in here and fixed him fast. Now it's up to Noose."

He lifts a vial. "Rose can plug him in the ass with this stuff. If he gets high enough, he'll forget that his kneecap was torn around." Doc lifts a shoulder. "If you'd brought him in later, it'd be a different story. Major reattachment issues."

"Instead of teeny-tiny ones," Noose comments in a dry voice, holding his index and thumb a millimeter away from touching. He snickers.

We look at him. He seems a little high right now.

"Do you know where Arlington lives?" It's the most important question of the hour, and I want the answer before he gets juiced with more drugs.

"Yeah." Noose's eyes tighten, and he clenches his jaw. "But it's probably just a fake addy. No *actual* physical."

"Come on, Noose—this isn't like you!" Storm blurts. "You would've had a contingency."

I raise my eyebrows. As do Doc and Noose.

"I'm not a fucking clown," Storm says loudly, clearly insulted. "I do understand the English language, ya know."

I hadn't actually understood.

"Listen, this broad isn't going to have a tile hung outside her door saying 'come and get me,'" Noose says in a voice that overrides Storm's. "She doesn't *want* to be found. She's doing something really fucking illegal—disgusting. I don't got the words for her brand of shit."

A lecture from Noose.

"Go to the addy. See what you can find. We lost the bitch because of the crowd of civvies."

"Got a look at her car, though," Storm says.

"Yeah, some piece of shit tin can," Noose mutters. "No plates? Just car description?" He squints through the smoke from his third cigarette.

Storm nods. "Neutral color, some kind of beige that the fancy-pants car makers are gonna call 'champagne' or some shit."

"So anybody's car color. Nondescript. Swell." I cup my chin, dipping my head down. I've got one man down and a flesh-peddling bitch off with the kid to parts unknown.

My head jerks up as the door bursts open, and Wring strolls in, eyes wild. They land on Noose. "Fuck me!" he says, gaze traveling up Noose's leg.

Noose raises a fist, and they bump. "What the fuck, Noose? Shannon just talked to Rose. Said somebody wasted your knee."

"Humpty Dumpty's men put him back together again." Doc chortles, rocking back on his heels.

Noose shoots him a hard look, dull, ruddy color bleeding at his nape and climbing his neck.

Storm is conspicuously silent. *Unbelievable.*

Doc and I exchange a look.

"What?" Wring's attention shifts between us, eyes narrowing at our not-so-subtle exchange.

"Lost the bitch. She pulled a fast one, got too many eyes on us. We couldn't follow her. Don't have dick." Storm explains machine-gun style, disappointment clear on every angle of his face. "I wanted to save the fucking kid."

We all did. And every kid after that one.

Wring grins to beat the band.

"What's so fuckin' funny?" Noose growls. "Doc"—he whips his head in Doc's direction—"shoot me up with some joy juice. I'm pissing vinegar."

Doc issues a soft snort and walks over to Noose's IV. He injects something into a small tube, and Noose flops back. "I can take bad news better this way. In pain, and all of the revelations bad—and my fucking fault—makes me want to kick in teeth." His eyes shoot to Wring, waving his palm around in an irritated figure eight. "Well, fucker?"

"I came late to the party."

Noose frowns. "We were three musketeers on this one, brother."

"Snare overrode Viper." Wring inclines his chin at me.

Fucking Snare. Always worried about security. Of course, that is what makes him such a damn good sergeant at arms.

Wring sweeps his heavy arms wide from his torso. "Saw you get your ass kicked. Stayed back."

The flush on Noose's cheeks screams back to life again. "Marvelous, dickhead. Make. Your. Point."

"Followed the bitch."

Every man in the room comes to attention as if the President of the United States just walked into the room.

"No shit?"

Wring nods happily. "Just a total coincidence."

Not much of a believer in those.

"So you let me suffer, thinking you didn't know a girl handed my ass to me."

Wring nods, still grinning. "All worked out, though. While you were getting the beat-down, I waited until Cupcake came to the parking lot with the kid. Followed her."

"She didn't notice your bike?" Noose asks, suspicion thick in his voice. "Because she's not a regular girl. She's sharp. Aware."

"No shit," Storm agrees.

"Nope, used the POS club truck."

"Hell, that thing sure earns its weight," Storm mutters.

I agree. Had it since I was a teenager. My first vehicle. Battery sucks, but I keep the engine tuned myself.

Fucking guys in their twenties couldn't find their ass with both hands. And forget something rudimentary like changing oil. Might as well tell them to perform their own sex change.

"Anyway," Wrings says, running a hand over his flattop of platinum hair, "she lives on the border of Kent and Renton."

"Addy?" Noose asks, slurring the word.

Wring's nearly invisible eyebrow lifts. He recites the address.

Noose sits up straighter, trying to shake off the drugs. "That's not the one I got."

"Yeah, bitch changed out her car plates too," Wring announces.

We all look at each other. I'm starting to see Storm's interest in torturing her at the moment.

"Probably got a stash of those too. Enabling twat." Noose flops back down after that pronouncement, launching more smoke rings at the ceiling.

Wring's eyes peg us. "She has the kid with her. Got to figure that out. Can't go charging in there and leave some kindergartner alone in a house. Could be Arlington's got company coming." He lifts his broad shoulders. "Or she arranged another handoff."

What a clusterfuck. "We can't let that happen," I say. "One of us has to take the kid, keep him somewhere safe until we get her to talk."

Everyone looks at me.

"No way. Not taking the kid."

Talk about having zero skills. *Fuck me.*

"We all have kids, Viper," Wring says reasonably. "You don't. You can play daddy."

I sort of want to kill Wring.

Doesn't help that all of them are grinning like assholes. Storm doesn't even have a place yet; he mainly crashes at the club all the time.

Club antics aren't for kids.

Doc's an old coot.

Noose is out and has twins under one year old. Wring's right.

And I hate it.

If Colleen were still alive, she would volunteer to take care of the kid until this mess got ironed out in a nanosecond.

But she's not, is she? It's just me.

And maybe that's not enough.

Chapter 6

Candice

Pulling up to my townhome, I roll the car into the shared driveway. The garage faces a slightly sloping driveway that leads to a well-kept '90s facade, complete with angular pitches and funky geometric-shaped windows beneath the eaves. I depress the button for the garage door opener, and as the massive door rolls up, I inch the Scion forward up the driveway and into my garage.

I relish the moment of complete anonymity. No one knows where I live. Every time a lease is up, I move. That's the price I pay for peace of mind. I'm always aiming for places that have six-month leases. That way, I can dust my feet off and rotate to the next locale. Sometimes addresses overlap, and I have to move out before the lease is up. It happens.

I don't pick up the tab, but the cost is high nevertheless.

Emotionally, since I haven't owned a home in my entire life, it's taken a toll. Just a vagabond, I go where the FBI wants me to be. Period.

I gave up everything women want—or are *supposed* to want. A husband, kids… Hell, I can't even bake a cake.

At one time, my compliance was necessary. Now I could choose. But I've gotten so accustomed to this life, why change it?

What life?

It's not like I've got a man. I don't even have any prospects.

I have Puck. And I haven't even seen him since we both began this detail from opposite sides of the fence.

I turn off the engine and put the key inside the console.

"Is this my new house now, Miss Candi?" Calem asks.

I click the button to close the garage door, and as it slowly lowers, I watch its progress in my rearview mirror.

"For now," I answer as the garage door taps the cement floor. Then I get out of the car and walk around to open the passenger-side door.

Calem exits cautiously, looking around. "Where do I sleep?"

There's no reproach inside his small voice. Only a question.

I close my eyes. *He thinks his home might be in a garage.*

I answer slowly, "I have an extra room for you to be in." I try on a smile. It feels forced. Too tight.

Calem gives me a similar one in return.

God. What a mess.

He's just getting along. Like he's always had to.

First things first. "Let's go inside." I start walking toward the door, which leads directly into the house. It has one of those convenient laundry-slash-mudroom transition areas.

Any house with doors that access the garage and are not integral to entry and exit to the main house are nixed from my consideration.

I would never give intruders an additional access point to where I sleep and eat.

After I've tapped my keyed entry sequence onto the numbered pad, it makes a low chime, disengaging the deadbolt. I open the door, swinging it wide until the solid wood is against the wall. No one stands behind the door. My senses take in everything as Calem stands slightly behind me, following my lead. It's obviously not his first rodeo where there's potential for danger.

Firstly, I use my enigmatic women's intuition, which, believe it or not, is a real thing.

I sense nothing. Smell nothing. See nothing.

Removing my gun from the handbag that's made for it, I hold it loosely at my right side, leaving Calem to my left.

"Miss Candi?" Calem whispers, voice trembling, his little hand hooked to the bottom of my bolero-style jacket.

"It's okay," I say back just as quietly.

Lifting the Glock 42, I sweep the weapon in front of my body. The barrel follows my eyes as they track all points of entry.

The ticking of the clock is loud in the otherwise-silent house.

After five seconds pass, I count off another ten. Frozen breath slides out of my starved lungs, and the tension singing between my shoulder blades recedes like a riptide.

Clicking the safety back on, I slide the gun inside my handbag, tight against the pocket where the mace resides.

"Are we okay?"

I sink to my haunches, tucking my flared skirt underneath my butt. I move his hair back again.

"Yes."

Calem's narrow shoulders drop slightly with the news. "I'm hungry," he announces.

That, I can figure out, but first—*Puck*.

"I'll phone my brother and let him know what's happened." I cock a brow. "Why don't you see what's in the fridge?"

I turn with a smile, knowing exactly what he'll find. My sweet tooth will become all-too-apparent in about five point zero seconds.

My landline phone on top of the end table is my archaic nod to the popular phones of the 1980s that are made of clear acrylic. The guts light up when the unit rings. I grab the receiver and punch in the memorized numbered code for my voicemail.

My phone doesn't ring at all. Except for when I get calls from one person. That concession was made long ago.

It's an out-of-date system as compared to the broad swath of technology the feds possess, but sometimes, backward things such as this are actually more secure. Counter intuitive but true.

I listen to the robotic voicemail voice as faint sounds of rummaging reach me from the general direction of the kitchen.

Missed call. Number unknown. *Puck.*

He's worried. I know this. I didn't phone him from a new burner because—surprise, surprise—things didn't go according to plan. Because I'm so anal, Puck has to be frantic about the missed time loop of communication.

"Miss Candi!"

I turn, semi-startled. I'd forgotten for a moment that I'm not alone. Smiling, I take note of the chocolate milk carton, Twinkies, and a huge canister of cashews scattered across the small peninsula countertop that separates my living room from the kitchen.

Food of champions.

I figure mid-life will challenge my slimness any second, but for now, some fluke of genetics, or just plain luck, keeps me thin despite all my efforts to mess it up. That and devotion for keeping a defensible body.

"Yes," I answer.

"You've got *gooood* food." Calem's eyes run over the things he could manage to get out of the fridge.

I walk over there, setting my handbag on the top of the fridge—somewhere high and difficult to reach, although Calem and I have already had the discussion on guns. Mine. Others. How they're never to be touched unless you're willing to use them. It had been more of a drive-by lesson than a deep one. Pretty hard to fit in discussions of weaponry during finger-painting time.

Nope, that had been a need-to-know as we were driving to the meet.

But I couldn't have a first grader see weapons and not understand some basic principles. And as an art docent, if I had to flash a weapon, there had to be a reason.

Personal protection was mine. And thankfully, society was cooperatively violent enough that I never did a handoff where a child gave the gun more than a one-second blink.

They simply believed it was necessary.

Reaching inside the fridge, I grab deli meat, cheddar cheese, and the condiments. Searching for something green, I catch sight of a hard red tomato, too chilled to ripen beautifully.

Oh well. Hauling all the stuff out, I say, "I'll fix you a sandwich, and you can have chocolate milk on the side. If you eat it all, *then* you can have a Twinkie."

"Ahhh," he moans.

I ruffle his hair. "Listen, I'm trying to be responsible here."

"What does 'respodible' mean?" Calem asks as he races to the other side of the kitchen and hops up on one of my stools, perching his small chin in two hands.

"Responsible means…" *Feeding a kid. Caring. Not hurting.* Sudden tears swamp my eyes, and sheer grit holds them back from falling.

"What's wrong, Miss Candi?" He's used to everyone imploding around him.

I'm not going to follow that trend. I dip my head, reining in my emotions and taking a deep inhale. I let it out in a smooth slide of breath. "Nothing." I hike my chin, meeting his large brown eyes. "Responsible means being there for something or someone… no matter what."

After about a half minute of contemplative silence, Calem says, "I like that word."

"I do too," I reply instantly.

Our eyes lock for a moment as a sort of primal and perfect understanding flows between us.

I might be older and a woman, plus an ocean of differences separate us, but in the end, I had an uncertain and terrifying childhood, and so does he.

Commonality glues us together.

I go about fixing the sandwich. I butter both slices of potato bread before adding mustard, mayo, and two slices of cheddar. Scooping the honey-baked ham out of the square plastic container, I fold three pieces on top of his bread, then I hack the tomato into the slimmest slices I can finagle.

"There," I announce, proud at my attempts as pseudo mom. *That's what moms do, right? They fix lunches, make sandwiches.* My eyes move over the chocolate milk and promised Twinkie.

Probably not all that other shit, though. My lips twist in a rueful smile. I've got to start somewhere.

Come to think of it... I go through the entire process again, making one for myself.

Calem inhales his and is already halfway finished by the time I get to eating mine. We sit side by side on two stools that are positioned underneath the countertop overhang, our backs to the small living room.

Calem swings his legs restlessly, and I perch my feet on the bar at the base of the stool. The stools will get left behind with all the other secondhand furniture I had fun shopping for.

Weird retail therapy, but one I enjoy. Maybe someday the stuff I buy will be mine for longer than a year.

Drinking the last bit of my chocolate milk, I lean back in the chair then let a honking belch go. "Excuse me," I say delicately, holding back a spray of laughter by a thread.

Calem doesn't have the same restraint and erupts into a gale of giggles. When he can finally control himself, he dusts bread crumbs from his lips and says, "Miss Candi, that was *so* disgusting."

He's thrilled, a wide grin showcasing his missing two front teeth.

"Yes, wasn't it?" I grin back, and he lifts his little palm in the air.

I lightly high-five him. "Whoever said girls couldn't belch as well as boys has not been hanging around the right girls," I announce haughtily.

Calem's smile is worth my uncouth behavior. Puck would not be impressed or surprised. That makes me smile.

Puck. Shit!

Racing to my room, I hear Calem calling after me.

"It's okay!" I yell back as I drop to my knees beside my bed and dig under my mattress.

It's not the best place to stash my disposable cells, but it's handy.

Getting one out, I turn it on. It takes a second to power up, so I walk back to Calem. He's already started plowing into the Twinkie. Sure looks good.

The cell beeps its readiness.

"What's wrong?" Calem asks, mouth full of whipped cream.

"I forgot to phone my brother."

"Oh, yeah." He takes a gulp of chocolate milk, sets it down, and mashes the last of the Twinkie into his already-full mouth. Kids are vultures.

I tap in Puck's number.

It rings and rings. And rings…

A frown settles onto my face. His not answering is really weird, and I don't believe in coincidences. Out-of-the-ordinary dots connecting usually mean something bad.

As I end the call, the screen goes dark. Tearing the cell open, I walk to the garage door.

"Hang on," I tell Calem then walk to my second fridge just a few feet away from the Scion. I open the door and grab a coffee can. Opening the lid, I'm assailed by the wonderful smell of aromatic grounds.

I stuff the SIM card from the burner inside the can. The dark goodness is a graveyard for hidden SIMs. After returning the can, I walk back into my house and go to a potted houseplant perched on top of an antique oak secretary, a unique piece of furniture from the turn of the last century. The plant is six feet above the floor, setting on top of the tallest part of the secretary. The ceramic pot is also vintage. Muted colors of orange, olive, and brown swirl around its exterior in a pleasing, bumpy texture. To anyone standing on the floor, the plant would seem to be growing from dirt in the pot.

But I don't have time to water houseplants. What I do instead is put a cutting inside a small fishbowl of water and place that inside the pot.

That leaves a two-inch space between the fishbowl and the pot holding it.

In this gap, I place the other half of the cellphone. Can't have anyone discover my brother because of my laziness. My fingers drift over the surface of the pot, and a moment passes where I have an intense longing to own something. Anything.

I turn away from the pretty pot and look at Calem.

He hasn't noticed my machinations. Instead, he's found my small TV and remote, expertly navigating the unfamiliar equipment. Plopped down on the futon that also serves as a couch, he's leaning back, swinging his legs as he does.

"Calem."

"Huh?" he says without looking, having found an old Bugs Bunny rerun.

The Road Runner is still running, I note. "I'm going to take a quick shower, okay? Can you hang tight for about ten minutes?"

"Yeah."

I walk in front of the TV. His eyes latch on to mine.

"Don't leave the house or answer the door."

His solemn eyes don't stray from mine. Calem nods.

We have an understanding. I swing a last glance around my locked house and move down the hall again. Worry over Puck haunts me as I remove my clothing, setting the bundle on top of the back of the toilet tank, and hop in the shower.

I feel gritty after my engagement with the biker. I can't wait to finally connect with Puck and ask him about Road Kill MC. I *know* a few in that club are privy to his status as an undercover cop.

Makes me wonder if that's connected with the biker at the park today.

Are they after him? Why else would they be involved? My suspicious nature offers a lot of speculation, which just makes me more anxious instead of less.

Shampooing my hair, I rinse, soap, repeat, and rinse again. I frown for a second then remember I shaved last night and don't bother with that.

Getting out, I wrap a towel around my long hair.

After the ritual of face cream, deodorant, body spray, and brushing my teeth, I pat my hair dry and fling it behind my back. Shivering a little, I pad naked through my room, the wet hair clinging to my chilling skin. I grab fitted yoga pants I use regularly at the dojo and a short-sleeved tie-dyed T-shirt. It's the rattiest shirt I own. Got it at a Jimmy Buffet concert when Puck and I were barely more than kids.

When we dreamed of living in a real-life Margaritaville.

I pull on wool-blend socks and sigh. *Feel like a human being.*

Slapping on a medic watch, which is a favorite for answering questions in the middle of the night, I walk out into the hall toward the living room. Trying to figure out what my next move's going to be, I wonder how I can explain the situation to my contact at Chaos—and the predator who works with them—without drawing suspicion to myself.

The idea seems simple in theory—I can point the finger at Road Kill MC. They had no right to be there for the handoff. In fact, I should be able to neatly pin the blame on their organization, stating that I didn't divulge the location of the handoff to anyone else.

That means someone has a mole in Chaos.

The second part of the handoff hasn't been missed, so it's still salvageable, thank God.

Smiling at the beginnings of a story that would stick, I continue down the long hallway toward where the sound of the TV is blaring. *He needs to turn that down.*

I slow, heartbeats beginning to stack like pancakes inside my chest. *The volume wasn't that loud when I was in the bathroom...*

Then my senses come alive like a decked-out Christmas tree just as a huge shadowed man comes around the corner. Male. Mixed race. Six feet, four inches. Two hundred forty pounds. Twenties. Red hair.

Hate-filled eyes.

The bigger they are, the harder they fall, my mind whispers. But my stomach coils in fear. "Calem!" I shout even as I'm ducking.

The guy lumbers into me, arms wide to swoop and grab. His muscles have had babies. There's no way to get his attention and halt his momentum with this kind of introduction.

Crouching lower, I stab his groin with my knuckles in a blistering strike, picturing my hand moving through his pelvis. It's not neat and pretty, but it's effective.

He makes a gurgling sound in his throat and begins to lean like a great tree toppling.

His hand shoots out in a last-ditch effort at a strike.

I lean away, tossing my hands wide to steady myself, fingertips brushing the walls at either side of me.

Calem, I have time to think before strong arms loop under my armpits from behind.

I kick both legs out in front of me, hitting the listing assailant in the chest with a perfect mid-torso impact.

He flies backward as I slam my head back, hoping to nail a forehead.

Too tall. I hit somewhere in the upper pectoral region. *Fuck!* I slam my foot into a shin instead. *Not wearing shoes.* Raising my fingers, I try to braille for eyeballs.

My hands meet air.

The unknown man is leaning his face away.

"A little help!" a deep male voice rumbles practically in my ear.

I plant my feet and lean forward, lifting whoever's behind me. Reversing our position, he uses his superior size to throw me against the wall with what feels like everything he's got.

Slapping my palms against the wall takes some of the impact, but not all.

I begin to slide down the surface, my bell rung.

A ghost of a man strides down the narrow hallway, backlit by light from the blaring TV set.

Military, my addled brain says. *Moves with stealth.*

He comes within range, and I go for the crotch with my foot. But I'm hopelessly slow, my vision doubling as I try to make a movement too swift after getting brained.

Yanking me by the ankle, he takes me the rest of the way down.

I lie on my back, staring at his silhouette. His hand gets close to me, and I bite it, trying for meeting my teeth.

He hisses, and his fist meets my temple.

Nauseating pain sweeps my head, and I begin to crawl away.

He easily lifts me from the ground and hurls me into the wall.

I can't protect myself. My reflexes are fucked six ways to Sunday. *Puck. Need you, brother.*

Gray fuzziness eats the hallway at the edges, and still, he comes. I frown. Now there are two men.

"Don't make me hurt you more. Stay down," the man with a military-issue platinum flat top and square beard says in a low voice.

A shrill *beep beep!* shrieks from the TV.

Calem.

My eyes find the man's glacial blue ones in the gloom. "Fuck you," I say without missing one iota of being in character, though my head spins and my heart constricts.

Calem.

Puck.

Slapping my palms against the wall, I push myself up. His hand is bleeding all over the carpet from my bite.

My smile must match my intent.

"Viper," the man says while his buddy covers his balls with both hands and moans a few feet away from his position on the floor.

"Do it."

He does.

My eyes flick to what has just appeared. A rope flashes from his hand, hitting me dead in the throat before I can stop it. The thing barely taps me. It's not hard, but it's precise.

Can't breathe.

I sink to the floor, my fingers biting the carpet as well-worn boots appear beneath my wilting vision.

Then there's nothing but a black so bleak, it's beyond dark, colorless.

Chapter 7

Viper

My left hand is on the wheel, and my right drags over my face. "That was fucking awful."

Storm's in the passenger seat, practicing deep breathing. "Whatever," he huffs, still clutching his balls. "I about died back there. I'm not gonna be able to have kids or something after what that bitch did." He shifts his weight and lets out a low groan.

Maybe. Candice Arlington is dangerous.

"Shouldn't have tried to hug it out after what you saw her do to Noose," Wring comments dryly.

"No shit, Einstein."

"I won't give you a brain duster for that, but the thought appeals."

Storm grunts.

"How's Arlington?" I ask, unable to shake my guilt over hurting a female. Done it before—in war. Feels wrong now, though. Or more wrong. Even *knowing* Arlington had a kid and was ready to turn him over to a Chaos Rider, who would then give him to perv central, doesn't make it much easier.

I think of the way she fit against my body when I grabbed her from behind. Like she was meant to be against me. Not to hurt.

To protect.

She was so light when I tossed her at the wall. The fragile, hurt gasp she made as she landed tears through me.

Fuck. Fuck. Fuck.

"Out cold," Wring says with a thread of satisfaction. "Got her trussed like a turkey. She isn't getting out of those bindings." His snort is soft in the blackness of the SUV.

"How hard was that love tap with the rope?"

Storm gives me a sideways glance. "The fuck, Prez?"

Wring leans forward between the two seats as I fly toward the house, using every back road there is.

Know 'em by heart. Born and raised in Kent, had the place out in Ravensdale damn near since before I was born. Been in the family for over a hundred years.

Wring's look is hard, a question in his eyes. "She's alive. I can calibrate a strike for anyone. She's a one-hundred-ten-pound female that's maybe five foot three. She got the impact necessary to stop breathing and elicit unconsciousness."

I barely catch his curt shrug in the rearview.

Wring gives a short laugh. "And it'll leave a helluva mark."

I remember her skin. Smooth like porcelain. My spine stiffens. "Can't question the dead."

"She's not dead. Nowhere near. But Arlington is gonna feel our engagement tomorrow," Wring says, flexing the hand she bit.

"Yeah," Storm chirps through a pant of pain.

Wring looks in his direction. "So are you."

"I won't fuck for a week with this dented-in dick I got."

Wring and I chuckle. "You'll be up to man-whoring in no time."

"Kid okay?" I ask.

"Yeah. Rider's following, remember?"

"Glad we got him out of the house before we started in."

Wring nods. "Smart to turn up the TV. Distracted her."

I shake my head. "She was going to amputate something on me. That's for sure."

"Be thankful it wasn't your prick," Storm mutters.

I take the turn off from Highway 512 to the long driveway that leads to the homesteader's cabin my folks bequeathed me, which was built by my grandfather's father.

Love this place.

Looks like it grew out of the ground. And though the water table in western Washington is high, the lay of this parcel of land keeps things high and dry. The cottage sets at the very top of a natural knoll. Dual copses of trees flank it like watchful soldiers.

That's probably why my great-grandpa did something really unusual with this place. It has a basement. Doesn't ever flood. They're not common in western Washington.

That's going to be Candice Arlington's temporary home. Though she doesn't know it. And she definitely won't appreciate my efforts of restoration.

Just finished the last bit only last week.

Working with my hands calms my nerves. Especially in the MC lifestyle. It's more than riding, getting laid, and partying.

There's a shit ton of nuts and bolts of the club that I handle behind the scenes. Lariat takes care of it with creative finances, and I oversee.

Snare guards our club.

Noose seeks out intel, always jonesing for the latest, the who and the why. That's how we got a bead on this kiddie ring of sick fucks.

Road Kill MC *is* a brotherhood. We're a team. Nothing short of that mindset will work. One percenter stands for that. Uncommon, but unified in the same end goals.

"Hope that puke festers by her front door." Storm laughs then grimaces, gently adjusting his junk.

"Nice DNA calling card, dumbass," Wring comments.

Storm's expression sours, his top lip pulling taut. "You ever get your balls tapped like that?"

Wring's silence is so long that we've pulled up in front of the tiny cabin and turned off the SUV before his soft answer is uttered. "Yeah."

His eyes have that faraway look they get when he's thinking about something in the past. Something bad.

"All right, so did ya puke?" Storm asks with the logic of the young and the lack of discernment to *not* ask that comes with age.

"Eventually."

Wring gets out of the car without another word, and Storm gives me a look, brows high.

"What's with that shit?" He hikes a thumb in Wring's direction.

I know it was the war.

Storm can't figure it out, but with one glance at the slightly lost look in Wring's eyes, I *know* there's been a time when he was helpless and vulnerable.

We all were.

Like Candice Arlington is now.

Popping out the driver's side, I catch Wring as his hand is on the handle.

"I'll take her."

Wring backs away, holding his arms up, palm out. "Whatever you say, Prez."

We stare at each other. "I can do it." I sound more like I'm trying to convince myself.

His eyes sharpen on my partially illuminated face, but he replies, "I know."

Storm limps around to our side of the rig. "God, I wish I felt better. I'd hammer that bitch."

I say nothing, but my guts tie into a nice tight knot at his words.

As I open the door, the interior car light flicks on, and I'm met with catlike golden eyes. Just a hint of green flecks.

There's no freaking out from Arlington.

She just surveys the three of us upside down. Her gaze rests on Wring the longest before returning to mine.

"Where's the boy?" she asks.

I laugh. There's no question of who we are, where she is, or if we're going to kill her.

All she gives a shit about is the merchandise.

Wow. And to think that I was feeling bad.

I'm a fucking fool.

Grabbing her by the armpits, I drag her out. The back of one of her trussed heels smacks hard on the car well, and she bites her lip to keep from crying out.

Have a feeling that when Storm is feeling up to things, he's going to make sure she makes noise.

I let her fall on the ground, and she sort of spins midair, landing on her back instead of her face. Groaning, she rolls off a sharp rock bigger than the others on my driveway and inchworms off it with a barely contained sigh of relief.

"Boy's fine. No thanks to you," I say in a voice like brittle glass.

Storm limps over to her and puts his boot on her chest.

Her eyes widen with an expression I can't read. Their gazes lock.

"Wait!" I say loudly, moving forward and grabbing his massive shoulder.

I'm too late to save the thing that happens next, though my last minute interference lessens it.

Storm steps down and gives a vicious twist, applying his considerable weight, and she cries out.

We all hear it.

The rib breaking.

I spin him before he can bear down more, shoving him away. "Fucker. Unnecessary."

Looking back at Arlington, I see hot tears roll down her face as she writhes inside the bindings.

Fuck.

"What?" he says, cringing as his nutsack gives a twinge. "Owed her that."

Wring says nothing.

Short breaths fly out and get sucked in as she struggles to breathe and control the pain while bound.

"Hyperventilating." Wring sinks beside her.

Arlington flinches away from him then gasps at the pain. "Calem," she whispers.

Beat up, with a broken rib and she's still worried about the money end. All business, I'll give her that.

"Please," she says, licking parched lips. "Don't—" She gasps. "Don't hurt him."

Hurt him? This crazy bitch. "We're not going to hurt him." I seethe at her.

"We're going to hurt you, bitch," Storm says, moving toward her again.

Arlington glares at him, almost as if she's sending him a silent message. Fucking hard as nails.

He hesitates.

"Hey," Rider says.

We pivot, looking at a brother who's one badass dude. He's got the kid by the scruff of the collar. "He's freaking out."

The boy's eyes are big and brown. Scared. "What are you doing to Miss Candi?"

"Shh, honey," Arlington says from the ground. "It's going to be all right."

Haven't heard a lie that big all month.

"Miss Candi?" Storm's hands turn to fists.

"Don't," Wring says automatically, never taking his eyes off the boy. Instead, he walks over to him and crouches low.

The boy's eyes move from Rider to Wring, and I can see his wheels turning. He's got no one to trust. And his gaze moves to Storm last. Probably reading the barely contained rage.

Looks like he might have some experience in that department.

"Hey, pal, this here is Viper." Wring says, pointing to me, and the boy—Calem—follows his finger, giving me a wary and distrustful gaze. Can't blame him there.

"Okay." He looks up at Rider. "Please let go of me."

Rider smirks. "You gonna wig out again?"

The kid blinks, seeming to translate the expression. "No." He looks at Arlington again. "I wanna be with Miss Candi."

Unbelievable. Miss Candi.

"You guys go. I'll get the kid and her in the house."

Rider just turns, taking me at my word, and Storm huffs, limping after him.

"I'll be back as soon as my dick is okay," Storm says over his shoulder, heaving a significant glance toward Arlington.

"You got this?" Wring's eyes ask if I *really* have it.

I nod.

He nods back then follows the other two men.

Arlington stares at me without expression, until the kid runs to her, flinging his tiny arms around her neck. "I thought they were the bad men, Miss Candi."

She cries out when part of the weight of his arm lays on her chest, and Calem stands, backing up a couple of steps.

I move then. Leaning down, I slide my arms under her body and lift her as the boy retreats, looking at me holding her. She groans at the movement and what it cost her rib.

Arlington's so light, it's like lifting a child. Like the ones she's giving to the fuckers.

I harden my heart at her fragile female face as it falls into my chest. Her breathing is labored.

"Don't hurt me in front of him." Her breath is hot against my chest, with a slight odor of mint to it, as if we caught her right after she brushed her teeth. She licks her lips again, then says in a soft voice, "Please."

I can't say I won't hurt her. It'd be a lie. I can't say everything will be all right. Another lie.

So I admit what I can. "Okay."

I walk to the house, and the boy follows. He follows me all the way into the newly refurbished basement.

Where Candice Arlington will be tortured.

Chapter 8

Puck

I'm in civvie clothes, driving a vintage 1968 Camaro. I don't look remotely like the biker I've been pretending to be for more than three years.

My sister's townhome is exactly as she described it—circa-1990s uninspired architectural styling. Triangle windows line the extreme slant of the peak of the roof. The windows appear like all-seeing hostile eyes, and a sense of foreboding washes me in a pour of sick adrenaline, drenching my body in a flush of alternating heat and cold.

I shouldn't be this reckless, but I can't stop myself. I roll up the driveway, slam my car into first, and leap out the door, not even taking the time to close it before I race up the walkway at full throttle.

I hit the front door on a sprint about the same time as *eau de* vomit smell strikes me like a whip. Leaning forward, I see spewed half-digested chunks of food decorate the bushes lining the border of landscaping that runs along the foundation.

Turning to the door, I punch in the numbers for Candi's house. "You never know when we might need each other," she said when she made me memorize the code.

I clench my eyes shut, wanting to know but *not* wanting to.

I knew this day would happen—when my sister would need me and I couldn't protect her. *I couldn't protect her from our own father. How can I protect her now?*

Lifting my chin, I square my shoulders. *Got to try.*

The keyed entry sings its acceptance of my correct sequence, and I open the door. Immediately, I smell Candi, and childhood memories fill my mind.

Scent is the most powerful memory trigger—and my sister doesn't change anything. She has the same taste in furniture, which she calls "funky chic," and the same taste in moisturizer and body spray. It smells like her. Like home.

Ignoring my emotions, I tear through the house, taking in everything.

A TV blares. I walk over and hit the switch on the remote to mute it, instantly cloaking the house in silence. A Bugs Bunny rerun keeps its frenetic pace across the screen, tossing chunks of disembodied light against the walls.

My body stills, and I listen.

The clock hanging on the wall ticks loudly, reminding me of the seconds I don't have my sister here and of the second part of the handoff just twenty-four hours away.

The buyer will have plenty of questions when the handoff doesn't happen as planned. The first will no doubt be: *Where the fuck is the boy?*

A Twinkie wrapper sits crumpled and forgotten on the coffee table. Tiny fingerprints are smeared across the glass squares of its top. Crouching, I give them a quick eye-measure.

Sure look to be the right size. I stand, mind whirring. *Why in the fuck would Candi ever bring a kid here?* Now I'm really freaking out.

Someone barfed in the bushes.

The kid was in her house.

My hands fist. *Where's my sister?*

Turning, I move slowly to a long, narrow hallway and flick the light switch on. Bright ceiling can fixtures explode with illumination, swallowing every shadow. My eyes leap around the long space.

This. This is where it happened.

Blood is spattered all over the '90s-era beige carpeting.

My heart starts banging inside my ribcage. Not thrown blood. Blood that just hung and dripped.

Two body-sized depressions mar the walls opposite each other.

I walk to the first and place my fingertips where a head struck, dipping into the deepest divot. I know it's Candi's.

Don't even have to measure, but my palm unerringly covers the indentation of a small skull.

With a sick feeling, I walk to the second depression. This one is more violent, the head impression isn't as deep, but the outline of the body is clear.

My sister's small body, heaved against the wall.

Sharp pride choruses through my system. *She fought them.* A small satisfied smile lifts the edges of my lips. There must have been a lot of men to bring her down.

Candi is the fiercest human being I've ever known. And whoever took her is going to die.

Slowly.

Don't you give up on me, sister. Stay alive, I say to myself.

To her.

Candice

He carries me gently, considering his plans.

Because make no mistake, I'm under no delusions as to where this is going.

The "Prez" of the Road Kill MC is going to make me talk. Somehow, it's hard to envision him working me over. More likely, it'll be the red-headed male whose crotch I sank my fist into.

I try to work through the pain of my rib to think coherently. I must be moving in and out of consciousness because I lose seconds as we travel through a cabin.

I've been hurt worse in my life. But that was a long time ago, and I'd forgotten how it felt to be in this much pain.

To feel this much fear.

A horrible calm descends, and right then, I decide I'll die. They're not getting anything from me.

I'll save Calem if I can.

My one regret is Puck. He'll never know what happened to me. I can't even say goodbye, and being robbed of that option is a raw wound to my soul.

A tear rolls down my face as my mind already resolves my fate.

"Tears aren't going to do diddly squat for you," the biker remarks.

I hurt, but I manage to roll my eyes up to look at him. The Road Kill president would be so handsome if it weren't for the fact he threw me against a wall, dumped me on the ground while I was bound, *and* kidnapped me, not in that order.

Yeah, that.

"I'm not crying," I gasp, "for coercion's sake or using feminine wiles."

"Smart girl," he says as we descend steep steps. The space smells of wood, paint, and unidentifiable construction smells.

New.

Funny what a person will notice under stress. Like how a thing of beauty can mask the evil therein.

With a casual flick of a wrist, he turns on a light, and warm illumination spreads across the low ceiling, chasing shadows out of the corners with beautifully warm and vibrant light. The space where I'll be held is surprisingly large.

Tongue-and-groove pine, stained natural, lines the entire ceiling. Wide windows intersect the top of the stone foundation, standing out in stark bones of wood and glass.

Moving to another door, he opens it with one hand then hits another switch, which makes a loud click.

Dim light filters into every corner of the area. It's a large bedroom with an old-fashioned metal bed. Squinting through my still-fuzzy vision as my head thumps with a fine headache, I just make out the headboard.

My grandmother used to call that style of bed a matrimonial. Ornate curves form in a gentle high arch, and the intricate metal "knots" spaced about a foot apart were designed to mimic flowers. A patchwork quilt, obviously done by hand, is thrown on top.

The Prez clears his throat. "Gonna put you down now. You try monkeying around, and I'll hurt you worse."

"Is that an actual word? 'Monkeying'?"

He shrugs and carefully lowers me onto the bed.

I seize his throat, digging my fingers around his esophagus like I'm mining for his spine. The pain the move costs me is instant, taking away my vision, breath—everything, leaving nothing but the agony.

Still, I hang on, though pain rakes claws through my chest.

The slap rocks my face back, and my head slams into a pillow instead of a wall. Stars burst in my field of vision, and I'm helpless to stop him as he yanks both my wrists. I scream while the sound of metal against metal clanks against the headboard.

Handcuffs.

My eyelids pop open, and my vision swims as I fight losing consciousness. Then I see a knife and tense, ready for the end—as though I've always been waiting for my death.

"Protect Calem," I command in an urgent whisper.

He slices through the zip ties instead of my body, but the metal handcuffs hold me to the headboard.

My breath slides out in relief to be free of the tight plastic bindings.

"What?" He rubs his throat, where I can make out the outline of my fingers running the border at the column of his thick neck. Without waiting for my answer, he points the tip of the blade at me. "Told you not to try anything."

I gasp and groan as breathing becomes a gift, and the pain is bright and white-hot.

His eyes are a gorgeous blue. Like a pristine body of water. They look at me like two blocks of ice.

"Had to try," I hiss through the pain.

"And look where *trying* got ya."

Yes. Look at that.

Another wave of pain lances me like a sword. Black wings of nausea and dizziness sweep through me. *Shit, not now.*

Yes. Now.

I turn my head, leaning as far over the side of the bed as the handcuffs will allow, and vomit onto the lovely new floor.

"Fuck!" he hisses.

I probably have a concussion after all the manhandling. Not the first time, though. I blow a strand of hair away from my face before it lands in my mouth, now fouled by throwing up.

My eyelids sink, and I hang off the edge of the bed by my wrists. Closing my eyes, I curl my legs against myself, trying to relieve the strain of my body against my injured rib.

The man is busy moving around. I can hear him mopping up my meal of sandwich and chocolate milk from earlier.

"Where's Calem?" I manage to gasp out, and a string of drool joins the mess at the floor.

"Safe," he says abruptly.

He's not safe until he's in protective custody. "Yeah, and this is safe?"

He's bent over as he finishes cleaning, but he turns his neck to meet my eyes.

"Safer than in your hands."

Not true. Of course he believes I work for whoever is trying to peddle children. I must maintain that guise no matter what. This man must never know my true identity.

Despair runs through me, scalding me as I realize the hopelessness of all of it. I can't incriminate Puck. Though he would see Calem safe.

I have nothing to use. No arsenal of weapons.

Nothing.

With a grunt of disgust, he slices the binding on my legs.

The cold flat tip of the knife comes to rest underneath my chin, gently tilting it up. "You try any of your martial art skills on me, little lady, and I will really hurt you."

The slap had been like a punch. And I think the only reason he didn't punch me is because I'm a woman.

I don't know why I feel this way, but I think, even though this man believes I'm a child pedophile liaison, he can't bring himself to truly hurt me.

If I were him, I would be dead already.

Viper

I didn't hit her that hard.

And that fact makes me feel like shit. Injured and bound, she still tried to take me.

The woman is brave. Corrupt as fuck, but brave.

"I won't try anything." Her skin has paled. Lips blue.

Some shock setting in.

I unlock the cuffs, and her wrists fall. Now the bindings are off. I flick my eyes to the bathroom where I just flushed the paper towels I used to clean up her mess.

"Got to get you to the bathroom."

"Water," she says, grimacing. Arlington moves to her side, biting her lip. Using her hand, she tries to push herself upright.

"Ah!" she yells, grasping her side and turning her face away.

Fuck.

"Let me get you there."

Her face meets mine full on, and my handprint is a red outline on the pale skin of a very delicate oval-shaped face.

Guts churning, I carefully scoop her off the bed and against my side.

"Stop," she says as tears roll down her face.

"Why?"

"Hurts."

"How about I don't give a shit?" I hike my eyebrows.

Her gorgeous golden eyes, shot through with vivid green, look into mine steadily. "Then please kill me. Don't let that other man do anything to me. Just kill me and take Calem to the police. Please."

I feel my frown. *Now* she's got me thinking. *Kill her?* I don't think so. Protect the kid—well, hell yes. That's a given.

"I might throw up again or pass out. At least, that's how it usually goes."

My face swivels to hers, and we stare at each other for a frozen moment.

I can tell immediately from her regretful expression that she didn't mean to say that particular comment and would do anything to take it back. In a quiet, slow voice, I ask, "How it *usually goes*?"

Finally, she nods. "It's not my first time."

Who the fuck has beat her up like this before?

Arlington shakes her head, then dumps it against my chest. Protectiveness surges through my body.

Fuck.

It's just how most men are hardwired: not to hurt women. It goes against everything for this particular man.

And lots of others. Except maybe Storm.

I'm in so much fucking trouble here.

"Dizzy," she whispers.

Right. "Okay, we'll shuffle to the bathroom."

I take a step, more or less hauling her beside me.

Then she just collapses.

I catch her, and she screams in pain as some part of me makes contact with her rib.

Fuck this. Bending, I put an arm behind her knees and her back then stand. Her head rolls to my bicep.

Thank God for working out. She seems to weigh nothing because I work my ass off to be strong.

And… because she's just that tiny.

I gaze down at her.

God damn, am I in a world of hurt.

Walking through the door of the bathroom, I'm really glad I spent the money in here, because I wanted a place all my own after sharing the main floor with every new patch-in who came along.

The bathroom is a mini-oasis, with a large standalone clawfoot tub, a walk-in shower, and a double-sink vanity topped with quartz. It was an extravagance not typical for a basement, but looking at fifty just around the corner, I thought it was a long time in coming.

I take Arlington to the sink and hold her weight, gradually sliding her down to the vanity top.

Gripping it with small hands—deadly hands—she says, "I think I can brush my teeth."

My eyes flick to a new toothbrush wrapped in cellophane.

"Toothbrush is right there."

"Thanks," she whispers, tearing off the plastic. She goes about brushing her teeth, fingers white with tension as though she's holding herself up against the counter.

Might be.

I can tell by the way she watches me she would rather die than ask for my help. Arlington swishes her mouth out with water from a cup and spills it down the drain. I hear her gulping at least two glasses of water before carefully setting it on the vanity. Our eyes meet in the mirror, and I see her thinking through her options.

Doesn't take her long to work out that she's too hurt to fight me, no matter what her skills.

Using her hands, she turns her body to face mine.

I stand, legs planted wide, arms crossed, and stare her down.

She holds her body stiff, because clearly her rib's injured and she doesn't want to move. Solid logic.

"I've got to use the bathroom."

Right. "Have at it." I swing a palm at the toilet. A fancy low-flow toilet with a smooth look that hides plumbing and a flusher gizmo on top of the toilet tank stands a short distance from the vanity.

Arlington's embarrassment is obvious. A dull sweep of red color rises on her high cheekbones, making her eyes glitter like citrine gems.

Hell of a lot better than that sickly pale look she had earlier. Was starting to worry me.

Which is a problem in and of itself.

Her eyes travel the five feet to the toilet. The blush intensifies. "I don't think I can use it," she looks down, "without your help."

Oh.

I walk over there and wrap my arm around her waist. She stifles a groan, and I loosen my grip slightly.

"Just get me there. Maybe I can lower myself down."

It's easy to get her over there. I lift the lid and step back.

"Can you not look at least?"

I nod, but my eyes move to the mirror to make sure she doesn't rush me from behind.

She doesn't.

In fact, Arlington can't make it. She tries three times, and on the third, she yelps.

I turn, and her soft black pants are to her knees. I'm looking at the prettiest pussy I've seen in a decade.

I get an instant boner.

Fuck me. I dip my head, looking away. But that dark-auburn patch of curls topping a perfectly smooth slit won't leave the dark recesses of my brain.

"I can't. I'm sorry." Her hand is at her ribs, her breathing labored.

Swiftly, I stride over there and take her hips. Naked hips. Skin smooth and silky.

Fucking dick nods in excitement. *Good Christ.*

Her small hands rise, gripping my shoulders. "Lower me."

I gulp hard. Feels like I just swallowed a bowling ball.

"Ouch!" Her hands slide to my chest.

My heartbeats start a rapid machine-gun-fire sequence, my mouth going dryer than a popcorn fart.

"I think you have to be down lower, to get me, to make sure you don't hurt me."

Hurt her more, she means. Find it interesting she doesn't say it.

I kneel in front of her.

My eyes are staring at her most intimate part. Her hands bite into the flesh of my shoulders. The scent of her pussy, the soft organic wonderful smell, fills my nose, and I have an almost insane compulsion to go down on her.

This woman sells children to pedophiles.

That thought helps, and I pull back into myself. Gripping her hips, I lower her to the seat, and our eyes meet.

Tears of shame scald her face, and I would be an idiot not to recognize the embarrassment there.

I stand and take a couple of steps back.

A stream of urine releases from her body, and she shudders in relief.

I turn away just enough to give her the illusion of privacy and to hide my expression of lust.

Things are getting fucked up in a hurry. That's the thing about life—a person can't predict shit.

Like wanting to have sex with a woman you've set your mind to torture.

Chapter 9

Candice

My rib feels like a shard of broken glass diving for a lung with every breath. As a matter of fact, that could be happening.

Every movement is agony.

That could be because he has me cuffed to the bed, my arms extended high and behind me. There's no way to ease the pain. I'm just a lump of burning agony. Worst of all, my muscles are seized. If I could just relax, I think the rib injury would take a more or less backseat to the immediate future.

We're on a first-name basis now.

Me and Viper.

I went pee and had some water. Got to wash the puke taste out of my mouth. Twice.

Now, I'm lying in bed, and he's watching me.

"Mister!" Calem calls from the top of the narrow, steep staircase.

Viper pivots toward the child's voice.

He probably forgot about Calem. A stab of panic lances me. I can't protect him. I can't protect me.

"Yeah!" he yells up the stairs, giving me a final look before turning his broad back on me.

A breath slips out, and I sag. I don't have to feign bravery. I just have to get him somewhere that I can exploit and get out of here. I take in his tall, muscular figure and feel despair trying to take over.

I can't let the emotion gain a foothold. I must get Calem out of here and to Puck.

He would kill all these guys if he knew the shape I'm in.

The wheels of my mind turn over the weapons I have at my disposal. I'm not dumb enough to not realize that Viper likes what he saw during our little toilet trip. Like every other red-blooded male, he got a load of the goods and wants a taste.

Figures, I think, mildly disgusted. But he didn't touch me inappropriately. His eyes did.

Hmmm. Difficult to follow through with hurting a woman you want to fuck.

I can use that.

Viper is halfway up the stairs when I spy Calem's little legs. "Where's Miss Candi?" he asks quietly.

"She's down here sleeping. We'll let you see her when she wakes up."

"Okay," Calem answers, but he sounds unconvinced.

Thank God. I don't want him seeing me bound and hurt. It'll shake what little stability he has right to the core.

"Hungry, partner?"

"Yeah," he answers with wary slowness.

119

Viper trudges up the stairs, clearly intending to rustle up some grub.

I don't know what time it is. My eyes hunt for food, proof of food, or anything. Nothing. The place is so new, there isn't even a clock. It's disorienting.

I'm hungry too. That tells me at least six hours have gone by. I need fuel. Carbs.

My eyes shut. *Freedom.* I need that most of all.

After a good half hour, Viper reappears, and we go back to staring at each other.

He's a clean-cut guy. Doesn't have some of the obvious signs of being MC. He's tall but not overly— maybe five feet eleven. His temples are beginning to silver, but he looks great for his age. It's apparent he works out regularly.

And Viper hits like he's done it before. Hence the finesse sufficient enough not to really hurt me. I know he could have done some damage.

I can still feel the sting of the slap on my face. Just another lovely wound to add to the others.

"Storm will be stopping by first thing tomorrow morning. Got the kid fed and in bed."

"Storm?" I croak. My throat is parched, but I don't ask for water.

"He's the guy you clocked in the dick."

Oh. Him.

Great, just great.

Viper's eyes run over my expression. "It doesn't have to be this way. If I never had to touch you in violence again, it'd make me happy." His eyes are sincere. I've had enough life experience and been on the job long enough to know a liar. "Tell me why you were trying to give this kid up. We know about the kiddie pervs."

I close my eyes for a moment, unsurprised. When I open them, his expectant gaze is latched on to my face. "I can't," I answer in a low voice. "And there's a damn good reason."

Our gazes stay locked.

"I will let Storm at you. I won't like it, but we need to know who's behind this, Arlington. Nobody comes into Road Kill territory and shits where we eat and sleep. Not happening."

I knew this. I also know what their goal is with me. Squeeze the middleman—in this case, the *middlewoman*—to find out who's running the shots and get at the source of the cancer that's metastasizing in their territory.

Chaos doesn't mind shitting where they live, I think with resignation. That's how we were able to set up our sting. We're *so* close to the head of this trafficking ring and taking down their house of cards.

So close.

I *needed* to do this final handoff. It was personal and a delicate balancing act to make everything appear to have gone through. The ringleader of the flesh trafficking wanted this specific boy. He was to meet with Puck personally.

Finally, we were closing in.

We still have time to make the rendezvous tomorrow. Puck does.

My mind trips over itself with thoughts of how to manipulate my current mess to our advantage.

"He'll kill me," I say in reply to finding out Storm is coming tomorrow.

"Maybe," Viper agrees, eyes hooded.

My gaze goes up the stairs. The child's welfare must be the priority. Maybe we'll lose the perp, but he's not going to have Calem Oscar if I can help it. "Please take Calem to the police."

Viper walks over to where I'm lying down, his eyes running down my body. He cups my waist with his hands, fingers almost meeting around it. I don't think I'm that small, but his hands are that large.

"What rib?" he inquires softly. His fingers splay, and the ring finger of his left hand brushes over the tender rib.

I flinch at the barest contact. Can't help it.

Viper's face doesn't change, but his eyes tighten, fingers gentle on my side.

"Gonna take your top off."

There goes Jimmy Buffet. And my dignity. "Raping me won't get me to talk." I'm disappointed. I thought all this torture and rape plan might be beneath him.

The young red-headed guy, I believe—but Viper seemed a little bit too refined for all that. I'd gotten a lot from him. That he was old-school, mannered, ex-military, and organized. He would have to be, running a MC as efficiently as I'd heard Road Kill was managed.

He chuckles. "I don't have to rape women." His eyes are steady on my face, his hands warming my bare skin. "I'd never do that anyway."

A tear trickles out my eye as I shift to one side. Viper rolls up the shirt until it's at my bound wrists. He leaves it there.

I put on an all-lace ivory bra because it happened to be the one on top of all the others. It's not practical like my tie-dye T-shirt that rests on the handcuff linkage or the athletic pants. A fluke of choosing.

His fingers trail down my arms, which are bound high above me. Calloused from whatever work he does, they leave an erotic trail in their wake before stopping beside my breasts.

This process of his featherlight touch on my skin *is* a form of torture: being hurt and bound while having another human being toy with my fear using tender fingers, coaxing my uncertain terror to new heights.

I crave it. I hate it. He can't possibly know that, though.

That it mimics certain memories. Most are saturated by fear and guilt, while the edges of deserved affection are in there somewhere too. The want of it anyway.

Viper's fingertips spread apart as he meets his hands in the center of my chest, thumbs resting directly beneath and between my breasts.

"Talk," he says quietly.

I shake my head.

He finds the injured rib with a finger and barely skims it.

I cry out.

Staying silent is so much harder than I thought.

"Why do I get the feeling there's more to this story?" He cocks his head, pressing slightly harder, and the sensation of broken glass grows more acute.

"Please stop," I breathe from between my teeth.

"Storm will do more tomorrow."

I do the only thing I can. I wrap my legs around his torso. Instinctive and natural, I use what I must. I won't talk, but I can't stand the pain, either.

If a man is thinking about sex, it is more primal than violence. Usually.

His smile is sly. "What are you doing?" Large hands grasp my waist as my legs squeeze him.

I breathe through the horrible pain of moving.

"Guess I should have tied your legs too." A stray dimple makes an appearance as he smiles.

This close to his face, I can see fine smile lines around eyes laced by black lashes and a square jaw that has a day-old beard. A dusting of silver like forgotten tinsel glints in the light.

Shaking my head, I say, "There's no reason to torture me. I don't know who the person in charge is, honestly."

I don't. But Puck would have known tomorrow, had I not run into Road Kill MC. Despair threatens to overwhelm me as its friend hopelessness beckons.

I struggle to calm the storms of my mind while ignoring the pain.

Viper's pool-water eyes search mine, and I put all my pent up frustration, fear, and determination into my own gaze. Naked before his scrutiny.

"There's other ways to torture it out of you."

No. "No rape, you said." *That*, I don't know if I could survive.

Viper nods. "It's very effective, but I won't sign up for that."

My shoulders ache as I slump in relief. I'm afraid I have a little Stockholm's syndrome. Or maybe it's the threat of the red-headed guy coming to hurt me that has me suddenly contemplating things I wouldn't normally entertain.

Because if there's one thing I'm not, it's compliant.

"I can make things better." His face goes still, emotions in plain sight. And I read from his expression that Viper is conflicted.

I would give a lot to know why, because right now, from his end, it's simple. He's got me where he wants me. Hurt me, and I talk. Or try to hurt me, and I probably won't. I'll just pass out instead.

Intrigued despite my fear and lack of options, I ask, "Like what?"

He captures my jaw with his hand, holding my face still. "The only way I want those legs wrapped around me is naked, with my dick impaled inside you."

I rein in my shock with a supreme effort. *Fuck him and maybe escape.* Or be fucked *up* by the guy who hated me on sight. Great options. But any choice is better than none.

"My rib is maybe broken," I remind him.

Viper nods. "I'll be very careful."

"Why?" My legs start to tremble from the exertion of staying in one position around him. My rib's killing me because it can.

I identify the ridge of his cock straining between my legs.

His thumb strokes my jaw. "Because I think you're lying. And… " Viper's nearly translucent eyes scan my body. "I want to fuck you." He kisses my lips softly, and the faint smell of mint and engine oil invades my nose. "And because I can't bear to hurt you again, or for anyone else to, either."

His forehead dips against mine as he rubs his cheek against the one he slapped.

I'm as confused as I've ever been in my life. This is a hard man. An MC president. They don't get soft when it comes to the club.

Calling out the pink elephant standing between us, I say, "You think I'm a pedophile enabler."

Viper's head rises, eyes never leaving mine. "It would *seem* that way."

I hold his stare, not backing down, seeing where this will lead.

Finally, he breaks the silence. "But I don't *believe* you are." He kisses my lips and breathes against them again with his next words, "I know you're something, I just don't know what yet."

After a few beats of silence, I say, "So we have sex, and then you let me go. I get Calem to safety, and it's done."

I dare to hope.

Viper stares at me so long, I'm sure he won't answer. Won't agree. Then he does, "Yes."

I just fed the devil a part of my soul, and he gobbled it—and me—right up.

Then I give him my answer.

Viper

I barely touch the rib, and she whimpers.

It's that noise and so many other awful, final things that happen between me and Candice Arlington that tell me the torture plan is off.

As if it ever had a chance. I should've known it wouldn't work the minute I laid eyes on her.

First of all, I have actual bona fide chemistry with a woman for the first time in a decade. Haven't felt this firestorm of desire since Colleen was alive. Sure, I've fucked about every sweet butt who comes through Road Kill doors, but fucking isn't the same as dying to be inside a woman—or to be with her. The raw *want* to hold a female so close that two people are one body.

Too bad that when I finally get hit between the eyes, it's by an accomplice to pedophiles.

When was the precise moment I knew Candice was someone other than who we thought?

When I was holding that knife.

I saw the expression in her cat-gold eyes. She thought I was going to do her. And what did she say in response to that realization?

Protect Calem.

Candice wasn't worried about her imminent death and her last chance to stave it off.

Nope. Her last thought was about the kid's welfare. And not just any thought. The last person Candice believed she would ever see was the one she told to protect the kid.

I don't know what part Candice Arlington plays in this intricate web of abusing the defenseless, but my gut says it's probably on the good side.

No matter how much she tries to pretend she's what we presumed her to be, there's goodness in there.

I see it.

Even when she was trying to beat the shit out of me, I saw her. Felt her. Who Candice Arlington really is.

Throwing her into that wall killed something in me that I can't get back. I should have bowed out then and let Storm take over.

I was gone before I started. Seeing her face in those photos did it. I just knew that anyone who looked like that couldn't be evil enough to do those things to kids.

I'm going to try to erase the damage we did to Candice with my body, then I can figure out who the fuck she is.

But no one other than me is going to lay a finger on her, and it isn't going to be to cause pain.

I lied to the brothers. Said I could hurt to get answers. That I could kill her. But at the end of the day, I couldn't do violence against Candice Arlington.

All I want is to sink into her. Injured. Scared. I want to wrap her in my protection instead of hurt her until she begs for mercy.

I'm looking for a different kind of begging from her.

I just forfeited the Road Kill MC—for a woman.

The very thing I vowed I would never do.

Chapter 10

Candice

Viper's lips quirk. "Got to release me." My legs fall to the soft bed, and I let a relieved sigh go.

"I won't rape you. This is a negotiation. You have sex with me, and I let you go."

"The other option is Storm will be here tomorrow to mess me up?"

He nods, but I see a shadow of something pass across his eyes like a cloud of uncertainty and I wonder at the brief emotion I glimpsed.

I can't deny that Viper would be the sort of man I'd go for if I hadn't been beat up, kidnapped, and facing likely torture with a side of worry for Puck and Calem.

However, my libido will take some coaxing. My headspace is skewed, too worried about Calem and Puck. I can't get out of here because I'm too injured. And I have secrets to keep. It'd be so easy to admit I'm FBI.

On the other hand, maybe that would mean death for sure.

As I watch him studying me, I can't see my death written anywhere in those pale eyes.

I see only desire.

Unless I'm really off base, I have to trust my instincts. And those are pretty finely honed.

Viper stands and walks away, saying over his shoulder, "I'll give you something good." His voice holds a touch of humor, and I frown, trying to shift my weight again. The rib sings, and I still. *God it hurts.*

He disappears into the bathroom, and my eyes follow him. Rummaging around, he closes and opens a few different drawers.

Viper comes back with two pills and a glass of water.

Cupping the back of my head, he helps me take a sip, and I swallow it.

Like I have a choice.

"That'll take the edge off the pain."

I lift my hands, clanking the cuffs, indicating my need for freedom. Suddenly nervous with the idea of what's going to happen, I lightly gnaw at my bottom lip, fingertips tingling.

Viper gives a slight shake of his head. "I'm going to town on your pussy. Don't need you trying to gouge my eyeballs out."

His eyebrows rise. The expression is part amusement, part explanation.

Oh my God. What if he hurts me? "What?" I ask, my mouth dropping open. "That is not part of the bargain."

This is not *Him*, Candice, I calm myself.

His eyelids drop to half-mast. "Listen, baby, I'm old-school. I'm a worshiper. Think the vagina is where it's at. And let me tell you, I'm no spring chicken. If I can't make you howl in three minutes flat, I've lost my touch." His smile is sudden, sure and vulnerable at the same time.

I close my eyes against it. "You threw me into a wall."

When I open my eyes again, I see that guilt lines his face. The palest blue of his gaze darkens to the color of a rioting sea. "I've never hurt a woman who I wasn't ordered to."

Military. There's one question answered, though it's no surprise. "You're the president of the Road Kill MC. *You* are in charge."

He nods. "And I got a gut feeling you ain't the one at the bottom of this. I don't know who is, but I don't want anything out of you but this—and that kid's safety." His hand cups the mound of my sex over my panties, and I go liquid. Which tells me how seriously fucked up I am.

Why am I doing this?

Oh yeah, for Calem. And to make sure Puck can capture the fucker responsible for hurting children.

But a little part of me knows that I want this virile, handsome, and fucked-up man to do everything he has planned. Just like he knows it about me, I'm sure he's not everything he seems to be, either.

Two halves of a fucked-up whole.

My idea of sex isn't really normal or vanilla anyway. And Viper keeps my wrists cuffed for more than he admits too. Somehow, on a primal level, he gets me. That should scare the shit out of me. Instead, I convince myself this furthers the end goal.

The lie sits all right with me. But sometimes lies that are fine in the moment come back to haunt a person later, like feral ghosts.

The can lights in the ceiling are dimmed to barely there illumination, and his eyes hunt mine in the darkened room.

"Tell me yes."

His hand is hot on the top of my most intimate spot. So close to my clit, a hard thought would put it there.

My heart feels like it's swelling inside my chest as I give a nod as the only sign of permission.

He rolls my yoga pants down from mid-thigh to my knees, folding my panties along with the movement, and I turn my head away until I feel them being tugged off and over my ankles.

My handcuffs clank softly against the metal of the headboard.

I suddenly realize I'm all warm and boneless. *The drugs.*

The rib has settled down, though, to a dull roar of mild throbbing instead of the shrieking agony it was.

I'm sure he'll attack the obvious, but Viper doesn't go for my pussy the way he'd implied he would. Instead, he lies down beside me, cupping my bare waist with his hand, and softly kisses my neck. Burying his face at the crook, he takes a deep inhale, breathing in the scent of my flesh.

I let out a surprised groan.

It's been years since I've been with a man. My job has been my boyfriend, and as Vince sears a path down the column of my throat then halts between my breasts, I realize it was a poor substitute. The road to my vulnerability has been paved by ignoring my basic female needs—my human ones. And that omission makes me all the weaker to what he's doing and what I feel, though I don't want to.

"Losing the bra," he says from between my breasts, and the day-old beard rasps against the tender skin.

"Okay," I breathe and almost forget my broken rib as I arch slightly so he can remove it.

The white lace cups loosen, and my breasts fall out. Vince swarms me, hands cupping breasts that are large despite how thin I am. He molds one in his right hand and squeezing, forces the tip up and high, laving it with his mouth and softly nipping the sensitive peak.

I start to pant, because breathing hard makes the sharp pain in my rib surface, and he smiles around my breast. "That's why I couldn't hurt you, knew it the minute I saw your face. Love your noises, knew you'd be fucking hot to be with, be inside of. Gotta have—" He sucks the top third of my breast into his mouth—hard—and I gasp, yanking my hands against the metal headboard, "All of you. Taste every bit."

His hands skim over my ribcage, expertly gentle over the tender area, and dive underneath my back. One large hand glides down to my rear and lifts my hips. The other lies flat under my back.

Vince moves over me, mouth hovering over mine, our noses almost touching. "Gonna bite my face off?" he asks softly.

Hadn't thought to.

I should have done a Hannibal on him, but I'm too dazed to think straight, and I shake my head, lips parting.

His eyes flick down to look at my mouth. "Fucked a lot of guys, Candice?"

He says my name for the first time, and I love the way it sounds on his tongue. But the question is so absurd, so out of the blue that I laugh. It hurts my rib, and I suck in an inhale. "No," I whisper.

His mouth lands on mine at the same time his hand leaves my butt and sweeps to the front of my bare pussy, and a finger enters me.

I gasp, hips bucking at the unexpected and delicious penetration.

Vince nibbles at my bottom lip as if he wants to eat every bit of me. Like a last meal. "Wet. Your cunt is so wet."

I kiss him back, and that taste of mint and vague scent of engine is more acute.

His finger pumps slowly inside of me, and it's amazing. I move my hips down against his hand and feel his smile against my mouth. "Perfect."

Then his mouth is off mine, and soft lips glide down from between my breasts to the divot where my navel is… then lower.

I gaze down at Viper, and somewhere along the way, he's lost his shirt, leaving only his bare chest. Strong broad planes of muscles and the outline of a six-pack are there, but he's not a super-cut man. He's all muscle.

The rhythm of his finger moving in and out of me never lets up.

My fingers uncurl around the metal bars of the headboard, hands dropping. The handcuffs give a sharp sound to the movement.

Vince's pale gaze is intense, never leaving me. It's as though we're the only people in the entire world.

Whatever he sees in my face takes us to the next level.

Withdrawing his finger, he cups my hips with both hands and draws them up as he bends down, curling his much larger body around mine.

I know what he'll do before his lips wrap my clit.

When they do, I think I'm prepared, anticipating anything. Carefully, he jerks just the lower half of my body into his face.

A loud moan sounds, and I realize it's me. I'm the one who's moaning. And I'm helpless. His hand squeezes my ass cheek, and his mouth is everywhere at once. Clit, labia, entrance. Repeat.

His tongue works my clit relentlessly, lashing it just so, and I'm sure I'll blow apart. Then the hand holding my ass sweeps to my back entrance and plugs me with a thumb.

I explode with a shriek, coming off the bed and gasping as my rib screams in agony, neatly piercing the drug haze and somehow inexplicably adding to the sharp pleasure of my orgasm.

Ribbons of pulsing sing through my core, milking his tongue and the thumb he pushed into me at the last second.

A low thrumming vibrates against my clit as he uses his voice against my most sensitive area, and I writhe underneath the pressure, coming again, my hips trying to dance on the mattress even as my rib feels like it's breaking again.

Instead of stopping the pleasure, my brain gets the pain and pleasure all confused, and the third orgasm leaves me breathless, the sensations all hopelessly crossed. Fused.

"That was so fucking hot." Vince licks my juices from his lips as he watches my scattered brain cells float back down to earth like lazy dust motes.

I only nod because I'm incapable of speech.

He removes his thumb from my ass, wipes his face with a sheet, then rises to his knees.

"Condom," I manage, but can't move a muscle. Viper stole my strength in ways he doesn't even understand.

"Bareback," he challenges. "Want to fill that hot pussy of yours to the brim with my cum."

Oh God. His hot words blaze through my skull like a brushfire.

He doesn't wait for my answer. Cupping my ass again, he tilts my hips up and lines up a sizable erection.

"Am I hurting you?" he asks suddenly.

I laugh—because of the ludicrous situation of my captor eating me out then fucking me. Because I want everything he's done and everything he's going to do. Because I know how sick that desire is.

Instead of trying to explain all that, I simply say, "No."

Vince takes me at my word and plunges his cock inside me.

What happens when a woman's had only a couple of lovers and the last one was over three years ago?

She's tight.

I groan because he feels good, but my body won't accept him, even though he tore three orgasms from me.

"Fuck, you're tight," he says, throwing himself forward. He catches his weight on his elbows, framing my face with his hands. "And gorgeous." He kisses my nose, stilling while halfway in.

I close my eyes, and he kisses my lids. It makes me want to cry.

And it makes a little of the scarring heal. The most unlikely event of my life makes ones I couldn't control a little less sharp.

Rocking into me deeper, he gets the last bit of himself in the last of me as I relax a little.

His tongue sweeps tears I didn't realize I'd shed off my face. "Don't cry, Candice."

"It feels so good, and I feel bad because it does."

"Stop talking."

He moves out of me then moves inside again slowly.

Again.

And again.

My pussy finally becomes relaxed enough to move with his thrusts, and the motion of our bodies is perfect, synchronized and natural.

"Can't last," he says, pumping faster as I lift my hips to meet his.

"Then don't," I breathe out as I meet him stroke for stroke, feeling that crushing pressure build inside me toward release.

My rib shrieks again as he rams his cock deep a final time and hits that spot deep inside me.

I arch, crying out at the pain the motion gives me, then shatter into a million jagged pieces of intense, raw pleasure.

The cords of his neck stand out as he buries his length, and I feel the throbbing of his hot cum filling me. I widen my legs to accept everything he pumps inside, and the rabid pulsing of my pussy sucks what he gives me deeper.

We are locked together in the endless loop of pleasure. His strong arms hold me tight against his body, and I feel wonderful.

Guilty. I'm horrified I fucked my captor and loved every second. Elated that I might have actually saved Calem. Ashamed at my methods.

Thrilled to be alive.

For now.

Chapter 11

Viper

Candice is exhausted. She falls asleep in the shadow of my body, arms still attached to the headboard.

The bed was my grandma's. Original to the house. It's not big because they didn't make them that way in those days. Marriage bed, she'd called it. Candice is the first woman I've had in it.

She's also the first woman I've had at the homesteader's cabin besides Colleen. The irony isn't lost on me.

Silently, I crawl backward out of the bed and admire the view of Candice Arlington.

She's a stunning woman, especially naked, which is my preferred state for females. I chuckle softly. Not an original thought, that.

I dumped my Levi's on the floor. Same style I've worn since junior high school, when I was a thirteen-year-old kid, jacking off to my old man's porn mags. Girls were a dream back then. A lot's changed since then, but the Levi's never go out of style. And they don't fall off my ass. Simple is how I like it. Mostly.

Lifting the faithful old denims off the floor, I hunt down the small key and extract it from one of the pockets before dropping the pants back on the floor. I unlock the cuffs holding Candice's sleeping form, and with agonizing slowness, I move her arms down by her sides.

She whimpers in her sleep.

I frown. Going back into a more natural position would hurt after being strung up like that.

But God *damn* if she didn't like being tied down when I had her.

My eyes run over her body. Lush tits. Beautiful pussy. She's a little thin for my tastes, but all that soft, pale skin covers muscle. The girl sees gym time—or martial arts time. That much was crystal clear when we took her from her place.

Candice was a hellcat when I came up from behind her. Could smell her fresh from the shower scent.

Smell her fear.

Turning my wrist, I check out the time—straight-up midnight. With an exhausted exhale, I walk around to the other side of the bed and, still naked, slip in beside her.

Candice Arlington can kick my ass. But for tonight, I want to pretend she can't.

The drugs I gave her are a special cocktail from Doc. Part pain meds, part sleep aide.

Candice hardly moves when I roll the hippie T-shirt down from around her wrists to just over her tits.

I tuck her in beside me.

I don't analyze why it matters if she gets cold or not—or why I shield her with my body while she sleeps.

Candice

"Miss Candi!"

The shrill young voice pierces the cocoon of warmth.

Protection.

Safety.

I try to roll over, and pain thrums through me. I gasp awake.

Memories crowd inside my head. My recent history of getting beat up, kidnapped and fucking the guy in charge of it all slides through my mind in a breathless handful of seconds.

My eyes slam open then close.

"Miss Can—!" The voice is cut off abruptly.

Arms that were secure around me leave. The bed depresses beside me, then the comforting warm weight beside me is gone.

I blink my eyes open, momentarily disoriented. Vince's basement space comes into focus, and I meet the stare of an enraged hazel gaze, like embers burning bright-green leaves.

The redhead. Storm.

Adrenaline thrills through me, and I jerk back, nearly falling out of the bed.

I suck in breath from the pain the movement cost me, and that hurts the rib worse. I want to put a hand to where it hurts.

I need both hands.

"What the fuck?" A gravelly voice says from right behind me.

Viper.

I know it'll hurt, and I do it anyway. Flashing my bare ass, I throw myself backward, coming away from the covers as Storm lands across the bed, reaching for me.

His reach is long.

Panic flares. *Can't make it.*

Strong fingers grab my shirt.

Shit!

He yanks me toward him by the collar, and I kick with everything I've got at the center of his body.

I scream, because the movement robs me of breath, and I pant, because breathing deeply isn't an option.

"Bitch!" he hisses, and his fist rises, looming for a frozen moment of time like a flesh asteroid.

Another hand captures his wrist midair. It's just as large, just as strong. A hand that was everywhere on my body just hours ago. In my body.

"Don't touch her," Viper growls.

I scoot against the pillows of the bed as a naked Viper squares off with the taller, and much younger, Storm.

Somehow, despite the size disparity, my money's on Viper.

"What the fuck, Prez?" he says in a voice gone low with anger. "Are you *fucking* her?" He sweeps his free arm at me, not bothering to look my direction.

Viper bares his teeth. "What if I am?"

Storm barks a laugh. "She's half-naked." Storm drops the arm Viper is holding and lets go. "Fuck, I'll take a crack at her if that's what we're doing—riding the pussy train." His eyebrows shoot up.

Rape. It's a multi-layered concept.

I exchanged my body for freedom, and a greater purpose. But that's different from someone *taking* something I own.

Grabbing my ankles, Storm jerks me toward him. He hurts my rib with the motion, and I scream, my fingers latching onto his throat with a vise grip, my other arm tight against my injured side.

But it wouldn't have mattered. Viper punches him in the temple.

Once.

Hard.

Storm shakes his head like a bull, trying to fling me away in the process.

I tighten my grip exactly as I'm supposed to.

Storm stops breathing, because my hands are that strong. I've worked hard to make them so.

"Candice, stop."

I find I can't. When a man means me harm, I must do him harm first.

It's just a Candice rule. I never bend it.

Viper sweeps me against him, and I have to let Storm go or risk taking him with me.

Storm has sunk to his knees. Hand at his throat, he gives Viper an accusing glare. "You hit me over a bitch."

Viper shakes his head; I feel the motion against my back. "I hit you because I'm not a rapist, and you're not gonna be, either."

He looks up at Viper. "You voted with the rest of us. You said we were going to make her talk and then get rid of her."

I must make some noise because Viper sets me down, and I can't get the shirt to pull down to cover my exposed female bits.

God.

Storm stares at me. Not at my face. At my vagina.

Viper notices and picks up my yoga pants, *sans* panties. "Put this on."

I do, as quickly as a person can with a broken rib. Not fast enough for me.

"What the fuck, Viper?" He gives me a look of blatant disgust. "Sleeping with the fucking enemy doesn't cover it, and what? You just had to get laid that bad?"

"No," Viper says. "We have the wrong woman, and things just…"

I turn and look at him, wondering at the pause in his words.

"Got away from us."

"You're saying this lethal bitch *let* you fuck her?"

I speak for the first time, hiking my chin defiantly. "I did let him fuck me."

Storm glares at me. "I want to end you. Cunts like you shouldn't be allowed to breathe air."

"She's not what you think, and we're going to let her go."

Storm's lips part. "I am not letting this evil bitch out of my sight."

We stare at each other, then I say, "I think you're overconfident. What are you? Twelve?"

He moves around the bed so fast, I barely have time to crane my neck to meet his glare.

I hold my position. Because I'm just that stubborn.

"You came into my home." I put my hand between my breasts. "Attacked me, and took a ward of the state who was in my temporary care. I reacted as I needed to." I lift a shoulder.

Shit, I've said too much.

His fists hang at his sides like hammers of punishment waiting to fall anywhere they can on my body.

But I'm not afraid.

There's nothing he can do to me that hasn't been done before. I will persevere.

I don't kid myself. Storm would do all the things his eyes promise if Viper wasn't standing at my back.

But the only male I really trust to protect me is searching frantically for me even as I stand here between two MC riders.

"And I watched you." He pokes me in my chest, hard. The gesture hurts the rib even though a foot separates the areas. "You took down a brother as you were trying to hand off a defenseless kid."

Viper steps between us, putting me protectively behind him. "That's enough. Don't ever touch her again."

I step slightly around Viper to take in the scene, and though he doesn't push me behind him again, his eyes flick to me in clear warning.

Storm meets Viper's eyes, and I feel like the valley between two volcanoes. "You gonna call church on this, Prez?" He says Viper's MC title with a sneer. "Because I got to tell ya, I think the guys aren't going to respect you even a little bit for this."

"This is my business now."

"So your business is tripping on your dick and falling into this pedophile bitch's snatch?"

He needs manners. Badly.

I take a step back and move around Viper, shoving Storm using all my weight. I don't weigh much, but training and momentum can do what lack of leverage and mass can't.

Storm staggers backward as I stop breathing from doing a stupid move like that.

Worth. It.

He roars like a demented lion and comes at me. I sidestep, taking the limb he offers as he strides toward me, and I sweep my foot.

Storm goes down and jerks me with him.

I move into the embrace, which is the exact opposite of what he anticipates. Slamming an elbow into his throat, I arrest my fall with my weight balanced on his Adam's apple.

He makes a sound somewhere between a cough and choking.

My rib is just a constant mass of grinding pain now.

Little feet race down the steps. For a moment, Calem's large brown eyes are round at the sight of a big guy on his ass, gasping for air. Then he's running to me and throwing himself into my arms.

I pick him up, doing a lot of my own gasping, hugging him.

He hugs me back, and it hurts so bad.

Feels so good.

"You don't have no clothes on, mister," Calem says to Viper.

Viper looks down at his body and snorts. "Nope," he agrees, crossing his arms.

He's wearing a wristwatch, I note. I laugh, trying to keep my eyes on his face.

His attention shifts to me. "That's incident number two"—he lifts two fingers—"that you've hurt one of my boys."

We stare at each other as Storm regains his wind on the ground.

"Only the rapists and woman-beaters. The rest you don't have to worry about."

Viper sighs. "He comes on strong."

Comes on strong? Now it's my turn to give him a disbelieving look. My rib is throbbing, and I'm starved. And Mr. Twatwaffle just got to his hands and knees. "That expression is too mild for him." I toss my thumb in Storm's direction.

"Probably."

Calem shifts in my hold, and I release him but draw him against my hip. "Stay close."

"I want to go, Miss Candi." He takes in the two men.

I look at it from his perspective. Two grown men, one naked and one obviously getting his shit together on the floor after a traumatic turn.

It's not a comfortable situation.

Viper points at Storm. "You stay away from her, and I'll take care of shit."

"That's a bad word," Calem points out.

"Yup," Vince says and grabs some jeans off the floor. He pulls them on, hiking them up, and buttons the fly, commando.

Storm stands, touching his throat. "This isn't over." His finger doesn't shake as he points it at me. "You're not going to keep running kids."

I can say this much. "I'm not. It's not what it looks like."

"Clearly," he says, gesturing at the bed with his hand. "It's so what it looks like, bitch."

"Get out." Viper jerks his chin at the door leading up the stairs. "We'll figure shit out later."

Storm gives me a final look full of dark promise.

I've seen plenty of those before. I have my own. I don't have to explain why I slept with his Prez. I would do it again.

Just not for the reasons I should.

Chapter 12

Viper

The front door to the cabin shudders in its frame as Storm slams it. The front porch steps creak, and a few seconds later, the engine of a Harley-Davidson Fat Boy bike roars to life.

Spraying gravel rains down, pinging off the steps as he flies down the long curved driveway that leads to the rural highway at the end of my drive.

His exit out of here is clear. What's not clear is why Storm came without Wring. Why he didn't text first. He's been a problem since patching in last month. Thought I could handle his style of posturing. Thought I'd seen it all. Dealt with it all.

Maybe not.

"Now what?" Candice asks.

I turn, still naked up top. Don't know where I left my shirt. *Whatever.*

I give Candice a narrow look. "You going to fight me?"

Sure the fuck hope not. I scan her body, wishing for round two.

The kid pulls on the hem of her stretched-out shirt. "Let's go," he whispers.

"Hey," I say, keeping one eye on Candice in case she tries to cold-cock me. I crouch in front of the kid. "Calem, right?"

He nods. He's got brown eyes the size of saucers in a cute face. Looks like he might have seen a few things in the past.

Probably why he got pegged by the ring of kiddie pervs—not enough folks giving shits about him to notice him disappearing.

"How about some breakfast?"

Slowly, he nods. "Ya got pancakes?"

I nod, and his gaze shifts to Candice. "Need to feed Miss Candi too."

He looks up at her. We both do.

She's tiny, even from my vantage point, crouched like I am.

"Okay." She shrugs. "With you two ganging up on me, what choice do I have?" But her face is pinched, eyes tight.

Needs more drugs.

"You scoot up there, pal," I say, "and we'll be right up after you."

Candice frowns, a question on her face.

Kid races up the stairs.

I stand, taking her into my arms before she can protest. Gently, I press my body into hers, pinning her against the wall.

"What are you doing, Viper? Just let us go. Don't try to sugarcoat what's happened."

I kiss the spot between her jawbone and collarbone. Lick it. Suck on it.

One of her hands makes its way into my short hair. "What are you doing?" Candice asks a second time.

"I'm not letting you go."

Sliding my hands under her ass, I lift her, pressing my cock between her pussy lips.

"I see that," she says breathlessly. "But I need to finish something, and I need Calem to do it."

My eyes open, and I pull her so close that a sheet of paper couldn't fit between us, touching my forehead to hers. "You're not actually working for these fucking pervs." It's part statement, part question.

"No! God no."

I hold her stare, the beautiful gold of hers unblinking. "What *are* you in this, Candice? Because I'm going to have to explain to the club why I was trying to clean up our territory and, instead, went with my gut and screwed you." I move my cheek against her like I'm scent-marking her. "And why I can't let you go, no matter who or what you are."

The moment of silence has weight, her body warm against mine.

"I can't say."

Slowly, I lower Candice to the floor. "Then there's nothing here if there isn't any trust." I move my finger between our bodies then rest a palm on the wall beside her head. Using my other hand, I pick up a piece of the darkest red hair I've ever laid eyes on, moving it between my fingers. Feels like silk. Like a woman that's not afraid of her gender. Candice might be tough, but her packaging is all female.

But I beat down a Road Kill brother for a woman we fingered as bad.

Fuck, I voted to torture and kill her. Said I was in charge of the doing of the deed. It chills me to the bone that I came *this close* to letting Storm and Wring handle it without my involvement.

I bend over her, and her hair smells vaguely of shampoo, me, and sex. The sex we had.

Pulling her into my arms, I admit, "I'm fucked up."

She pulls away just enough to tip her head back, meeting my eyes. "Not as fucked up as I am."

I search her eyes like I'm mining for treasure. If Candice Arlington is a liar, she's a damn fine one. My instincts haven't steered me wrong yet.

My fingers thread her hair, balling it into my fist, and I pull her forward, my lips crashing into hers.

Groaning, she slides her arms around my neck.

Finally, I force myself to pull away. "If you leave this place, I can't guarantee your safety. Every brother wants you dead. They think you're deep in this."

"I am deep." A single tear slides down her face.

I grip her upper arms. "Fucking tell me what the hell your role is in this."

Candice shakes her head, looking down.

"They got something on you? What is it?" *Fuck it.* "Let me protect you."

Leaning down, I put my face close to hers. Releasing her arm, I bang my palm against the wall, shaking a picture not far away. "Goddammit! Let me help you." My voice lowers to a growl.

What the fuck do they have on her?

She cups my face, and something deep inside me begins to unravel—disconcerting as fuck.

"I don't need a white knight, Vince Morgan. I need you to back down, give me time."

Running a fingertip down her neck, I slide it between her breasts. "How much time?" I whisper.

"Enough."

Our eyes lock. "Can't promise anything. The men want what you know, and they want you dead." I stick a thumb between my pecs.

"And you?" A mahogany eyebrow arches, and I have a sudden strange sensation that I've seen her before. Can't shake it. The expression niggles at my memory. I'd never forget it, though. Meeting her. I dismiss it.

"And me *what*?"

"Do you want me dead?" she whispers the question like she's afraid of the answer.

This one's easy. I shake my head. The idea of this vibrant woman not breathing makes my guts a hot, slick mass inside me. Somehow, the intensity of emotion I feel for Candice reminds me of Colleen.

And that scares me more than all of it together.

That's when I know there might be such a thing as love at first sight. Like my body chose for me. Then my brain reluctantly followed, and like a fucking traitor, my heart decided.

Unfortunately, it's not all about me. It's about what's on the line. I am the president of the Road Kill MC. It's not just a title. It's a duty.

I know what I have to do.

God knows, I don't want to. But it's the only thing I can do for now.

"No. I don't want you dead," I answer truthfully. I don't have the balls to tell her what I really want. Don't have the balls to admit it to myself.

Tension eases from her shoulders.

"Come on." I take her hand. "Since you're not up to kicking my ass, let's go eat pancakes."

Candice doesn't say anything, just takes my hand and follows me up the stairs.

Candice

I'm terrified.

Not of what might happen, having a broken rib, or the mess with Storm.

The fear comes from how I feel. How Viper makes me feel. That's why I need to get the hell out of here.

I don't want to do what I must. But I will.

Vince moves around the kitchen without a shirt on and barefoot. Confident.

He's hot. Virile. He's everything I thought I'd never find in a man, and in the most unlikely of places.

If someone had told me I would have scorching chemistry with a man that was part of—*no*—in charge of a motorcycle club, I would have asked them how much crack they'd been smoking.

Not even the explanation of them keeping their territory undefiled is enough to justify their processes. The FBI suspects Road Kill of gunrunning.

As I watch Viper make pancakes for a woman he kidnapped, I try on the perspective of him as a biker. And can't make who he's been with me fit with what the reality is. That's when I know I've made the one, critical mistake.

Caring.

I only see the human being, not the suspect.

Sadness wells up inside me, with no place to go. When I close my eyes, I can still feel his body moving inside me. The expression on his face was brutally tender. A mixture of lust, sadness, and joy. I don't know why he has that mix of emotions, but it was like I was looking in a mirror.

Like Viper finally found what he was looking for, and in the process, so did I.

"Hey," Viper says, plopping a stack of pancakes in front of me, "you okay?"

I shake my head, saying what I can. "Rib hurts like hell."

Fate is a bitch, my mind whispers.

Viper snaps his fingers. "I'll take you to Doc. He'll tape it. Make it feel more stable." His eyes meet mine. "There's no fixing the rib if it's broken." He looks out the window, eyes to the drive. "Goddamned Storm."

"Yeah, I know." *Of course I do.*

Viper's eyebrows lower over his eyes. "You been injured like this before?"

I cut the pancakes instead of looking at him. "Yes."

A couple seconds of silence beat the hell out of the moment.

His large hand flattens beside my plate. It's blurry through tears I won't shed.

"Want to talk about it?"

I pour the syrup over the stack and watch the pat of butter mix with the amber liquid. "Not really." I take a shallow breath, memories assailing me.

"Little slut, you come, or I'll break another one."

My pussy seems to accept the command, and deep pulses shock me as I lay beneath his pounding assault. Too tired to breathe.

Too exhausted to fight.

Like Pavlov's dog, I know what happens if I do what he says, and I want the reward of his absence with such raw need that my body does what he says so I don't have to think about the horror of what's happening to me. So I can escape it.

So he'll go away.

There's nothing as good as that.

Then Puck's there, dragging our father off me. Puck gets beaten, saving me from round two and another broken rib.

That time.

Eventually, there comes a time when Puck's the one doing the beating, and our horror of a sperm donor never touches me again.

Then Puck takes me far away from that man. The man who helped create me.

The man who murdered me without a weapon.

Murdered us both.

I stuff a bite of pancake in my mouth and mechanically chew it.

Viper lifts his hand, and he comes around the counter, slowly spinning the stool I sit on. Gripping the sides, he cages me with his strong hands, staring into my face.

I swallow the load.

Releasing the stool, he captures my face in his hands. "I don't know what's wrong, but I know there's something in there." He presses a soft touch to the center of my forehead. "Something I want to make better." His eyes catch mine again. "Erase."

His pale-blue eyes hold a care for me inside them they shouldn't.

He has no right to care about me.

Never in my life have I wanted so badly to cry. My throat and the backs of my eyes burn with tears. My soul's on fire. Fire to have someone besides my brother love me and not hurt me.

I put myself back together in pieces, like picking up shards of glass and gluing the whole mess back together again.

And Viper watches it all. "No, goddammit," he says quietly. "Don't you hide from me, Candice Arlington."

"It's Candi," I say softly.

He drags me off the stool and into his arms. I let him. And a part of me dies, thinking about what comes next.

Because it has to.

This is bigger than me. It's bigger than all of us.

I have his trust. Because he's just that instinctive. During the short time we've known each other, Viper's read something in me that no one else could. And now he's going to regret that, second-guess himself.

I hate that he will. For the first time in my life, I've felt something real. And I want to grab at it in case that beautiful thing disappears.

But it's like smoke in my hand.

Turning my head, I lay my cheek against his bare chest. "Thank you." My voice only trembles a little, but the sincerity of my gratitude is completely genuine. So deep, there's no end.

He steps away, and a slight frown mars the space between his eyes. "For what?"

I tip my head back to look up at him.

For what. "For believing in me."

His laugh is rueful. "Never had much of a choice. You kinda ran right over the top of me."

"Yeah." I know exactly what he means.

Chapter 13

Puck

*C*andi, oh my God! I can't find you. I slam my fist on the wheel of my car and scream my rage into the tight space.

I'll kill the fuckers that hurt her.

She's more than family. Candi's my best friend. My partner in crime—against crime. My confidant.

The only blood worth having.

"Jesus, how did this job get so fucked up?"

I toss my head back against the car seat, taking deep breaths. Drumming my fingers lightly on the steering wheel, I try to think things through.

"She was on her way to the drop with the kid."

My head jerks up. I grab my cell and utter into the voice-to-call feature, "Mule."

It rings.

I pray that somehow Candi can answer.

More ringing.

My heart sinks.

Fuck.

I tap End Call.

Clenching my eyelids, I grate, "Mover."

It rings and is snatched up almost immediately. "Mover," his smooth baritone answers.

What is it with people who answer the phone and say their own name? Is it an ego stroke or what?

"Mule's late for the switch."

"I'm sorry. This isn't the best time to discuss recipes."

Read: Cell's not secure.

Fuck me running.

"I'm missing a key ingredient."

After a heartbeat of silence, Mover says, "I've just been made aware."

"Let's talk about the cooking in, say…" *Right now!* "As soon as I can get to the club."

"I am at your disposal."

I bet.

I tap End Call.

Feeling numb, I back out of Candi's driveway and head over to the Chaos Riders Clubhouse. I won't be undercover after this stint. I'm never doing it again. Candi and I will *not* be used by our respective law enforcement entities ever again.

Shit just got real.

We've lost ourselves. And now she's in trouble.

We were only able to be what we are today because the file on the shit that happened when we were young is sealed. We both squeaked by psyche exams, somehow.

Probably were so determined to get over our past, we faked it until we made it.

Hang on, Candi. I'm coming.

Viper

She's hiding something.

Not the sort of thing a person would assume. It's about more than her real role within this rat's nest of crime against the kids.

It's something about *herself*. On a personal level. But I've done all I can in our brief acquaintance to fuck things up *and* make things right.

Sort of contrary.

I loaded up on a plate of carb discs. And that kid? Holy shit. He ate almost as much as me. Couldn't believe it. Took down an entire bottle of my best maple syrup between the three of us.

Finally, I stretch, giving Candice a circumspect look. *She gonna bolt? Or will she decide to stick around.*

Fuck it, as Noose says. "I'm going downstairs. Going to toss my shit on."

Calem looks at me.

"Clothes and shoes," I expound.

"Everyone saw you naked, even Miss Candi." His small eyebrows pop.

Marvelous. "Well, all my stuff was on the floor."

"Why was it on the floor?" Calem sets his fork on top of his plate, giving me his full attention.

Shit. "'Cause I was working on getting changed."

"Huh."

Candi turns her face away, hiding a smile.

Glad I can be amusing. I'm just amusing the hell out of everyone. In fact, why haven't the three musketeers—or four, if I count Snare—been blowing up my phone with texts?

I pat down my jean pockets.

Ah. That's why. Phone's downstairs on my nightstand.

"Stay here." I point at Candice.

She lifts her palms, trying to look innocent.

I think of going to town on her delicious pussy.

Our eyes lock.

Nope. Beautiful. Mysterious. *Not* innocent.

"I'll be waiting."

I'm back up there in about five seconds—boots and socks in one hand, cell shoved in my back pocket, and shirt slammed over my head.

"Nice shirt."

It's solid black but faded from wear. Scrawled across the front in fancy cursive lettering it reads Fucks Given, with a fat arrow pointing to the right underneath the two word phrase.

We both look at Calem.

Maybe he's too young to sound that shit out.

Gingerly, Candice slides off the stool, hand going to her side.

"Need help?"

A smile quirks her lips. "I'll be okay, just moving slow. That thing with Storm didn't help."

Yeah. "Know it. Had a different agenda before…"

Candice says, "Before?"

"Just before." I don't offer additional explanation. Fuck, there's no explaining anything, especially when even I don't know what the hell I'm doing.

Sitting down on the edge of the oldest couch in the universe, I pull on my socks, stuff my feet into my beat-up black boots, and zip.

Standing, I shrug on my cut I always hang on a wire hook right next to the door leading down to the basement.

"You'll freeze."

"We're not going on a bike?"

I shake my head then jerk my jaw toward the kid, who's commandeered my ancient TV.

Fucking kids and tech. It's like they're born knowing how.

There was about ten text messages on my phone and two missed calls.

Half are from Noose.

If anyone can find out more about Candice Arlington, it's him.

And I've got vested interest now.

"Come on," I say and walk to a dinky closet my grandma would've called an armoire. It holds shit like coats and that. But it's worth much more to me because it's a family piece.

Opening the cabinet door, I jerk a puffy coat off the hanger.

"It's not that cold," she protests.

Ignoring her, I thrust it her way. "Humor me. Just put the thing on."

That's all I need—a starving, cold, unsatisfied female. Come to think of it, I've ticked off a lot of things on the do-right-by-a-woman boxes.

Except throwing her into walls. That shit'll haunt a man.

Candice slips on the charcoal-colored jacket then flaps her arms up and down. The sleeves are about half a foot too long. The length hits her mid-thigh.

"This yours?"

I nod. "Don't wear it much. Mainly for doing outside work around here."

She looks around for a full minute, and though I want to get the fuck out of Dodge, I wait through her perusal.

I'm already catering to the Power of the Pussy. *Swell.*

"This is so real."

Okay. Not what I was expecting.

Candice looks at me watching her. Blushes. "I mean, it feels like this little house just grew out of the ground."

Kind of did. "My great-grandpa built the entire thing with one cedar tree."

Her head whips to mine. "Really?"

I nod.

"That's really something."

I nod then say quietly, "Let's go."

She touches the injured rib absently and turns to the kid. "Let's go, Calem."

He shuts off the TV and walks over to her. She takes his hand.

I stare. Can't help noticing her hands are barely bigger than his.

But I remember perfectly what they felt like on my throat. And the clear image of them pinching Storm's throat.

I'm clearly insane.

And there isn't one of the men that won't question my rationale about Candice Arlington.

Hell, *I'm* questioning it.

Hardcore.

Candice doesn't like the blindfold, but I have to do at least that much.

Instead of complaining like I expect, though, she peppers me with questions about the house. My family.

I try to keep my eyes on the road instead of her lips. Harder than I think it'll be.

She seems strangely interested in all my history but doesn't ask any questions about the club.

Not one.

By the time we get to the club, I'm talked out. Especially with what I know will be waiting.

But first, Storm's going to get a first-class dressing down.

That fucker is not going to be the circus trainer in my act. If he ever comes to my house unannounced again and doing the helicopter with his dick, I'll fuck him right up—brother or not.

I slip out of my souped-up black SUV and walk slowly around to the passenger side to take off Candice's blindfold.

"Stealthy." She blinks in the bright sunlight, shading her eyes with a palm.

"As I already said, at best, we have an uneasy alliance."

"At worst?"

My eyes trail to the front door of our refurbished World War II bunker. Sun glints off the top, sprinkling diamonds of light everywhere it refracts. The old ladies insisted on a greenhouse thing.

They made good on it, too. They got after the perimeter of the club too, river rock creating a loose border, and wildflowers blooming between building and stone.

The guys bitch about the vagina look, but I chuckle. I'm old enough to appreciate the beauty—and damn happy I didn't have to do it.

I have plenty of jobs. Wrangling the boys is like corralling headless chickens.

"This had to be you." Candice takes in the details that personalize the club.

I like old shit. Repurposing it, restoring it and enjoying the result. Then I'm on to the next project.

I'm not liking how insightful she is. There's also something so unique about *what* she notices.

I'll add being bright to the list of things that are beginning to stand out about Candice Arlington. It doesn't give me answers—her attributes only deepen the mystery. That only makes me more, not less, determined to find out who she is.

Finally, after studying the structure for every bit of three minutes in silence, she asks, "Is this going to be an interrogation?"

Can't lie. "Yes."

"Okay." The wistful longing leaves her eyes. Indifference slides in, taking its place.

"Is he going to be okay?" She looks to Calem, and he's already tumbled out of the big rig and puts his hand in hers.

"Yes," I turn to her. "I've already told you Road Kill's stake in this. Nobody's going to piss in our Wheaties—or hurt kids."

We're at the front door. "There'll be an old lady here." I jerk my jaw in the direction of the door. "One of them will watch the kid—Calem."

Candice turns back and surveys the SUV, an oddity with all the bikes lined up on either side of the only non-bike in the parking lot area.

Straightening her spine, she turns back to me.

I notice her eyes tighten from the pain as I open the door for her and Calem. As we step inside, the noise is the usual slap in the face.

Chapter 14

Candice

I'm trying not to analyze my actions. But it's not going down easy.

I fucked up. I'm not so deep undercover that I had to have sex with the president of the rival MC that I'm using to locate a human trafficker. *Nope.* Wasn't that desperate. Didn't have to play that card.

I won't lie to myself.

I wanted him. *Viper.* Plus, he offered my release in exchange. And I trusted he would let me go.

Dumb or intuitive? We'll see.

However, here I am, supposedly to get my rib taped. But now that medical "fix" has become the vehicle for his band of badass bikers to give me the third degree.

I'd rather not see Storm again. There's only so many ways a woman can surprise a man who outweighs her by a hundred pounds. No matter my skills, I'm still small. And that disparity is never more glaring than when I'm in the middle of a hand-to-hand situation.

A young woman runs up to us wearing a leather cut like the other bikers, but fitted to a woman's figure.

I know she's an old lady because of her clothes. Usually—but not always—the old ladies have an air of sexy with a streak of slutty. The club whores of the MC persuasion just can't seem to get there. It's all slutty with a streak of cheap—and that's being kind.

This girl has straight long platinum hair and pale-green eyes. A little boy, maybe somewhere around eighteen months or so, rides her slim hip. Her vest has a patch that reads, Wring's Property.

"Hi," she says. "I'm Shannon." She looks at the little toe head on her hip with eyes so light blue, they're almost white, and a pang of sadness tinged with regret shears through me before I can stop it. "And this is Duke." She smiles at him, and Duke gives a toothy grin back.

"That's quite a name for a baby," I say, smiling despite the circumstances.

She nods. "You haven't met the dad." Shannon gives a slight eyeroll as she waits for me to tell her who I am.

The silence swallows the moment, and I finally say, "I'm Candi."

Shannon's face jerks back. "You don't look like a Candi."

"I get that a lot." I smirk.

"I like your real name," Vince says.

I turn to him but don't tell him Candice actually isn't my real name. "Thanks."

"So…" Shannon says slowly, eyeballing Calem, me, and Vince, an obvious question on her face.

"Candice was hurt. Got in the middle of something." Vince's explanation is economical. Sufficient. Not a complete lie as lies go.

"With Storm," I add.

Vince gives me a sharp look.

Like a perfect volley, I give him one that says, *Tough.*

Shannon's nose scrunches. "Storm," she says with distaste.

"Shannon," Vince says like a warning.

Hmm.

She holds up a slim palm. "I know, I know—he's a *brother*." She tacks on pointedly, "Now."

But I can tell somebody's not loving Storm as part of the troupe.

Vince ignores the undercurrent by smoothly changing the subject. "Would you watch Calem here for a little while?" Vince touches Calem's shoulder.

Calem's too busy trying to look everywhere at once to notice.

"I'd love to." Shannon's face lights up as she turns to Calem. "Hey," she says to get Calem's attention, "have you read *Where the Wild Things Are*?"

Calem blinks up at her, shaking his head.

Probably never been read to in his short life.

"I used to work at a library and read to kids just like you. They really liked that book. Let's go read that." Shannon doesn't take no for an answer, taking him by the hand.

Calem lets himself get hauled away.

He only looks back at me once.

I pause, give a wave.

"We'll go see Doc now."

Viper doesn't say anything more, just turns and walks toward the back of the building.

I follow.

I've got to call Puck. I've been missing for hours now. But how can I do anything right now?

At least the handoff time hasn't been compromised yet. Though it's only hours away. If I can't get with Puck, we won't be able to swing it.

Who am I kidding, thinking I can make a sting work when we've been compromised to death? Still, I hold out hope. I wanted this guy so bad I could taste it. Or maybe it was that Puck and I wanted the closure.

Vince knocks on a door that has the name Doc on it, with a red placard directly underneath the lettering that depicts McDonald's golden arches on first glance, but really is a parody.

Classy. This is the guy who's going to fix me. Ah-huh.

Vince walks through, and Doc pushes away from a desk with an enormous computer screen on it.

He seems flustered, finger-combing a shock of white hair back from his face. "Hey, Viper."

"Doc."

His slightly buggy eyes take me in behind glasses too large and round for his face.

I must look worse for wear. My yoga pants are dirty, and my Jimmy Buffet tie-dyed shirt is stretched at the neck from that loser Storm.

Doc chuckles, checking out my T-shirt. "I went to that concert." His eyes narrow on me. "That was forever ago. You don't look old enough to have been there."

I inhale as deeply as I dare then let it out slow. "I am—I was."

We stare at each other and Doc cocks his head. "What's wrong with her?"

"Doc, this is Candice Arlington." Viper stumbles awkwardly over the next fact. "Think Storm broke her rib."

Doc's bushy eyebrows sail almost to his hairline. "Why would he do that to a woman?"

Why indeed.

Viper downplays it. Or tries. Pretty hard to explain that kind of treatment. "There was a mix-up, and some reactions got away from people." Clearly, he's not going to explain the trafficking to Doc. Must be above his security clearance.

Viper and I exchange a loaded glance.

Doc sharpens his expression for a moment then turns to me again. "You go by Candice?"

"Mostly."

"I'm Doc," he says, putting out his hand.

I'm careful with shaking. Rib seems to hurt worse as the day goes on. Feels like someone shredded my side.

Taking a deep inhale isn't an option.

"I can tell you're in a lot of pain just by the way you're holding yourself."

"Yeah," I say.

"I have some class-A narcotic action that will dull that shit. Dial it down so it's not riding you like a monkey on crack."

I blink. He does have a way with words. But I can't have drugs and stay sharp. Not if I'm meeting a bunch of pissed-off bikers. Viper offered painkillers earlier after pancakes, and I declined.

If my inhibitions fail me, what if I let something slip? I could compromise the investigation—and Puck. "Thanks…" I hesitate, thinking about how great the pills that Viper gave me were. Just a little bit of time nearly pain-free is tempting. "But I don't think so," I finally say.

"Candice," Viper starts, "let him give you something."

I state the truth. "I can't protect myself if I'm high on medicine." And by God, I've clearly needed to "bring it" lately.

He turns me with gentle hands until we're facing each other. "Do you think any of my men are going to hurt you?"

I've never had this kind of eye contact before. Aggressive. Intense. Sincere.

Lingering like a caress.

I close my eyes against what I see, too scared to believe. I don't know if I can survive the erosion of the careful walls I've erected around the castle of my heart.

For anyone.

But he's doing it, stone block by stone block. Viper keeps doing things that make me question everything I've always been sure of.

"Let's see what we have here," Doc interjects quietly, looking between the two of us.

"Okay." I sound as weary as I feel.

Doc leads me to a classic exam table. Clean white paper has already been drawn over its surface and pinched at one end with a bar made for holding the paper in place.

"Can you get up there?"

I nod, carefully hiking a butt cheek up. I press my palm into the platform and heave.

Gasping through the pain, I try to do a version of the movement on the other side but can't.

Viper is suddenly there. He slides his palms underneath my ass and lifts me easily, gently scooting me back.

"There, stubborn wench." He winks.

I smile.

"Okay, Prez." Doc moves up beside him.

Viper reluctantly retreats, and Doc takes his place. Gentle hands work underneath my shirt. When he gets to the rib, I flinch, and his fingers still.

"Not a bad break," he says offhandedly.

"What?" I scowl.

He harrumphs. "It's a fracture. They hurt about the same but heal up much faster. You'll feel better in about three weeks."

Doc rifles around in a drawer next to the table and gets out a stiff, gauze-like material, which he uses to wrap my rib. "This doesn't work anymore. Only time heals ribs. But it'll feel stiffer—allow movement. Or some movement."

Three weeks.

Closing my eyes, I sort of sway at the thought of this level of pain management for nearly a month.

"Candice," Viper says in a low voice.

Without opening my eyes, I say, "I have to do things. I can't afford to be injured."

"Tell me."

My eyes open, and we stare at each other. "No."

He slams his fist on the table, and Doc takes a couple of steps back.

Wise man.

"That's not going to be good enough for my men. They'll want to know what role you play in all this debauched bullshit."

I lean into him, our faces nearly touching. "Then they'll have to kill me to do it."

"Fuck!" Viper yells and spins on his heel, pacing the small room, giving me his broad back.

"Who is she, Viper?" Doc asks. "Who'd I just patch up—that Storm lost his cool so badly he fractured her rib? I'm kind of old-school for beating on women. Doesn't sit right."

"That's just it," Viper says to Doc, but he looks at me, "I don't *know* who she is."

Doc shakes his head, wispy hair creating a crisp halo effect around his head. "This ain't good."

I dismount from the table very carefully. The rib squawks, but moving is easier with it taped. Maybe this will see me through the worst of the next grueling set of circumstances.

I just have to get through this last handoff—if it can be salvaged.

"Where do you think you're going?" Viper seethes, blocking my way to the door.

"You've called church, right?"

He gives a terse nod. "Let's face the music."

A rattling sound comes from behind me. Doc is holding up an orange bottle with pills inside. "I wouldn't face that firing squad unless I was lit up like a firebug."

There is some logic there.

But can I trust Viper not let them pound me? His eyes are steady on mine.

He was so tender with my body that I *cannot* envision him watching me get abused, but stranger things have happened.

Like when the one man in the entire world who should have been my champion, my protector, *was* my abuser.

The sooner I get this over with, the sooner I can get out of here, pick up a burner, and phone my brother.

Doc hands me a bottle of water and two pills.

Viper glowers.

I toss them back, swig it down, and brush past him toward the door.

His hand lands on the nape of my neck, and he's so much larger than me that his fingers almost meet at the hollow of my throat.

Our gazes collide.

"Let me get the door for you." He opens it, sweeping it wide, and releases my neck.

"I'm old-fashioned that way, Candice," he says to my back. "I'll always open the door for a lady."

His voice is a slow, lazy drawl. But his words burn themselves into my brain like acid, trenching my consciousness, tears filling my eyes.

How long has it been since anyone *saw* me?

Got me?

Treated me like someone with value beyond serving their purposes?

A man who runs a bike club. That's who.

I swipe wetness from my cheeks and slow. When Vince makes up the few strides that separated us, he walks beside me.

Like an equal.

And I can't feel worse.

Problem is the Bureau comes first. And I must finish this. I just wish, just one time, that *I* could come first.

We move through the center of the club, and at this time of day, it seems to have more of a family atmosphere. I see Shannon reading to Calem, her toddler at her feet.

Other old ladies are chatting away. But when I walk by with Viper, they stop and stare.

It tells me a couple of things.

One: the president gets noticed.

Two: he must not take a lot of women through the club.

Ignoring them as best I can, I make it all the way to the other side of the building. Vince goes to a solid wood door, opens it, and strides through.

I follow him and am met by a sea of hostile eyes.

Worst thing? I'm starting to feel the effects of the drugs. It's great that the pain's receded. But my smart ass mouth has even less of a filter.

And the result of that might be more than I can recover from.

Chapter 15

Puck

My anxiety about Candi is making me rash as fuck. *I know this.*

If there hadn't been blood and puke at her house, I might be able to calm my tits.

So I'm sweating literal bullets as I cruise up the driveway to the new Chaos digs.

We had an old building before we got made. Cops swarmed up our ass like a hive of angry wasps, stinging and sniffing around until we had to change the profile of the club. Of course, they didn't know I was one of them.

Mover spearheaded a mess of a relocation and putting the club back together again after the flesh trader, Ned, was killed.

Because Mover's a feebie. Good for him. Well, it's time to confer on the hard facts as they sit now. We've never spoken about our mutual purpose because we haven't been granted the clearance to work together. Though the mutual purpose is different, when it comes to Candi. She—I'll break rules for. Especially with kids at stake.

It's unbelievable to me, but that's big government. Supposedly, you have two lawmen working toward the same end goal.

But can we share information?

No.

Can we team up?

Hell no.

So addressing the case directly would mean breaking all the unspoken rules in the world.

But Candi's in trouble. And there's no life for me without her in it.

I park the Camaro and slip out the door. Slapping my hand on the manual lock, I close the door then stuff the keys into my jean's pocket.

Striding to the door, I can't help but notice the similarities between the rival clubhouses of Chaos and Road Kill. Yeah, I know where Road Kill MC has their clandestine meetings—"church."

Definitely picked the right club. Don't think Road Kill is doing much but gunrunning. And in today's world, that's almost not important enough to worry about.

Sex trafficking is the hot ticket now. It's the criminal offense that gets all the law entities spun up and engaged.

Actually, it should've always been the focus. Saving the future generation *now*, before they're running the country and all fucked up because we didn't give a shit when it mattered, has to be a good solution. *Let's be preemptive, guys.* Let's do the right fucking thing for once.

I open the solid steel door, and it swings outward slowly, revealing the beating heart of the club.

Looks like a heart attack waiting to happen from where I stand. But I'm used to the decadence of the place, where at any moment, there's a half-naked female draped over furniture or getting done by a brother.

Alcohol flows like a river. Music is so loud, it vibrates through the soles of my boots.

And secrets are guarded like a living, breathing treasure.

I wade through the bodies of people having sex or boozing and remain focused on the door at the end of the building. Easy to see despite the smoke haze, it's also solid steel. And soundproof.

Thumbing the latch, I push it open.

Mover sits at the head of a long table.

The table doesn't have any significance like the others at some MCs. It's just a meeting table for bodies to sit around—sixteen in all.

The banquet size suits the length of the room. Made of brushed aluminum, it's light and doesn't rust, so cigarettes and booze rings don't mar the surface.

"Puck," Mover says in partial greeting, loosening his tie.

He has a fantastic bike, but he's always meeting buyers for every illicit thing he can think of—and things he can't. Mover believes that, somehow, if he dresses formally, it makes him better.

I know the lie, though. I've lived it.

My father was rich. And having more money didn't mean he was more handsome or better than the rest of humanity.

It just meant he could do more harm, hiding his filth behind a polished exterior.

"Mover," I return in clipped greeting.

There's another brother standing next to him. Figures it's got to be the one I hate the most.

A couple of bikers were taken out a few years back when a young woman escaped. *What was her name? Oh yeah. Sara.*

She was very resourceful. Too bad she didn't get to this dirtbag.

Dave, aka Dagger, wasn't around to get killed. He was out scouting new female flesh at the time. He'd taken a leave of absence for almost a year after that handy debacle. But here he is, like a bad penny, just tarnishing up the whole fucking place.

Dagger had a case of acne when he was a teenager, and the pockmarks litter his face like empty craters. His hair is somewhere between true black and brown, swept back from his face like a wash of dirty coffee. His eyes are the same mud-brown color as his hair.

Right now they're narrowed on me like two, hate-filled slits.

Feeling's mutual, douche.

"Dagger, I think Puck has some pressing items to discuss."

Another thing I can't stand about Mover—he's a fucking four-dollar word user. It's not so much that he uses words beyond my ability to understand. It's the way he forms his sentences.

Like his shit doesn't stink. Haughty fuck.

"Yeah, that's right," I say, neatly dismissing Douche Nozzle Dagger.

He glares, walking toward me like a swift current.

Our chests stand a hard thought away from contact.

"You got a problem?" he grits.

Fuck, so many. Beginning with my sister being MIA. "Yeah, but not enough time to deal with them all."

"Dagger," Mover says with a bell-like warning in that one word.

He turns, giving Mover a few seconds of attention. "Fine, Prez."

Dagger turns back to me. We're eye-to-eye, and at over six feet, he's a tallish man.

Unlike me, he's not lean and athletic. He's just big, heading toward fat, but in the meantime, there's enough size to be a problem. And I don't fucking need another one.

My feelings are very close to the surface, like a ripple of water away from rinsing my carefully maintained exterior.

"Sometimes, there ain't gonna be anyone but you and me, *Puck*," he says with such force a tiny bit of spittle beads on his lower lip, and his thick tongue swipes over the area.

My revulsion kicks into gear. "Anytime, Dagger. You name the time, the place—and we go."

Dagger's hands ball into fists at his side.

"Children," Mover says in a droll voice.

Dagger's eyes tighten, but he steps back, then clips my shoulder as he brushes past. He slams the door on the way out.

Dick.

Some clubs have men who are truly brothers. The camaraderie overtakes the petty differences that are always there between human beings and the testosterone-fueled MC life.

Not Chaos Riders.

Of course, because their very purpose is to go against authority and because they have rules only one percent of the population follows, biker clubs are probably the height of dysfunction. But if there's one thing I've always believed in it's that normal is a setting on the dryer.

I catch Mover's eyes as soon as Dagger is through the door and gone. "We need to talk."

Mover leans back in a seat that swivels and is comfy for his kingly ass.

"Oh?"

"Yes, I had things to say earlier—"

"I was indisposed."

I plant my legs apart and cross my arms, teeth clenched. "What is that supposed to mean?"

His lips curl.

Heat flows through me. I'm not one of those guys who gets pissed without a physical outlet. Plenty of shit will happen if I get pissed off enough. Like now. "I know what the fuck the word means, Mover—and I know you weren't taking a growler."

He pushes with his feet, rolling the chair backward and gaining enough distance between us to stand. "No. But I was cinching a delicate deal, and you know how I detest cell communication." Walking slowly around the end of the twelve-foot-long table, he drags a trailing fingertip along the surface. "Cell devices—so untrustworthy. So easily compromised."

In that, we agree.

Of course we would—seeing as I'm a cop and he's FBI. And we're so deep undercover, we can't see daylight.

Mover's eyes find mine. His are a strange color somewhere between gray and blue. Slate. Hard like flint. Cold like steel. Just enough blue to make them glitter in the low light of the room.

"I assume there's been a problem with the merchandise?"

This is the hard part. "Yeah. Bitch didn't show."

"You can drop the act, Puck. It's just us."

He can't know Candi is my sister. "This isn't an act. We might have different directors in this little orchestra we're playing in together"—I swing my finger between us—"but our goals are identical."

He lifts his chin, bare of whiskers. Another novelty of a MC president—no beard. "True."

"The bitch," I say with emphasis, "because that's what she is, *didn't* make the drop."

Mover stills. "This was the final piece of the elaborate puzzle. The one thing that would nail this bastard to the wall. We may be disallowed from working directly together, that's true, but we wished for the same outcome."

I just said that. My shoulders sink. Maybe there *is* some commonality, after all. Maybe I've grossly misjudged Mover because feds and cops don't mix— oil and water. "Yes," I say, unable to contain my relief. "The perp identified this kid specifically for the man pulling the strings. The one in charge of this sick ring wants *this* particular boy."

"Calem Oscar," Mover says, almost absently, lines of clear disgust marking his face like brands.

Yanking my hair tie from my nape I snap the elastic band between my fingers. "Got to find the woman. She's the key to all this." My palms dampen.

"I do wish that Vince and I could come to terms finally." Mover states out-of-the-blue.

"Does he know your role?"

Mover shakes his head. "Not fully—though he's very aware that I'm an undercover law player." His eyes lock with mine. "That you are."

I search his face. "You know something." He just switched gears from Candi to the Road Kill prez.

Mover smiles. "It is an interesting feature you possess, Puck—ascertaining the thoughts of others so quickly."

Right away, his words spark a memory.

"Puck! Get that whore of a sister to me right now."

The force of the blow rocks my fourteen-year old face back, blasting blood out of a nose hit too often to heal in between strikes.

Candi is no whore. "I don't know where she is," I seethe, spitting blood onto the imported marble flooring.

He stares at my face, searching for the lie. I know from experience that my face shows nothing.

I stare back, giving away nothing.

"I can't tell if you're lying anymore, Puck." He grabs my throat, hauling me close, and I go up on my tiptoes so I don't get strangled right then. "Can you tell if I am?" His mouth makes a cruel sneer.

Yes, I can tell.

Because the truth is so seldom and everything is mostly lies, discerning others' thoughts becomes basic deductive reasoning.

"Where did you go?" Mover's eyes scrutinize my expression.

My gaze shifts away from his probing look. "Just remembering." My purpose floods me. "Tell me what you know—for once, I don't want to pretend. I want this to be over."

"Only if it benefits the end. After all, the woman isn't important. Only the boy. It's he who will see this vile human apprehended. The boy's presence is the key."

I know this.

I also know Mover isn't aware Candi is deep undercover. That's not the way undercover works, even within the same law entities.

"I have a mole in Road Kill MC. Somehow, they intercepted Dagger for the handoff. He's looking into it."

Stepping back, I shake my head. "What? Dagger— what—didn't show up?"

This is what I was worried about.

"He showed up and was promptly bludgeoned for his efforts. Woke up a short time later with quite a lump." Mover raps his knuckles on his head.

"How's Road Kill MC involved?"

"He woke and managed to get to the rendezvous just as a crowd of civilians was flocking around the riders like disgruntled birds. Those dots were simple to connect."

Great. Witnesses. I grab my chin, rubbing my thumb over the day-old stubble. "It's got to be a territory thing."

"No doubt they've got the same intel we do, and they're attempting to squelch the child trafficking in their own way, for entirely different reasons."

"Yeah." I sigh, tearing my fingers through my hair and retying it with an irritated tuck and pull. "They don't want a load of bullshittery moving in and fouling up their backyard. That's what it's really about."

Mover's neatly shaped pewter brows sweep low. "And do *we*?"

"Fuck no," I reply instantly.

Our eyes meet.

He spreads his arms, the cuffs of his jacket sliding up to reveal cufflinks, the gesture clearly saying, *"Exactly."*

So Road Kill MC has Candi.

They have my sister, and they don't know she's FBI. They think she's the mule for this operation.

"I need to go," I tell Mover. A surge of pounding adrenaline streaks through me like molten lightning, making my feet and hands tingle.

He gives a slight shake of his head. "We need the merchandise at the meeting point. It's a rough handoff without fanfare, but given the circumstances of the botched initial engagement, there's a chance to salvage this if the woman can be located and the boy presented."

Mover lifts his hand and makes a fist. "We are this"—he puts his index finger and thumb nearly touching—"close to reconciling this, Puck."

In this moment, he's not a fed, and I'm not a cop anymore. We're just two men wanting the same thing.

Protecting the young.

Chapter 16

Viper

I lightly touch Candice's arm. She halts. Letting my instincts fan out, I take in the feel of the room. Pretty hostile.

Storm half-stands from his usual chair, eyes on Candice.

I point at him. "You're already on my shit list. Don't dig it deeper."

He reluctantly plants his ass again, sullen eyes still glued to her.

Noose is perched against the wall, one boot on the wood paneling, obviously favoring his knee.

Ignoring his hooded eyes, I haul Candice by the arm behind me as I make my way swiftly to where I usually sit at the head.

But I don't sit today. I stand, and Candice stands beside me.

Voices erupt all at once.

Picking up the beat-up gavel, I whack it once on the wooden disc on the table.

The rumble of chatter settles then stops.

"I think I'm speakin' for most when I ask: what in the absolute fuck, Vipe?" Noose's charcoal gaze meets mine.

This is where internal fortitude gets tested. I'm going to really fuck with my men now. I know I'll be fucking with me too before the words ever leave my mouth.

"I'm throwing down for Candice," I announce in a low, clear voice.

Candice tenses at my words, and I don't react.

Noose's boot falls with a thunk, then he slowly walks to me, the barest limp marring his saunter. "Are you fucking insane?" he asks in a loud articulate voice.

"Stand down, King," I reply, using his last name for the first time.

I'm not sure we won't go.

It's Candice's reaction that's interesting, interrupting the growing tension. "You don't need to do this, Viper," she says in that calm way of hers I'm coming to love.

Thing is—I do love it. For reasons I can't even make sense of. We fit. We work. And I haven't had that happen but one other time. My gut says she's innocent, and that deep, core-level intuition has never let me down. In fact, listening to my instincts has saved my ass more times than I can count.

The brothers will have to trust me.

"Viper, *not* this woman. Anybody else—hell, pick the nearest working girl—and we'll back you," Wrings says.

Candice centers a hard stare in his direction.

"Nice throw," she comments to him icily.

A memory springs to the surface of my brain—Wring tossing her into the wall. After I did the same.

Shame melts my guts.

"I can do better than that, cupcake." Wring winks, unfolding his arms and letting his arms drop. He puts his blade down on the wooden table.

Candice, with a fractured rib and definitely the worse for wear, straightens her spine in a way that's got to hurt. "But I didn't quit."

His striking bright-blue eyes slim down on her. "No. You didn't."

"I don't need your protection, Viper," she says then faces the group of men. I cringe mentally before she goes on with, "I have a role in this. And…" She meets their eyes. Every pair hates on her, especially Storm's. "I can't say what it is."

"You're nothing but a cunt with purpose," Storm says.

I step away from Candice and closer to Storm. "Cut the fucking commentary unless you want me to clean your clock again."

The men look at Storm.

Then their incredulous expressions shift to me.

"Viper take a swing at you?" Lariat asks, his face whipping between us, black eyebrows jerked high in surprise.

Storm crosses his arms, sliding his jaw back and forth. "Yeah."

"Why?" Wrings asks, shock ringing in his tone.

Storm cocks his head at Wring. "'Cause you weren't answering your cell, so I got my ass over to Viper's place as soon as I could. Found them in bed together. She's flashing her snatch, and he's protecting her."

The men look back to me.

I don't say anything. I owe them an explanation I don't want to give. One I can't.

"She must have some kind of golden pussy to make you go back on what you said you'd do," Wring says, flicking out his switchblade and going after his nails again. His eyes don't stray from my face, despite grooming his nails.

Candice does have a golden pussy. Scratch that—it's platinum. That and more. It's the *more* that freaks my shit right out.

All women have vaginas, but not all women have our love. And I don't feel like men have a choice with who they end up loving. The two camps are not the same animal.

"Listen, all of you." The woman has brass balls. "I have something to finish here."

Candice looks at me with her golden eyes, and I remember pushing into her and watching those cat-like eyes half closed with pleasure. Something deep and irretrievable shifts inside me, like my fucking heart is falling inside me from a look and a memory.

Nobody to catch it but her.

I suck in a painful breath, realizing the brass tacks of my situation.

And it's pretty simple: I'm in fucking trouble here.

She looks away, finishing her thought aloud. "And you need to let me do what I need to. Trust me. I can't say what the process is, but I need to see this through with Calem and the handoff."

"They have something on you?" Lariat asks, insightful as always, echoing my earlier suspicions.

"No," she says, looking at her clasped hands.

"I don't trust this bitch as far as I can throw her," Snare says.

She lifts her chin. "I've already been thrown. And you're right—I am a bitch."

Wring smirks.

Candice turns to him and says in a level voice, "You weren't even the twentieth in line, bucko."

Wring scowls, pausing his relentless nail cleaning as their gazes clash.

I laugh. In the middle of all the tension, a bubble of laughter erupts out of me like a volcano looking to spew lava.

Startled, Candice turns to me and laughs too. Then she gasps, her hand going to the injured rib.

It's difficult not to look at Storm, the cause of the injury.

Instead, I think about her words. Wring and I weren't the first men to throw her.

What is Candice doing where she's been forced to be that fierce? That defensive. Most women would give up faced by three men.

She didn't. What kind of life does Candice Arlington lead?

A dangerous one, my mind instantly supplies.

"I don't have to accept this," Storm says. "I don't give a shit that I just patched in or not."

He stands.

I stare down each brother. "Any of you feel froggy enough to jump on my lily pad, do so—or get the fuck out of here. You walk now, you walk forever."

They all meet my eyes.

Like usual, Noose settles things in his harsh, unadulterated way. "Fuck it, you've never done us wrong, and if you think…" He narrows his eyes to my left, pausing over her name. "Candice has got a hidden motivation other than handing over children to pervs, I'm game."

Noose feels around on his cut for something then jerks a box of smokes out from his interior pocket, the leather creaking as he settles the cut back into position. Flipping the lid back, he clips his lips around the cig then brings up his lighter. "But—" He cups his hand around the flame, and it blazes at the tip like a sinister tangerine eye. "If she turns out to be playing you, I'll kill her myself."

His eyes move to hers. "Because if you're playing the prez, then you're playing all of us." His hand spins a lazy circle at the loosely assembled men. "And that gets you a knot necklace, sweet thing."

"Amen," Storm says under his breath.

"I saw what you can do," Candice says quietly.

He points his cigarette at her. "And I feel like someone ate my kneecap and spit the wad back in the general direction of my leg."

Candice's exhale is hoarse, her shrug, slight. "You came at me with the rope. I defended myself."

"Ah-huh." Noose shoots a perfect ring toward the ceiling.

They glare at each other.

"Now what?" Lariat asks, leaning forward and putting his laced fingers on the tabletop. "We thought Arlington would lead us like pied pipers to perv boss, and we'd chase these fuckers out of here." His dark eyes roam my face. "Now our president has decided to forgo that pleasure for pussy."

"Property," I correct. Pussy is like weeds that crop up everywhere. Property's like the peace rose. No comparison.

"You *hated* when complicated pussy mixed shit up in the club," Snare reminds me. He looks at the three former Navy SEAL musketeers and nods in their general direction. "Even Trainer couldn't manage to do someone easy."

"Fucking trend," Rider says.

"Epidemic," another says from the peanut gallery.

"You fucking morons all have balls and chains the size of the moon, and for the record—that shit will *never* happen to me," Storm says.

"No woman would be with you. You're too broken to fix," Candice says with terrible precision, waving the red flag before the bull.

He lasers his hazel eyes down on her like a firing squad. "What in the fuck would you know, ya stupid twat?"

"All right," Wring says, whacking the back of Storm's head.

They stand at the same moment, and the tip of Wring's blade bites into the tabletop.

Storm's hands curl into fists. "Don't fucking do that ever again."

Pushing out his chest, Wring plows it into Storm's. "Stop disrespecting Viper's property."

Wish I could give Wring a raise if there was such a thing as salary in the MC. But there's not. Just loyalty.

Storm swings his heavy arm toward Candice. "She's *not* his property. She's giving kids up to sick fucks to abuse. Candice Arlington is robbing human beings of their *lives*."

I blink. Didn't think Storm had it in him.

"I'm not," Candice says in a low voice.

Storm's face whips to her. "Then tell us the fucking tale. Otherwise, all you are is some walking vagina that the prez is gone over."

"Stop talking, Storm," Noose says in his final way.

"Yes," I agree. "Every one of you men know what it is to find property. A woman doesn't always get presented to us like a perfect gift with a neat bow on top. And that was certainly the fucking case with all of you." I swing a finger at the others, all of them with complicated history.

"I know what property is," Candice says and turns to me.

Don't. I have time to think before she says it.

"I'm nobody's."

I read the pain in her eyes from those words before she masks it with uglier ones.

"Not yours. Not any man's. Ever."

My gut feels like it's been kicked, and all I can manage is neutrality because I just laid it all out on the fucking line in front of my men. For her.

And she doesn't look so lily white.

"So if you don't want to be Viper's property, you're free game, sister," Lariat grins, standing. "You're just a woman with more mystery than truth. All of it black as tar."

"Yeah," Storm says, a broad grin spreading across his angry face.

Her words are still stabbing at me like sucking little wounds, beginning to bleed me like happy leeches.

Candice Arlington would rather be beaten to death by a bunch of bikers than show a bit of softness. But I saw what she tried to hide.

Her silent call for help.

She doesn't even know she threw out the SOS. Just did it desperately, like a Hail Mary.

And I caught the signal. Because I was looking for it.

She's never had anyone really throw down for her before. And I'm not talking MC life. I'm talking someone having her back. It's clear to me.

And I'm not taking *no* for an answer. Candice Arlington is mine. Even if she doesn't know it. Even if she doesn't want it. Even though I didn't realize, until that very moment that I wasn't ever going to let go.

Candice backs away from me, hands loose, breathing even.

She's ready to fight them all.

All fourteen of them. Pride and surprise wells inside me. Something fashioned this slip of a woman into hard lines even though she was soft against me.

And I want that again. And again. More than I want anything else.

Even more than the club.

That's where I've really fucked up.

"Anybody touches her, and I'll kill you," I say. "No questions asked."

The men look at me. Take my measure. Understand that I'm as serious as a heart attack. "I'd never hurt another man's property." My gaze sweeps the room. "And I expect you to protect Candice."

"Fuck." Noose swipes a hand over his tightly bound hair, "You're not fucking around."

I shake my head. "Were you with Rose? Did you with Rose?"

Noose blows out two rings in a row. "Hell no. Got after anything and anyone who thought to even breathe around her. That woman owns every chamber of my heart. I'd fucking bleed for her."

That should make the men laugh. Prompt smart comments.

No one says anything.

Probably because there are a few brothers who have the same disease of the heart.

Like the terminal case I just caught.

Chapter 17

Puck

Wearing a gun at each hip, I feel like one of those old-fashioned gunslingers.

Can't blow my cover to Road Kill MC.

My bike is warm and hard between my thighs. The comforting rumble is an abiding white noise and vibration I never want to give up.

In a lot of ways, I'm more biker than cop now.

That's another excellent reason why Candi and I need to give up our careers. Neither of us know who we are anymore.

Can't find ourselves.

I knew where Candi's place was because we have trackers on each other's cars. Hers wasn't engaged, so now I'm relegated to using the shitty intel from Dagger that will hopefully lead me to my sister.

Otherwise, it'd be a deathtrap to show up at a rival biker's club unannounced.

I'll be announcing all right.

Hell, I'm not supposed to *know* the location. I'm taking such a large risk by walking into this club that I don't want to think about it too closely.

Doesn't matter anyway. Only Candi's welfare does.

Rolling up the freshly asphalted drive toward Road Kill MC, I wind to the top.

I back into an empty stall at one end of a gleaming row of bikes. It's the easiest position to scream out of if I need to. My eyes sweep the structure with nothing more than a cursory glance.

I might have admired the building if I weren't so fucked up in the head about Candi. Right now, everything I take in is more about taking note of entrances and exits. *Can I get out if she's there?*

If Candi is here—by some miracle, does she have a weapon?

I swing my leg over my bike seat and straighten my spine as I walk toward the entrance. *We'll find out.*

A prospect is just coming around from the back—probably taking a leak in the dense forest that encroaches the rehabbed building from every side—and spots me.

There is a moment of comedic pause before he sees the Chaos Riders cut I'm wearing.

His face shows every emotion right before he kind of goes bat shit.

His hand rises to his mouth, ready to do a sharp whistle.

I pull my gun and shoot his foot.

I'm committed.

He drops to the ground, holding the injured foot, and for a moment, I feel bad about it. Then I remember that nobody and nothing matters but my sister.

He opens his mouth to scream, and I say, "Don't make a noise."

I'm the only cavalry Candi has, and I'm not going to let Fucknuts here wreck it.

I bet her only fed contact is trying to raise alarm bells over her missing the meeting. But they'll be too late.

Leaving the prospect moaning on the ground, I hit the lever on the door and give it a yank.

Nothing.

Shit.

A numbered pad softly glows to the right of the door.

"Number?" I bark at him.

The kid's probably pushing twenty-one.

He flips me the bird.

I move the gun so the barrel is the only thing filling his vision, and he rattles off the number.

I punch it in with my free hand while keeping the weapon rock steady. With a chime and a sigh, the bolt gives, and I throw open the door.

Turning to the writhing prospect on the ground, I say, "You're never going to patch in, numb nuts."

I show him my back and walk through the threshold, letting the door close behind me with a slam.

As I anticipated, the place is booming with loud music, effectively having muffled the gunfire.

Several things happen at once.

Two prospects get a load of my cut, which I make no attempt to hide, and start shouting.

I lift the gun and that's a better message than my one word.

"Quiet," I say in the loudest voice I dare. It carries.

A couple of kids cower way at the back of the building by an attractive Nordic-looking blonde.

Calem Oscar is one of the children.

My heartbeats pound against the inside of my ribcage. Maybe—just maybe—if the child is here, Candi is too.

I stride over to them, waving my gun like a flag at any male who draws nearer.

"Don't get clever," I say, cruising through the center of the building and casting the net of my vision wide, taking in what it can.

The blonde puts the two older kids behind her and shields a baby with her hand. "Please…" Big crocodile tears crawl down her face. "Please don't hurt my baby," she whispers.

"Not here for that," I reply, then my eyes find Calem.

His gaze moves over my arm, then he asks uncertainly, "Puck?"

I look down where his eyes just were and see my old tattoo of a hockey stick and puck. I nod. "Yes."

He comes out from behind the young woman with the baby and holds out his hand. His eyes flick to the gun then back to my face.

"Hang on to a beltloop, Calem."

Doing it without question, he asks, "Are we going to save Miss Candi?"

My face snaps to his for a moment, then I'm back to wondering what Road Kill rider is going to launch on me while we're discussing shit. "Where is she?"

He tugs me in the direction of an unmarked door at the back.

Good place for church. A smart move for anyone thinking to invade the club. Labeling the door "church" would just be inviting a mass killing if someone with hostile intent showed up during church.

They would just bust in and spray bullets. Take out the entire club hierarchy in a few seconds.

The Chaos Riders clubhouse has a similar door, which is soundproofed. I can't be sure Road Kill's is, but I'm betting on it.

I turn, grabbing Calem, and spread the range of the gun outward.

Several men had creeped up behind us.

They raise their hands as we back slowly toward the door.

The blonde hides an older kid underneath a table then crawls underneath herself with the toe-headed baby. Tears streak her face and what little make-up she was wearing is gone, leaving her face pinched and pale.

If my sister's life wasn't at stake, I would feel like a dick for scaring an innocent.

I keep moving until I feel the knob beneath my hand. I turn and push it open at the same time, slamming the thing against the wall in case someone's tucked behind the door.

They're already shouting, or they would have heard my entry and been more prepared.

The door starts to come back, and I kick it shut, sliding the latch by feel as I sweep Calem behind and against me.

A body lands on it in the next second, but they can't get in. It's just me and the Road Kill MC men.

My breath is one searing mass inside my lungs. Burning me up as my eyes search the room.

Then I see Candice.

And she sees me.

The look in her eyes—there will be no forgetting it as long as I draw air.

Relief.

Love.

And the best part: an expectation met.

Standing tears cloud her jewel-like eyes. And I know right then that Candi understood—down to her marrow—that I would come for her.

"What the fuck?" a big guy with kinky red hair roars, his eyes wildly roaming over me, the kid, and the gun. Then he launches himself across the table… and into the pathway of my gun.

The gunshot is loud in the small space, making a dull thud when the bullet plugs the guy playing Superman right in the thigh.

Calem screams, high and piteous.

Fuck.

I lift the barrel higher, swinging the end at all comers while a blossom of blood sprouts from the guy's leg. He howls, clutching at his thigh.

"Stay put, fellas."

"Puck?" Viper says. He's king shit of Road Kill MC, and for being a gunrunner, he's probably not a half-bad guy.

Can't help my eyes going to Snare, Noose, and Wring—who know I'm a cop.

Will they reveal that fact now?

What will I do if they do?

Fuck it. Don't care. I look at Candi again. "Give me Candi."

My stare is unwavering, and I lift my left arm, wrapping my left hand around the gun and letting my right fall to my side. Can't hold it up forever.

Thank God that the only thing the old man ever gave me was true ambidexterity. Because, God knows, there wasn't anything else but daily terror with a healthy dose of guilt.

Viper pulls my sister behind him and crosses his arms. "No."

What the fuck? Surprised by that answer, I almost lower my gun.

Time slows. I force myself to take in everything happening in the room. The big guy on top of the table, bleeding and writhing.

Wring's got a bandage on his arm, but what looks like teeth marks peek out at the edge.

Flicking my eyes to my sister, I snort. "Your work?"

Her eyes crawl over Wring's arm, and she nods.

"Give me the girl, or I start shooting brothers one at a time." I lift my chin. "Head shots."

I'm sorry that Calem would witness what I might have to do, but things just got real.

Noose's eyes widen. These guys aren't sure who's side I'm on or if I'm even the cop they knew me to be a couple years back. Sometimes I wonder that myself. When it comes to Candi, I'll do a hell of a lot.

"Fuck, you're goddamned dead," a rider I don't know says.

Eventually.

"I let the blonde live," I quirk my eyebrows, giving Wring my full attention.

I saw her cut before she got under that table. She's his property, and I know exactly what an MC man feels for that.

He flips a blade ceaselessly, a vein presenting itself in the middle of his forehead. Wring takes a step forward, but Snare, the one with the twisted scar on his face, holds him back. "If you touched my property, I *will* kill you, slow."

I would do a lot to get my sister back. I've already done things I'm not proud of to protect her—as she has for me. But I do draw the line somewhere.

One of these fuckers, or more than one, hurt Candi. She's injured—I can tell by the stiff way she's holding herself, the hand she's laid on her ribs without even realizing it, and the tightening of her eyes when she takes a breath.

I shake my head, but my voice holds the soft menace of my intent. "I don't hurt women or children—unlike some fuckers."

Wring shifts his weight. "Arlington's giving kids to pervs. She's part of a kiddie-trafficking ring in our territory."

"Unacceptable," Noose says, folding his arms across a chest any gym rat would envy.

The big guy on the table groans, trying to stop the flow of blood and making a huge mess in the process.

"Yeah. I know."

Noose jerks his face back. "I know who you are, Puck—and I gotta say—you're not making even a little bit of sense. And by the way, shooting up brothers is a good way to die."

"I'll die later. Could've gone wild out there. Your shitty prospect coughed up your code after I shot his foot." I nod at their looks of combined disbelief and anger. "My advice? Don't patch that fucker."

My eyes move to my sister. "Candi, come on."

She moves out from behind Viper, who looks like he does serious gym time too.

He stops her with a hand on her shoulder. "Don't go with him."

Turning to him, she does something that almost makes me drop the gun for a second time in the space of five minutes. Rising on tiptoe, she holds both sides of his face. "Forget me." She wraps her arms around his neck, and I barely hear the next part. "Thank you."

He snaps his arms around her. "I threw down for you."

Holy fucking shit. No *way.*

"I know." She sinks to her flat feet, extracting herself from his embrace as she backs away. "We're together." Her palm waffles between me and her as Calem's small hand clings to the bottom of my cut.

"What?" he asks in a low voice of clear shock, then eyes like blue glaciers fix on me.

What the fuck happened with the prez of Road Kill MC in the last twenty-four hours? From the look of it—a goddamned lot.

And none of it good.

Damn. Candi just tossed me under the bus. Of course, every male in the room is going to think we're *together* together.

"Did he hurt you?" I ask her as she makes her way to me with agonizing slowness.

Her body tenses. "Viper?" she asks, staring at him as she walks backward toward Calem and me. "No. Never."

The way she says it has my grip tightening on my weapon.

"Then why the fuck are you crying like he did?"

Because I know my sister's voice when she's upset, when it's so loaded down with tears that it sounds like a river of grief without an end.

I fucking know that like taking my own breath.

Viper makes a move to close that distance she's gained.

I raise my weapon and give it a nod.

He stalls.

"Don't hurt him, Puck," Candi says, reading everything just from Viper's expression.

I want to. God knows, anyone who's been involved with my sister and returned her to me injured sort of deserves to die. I don't even know if my curiosity over what's happened is enough for me to want them to live long enough to get the answers I so desperately want.

When Candi's backed up against my chest, I lean over and, without taking my eyes off the men, kiss the top of her head.

Can she feel my abject terror at thinking I'd never see her again?

Yeah.

She reaches behind herself and squeezes my weaponless arm.

"Let's go," she whispers.

"You'll be hearing from me," Viper says. He says it for my benefit, but his eyes are on Candi.

I shake my head. "No, you'll be hearing from us."

"I'm so sorry, Viper," Candi says with a hitch in her voice.

Viper's eyes narrow on me with a promise. Then I lead Candi and Calem out the way I came in, flanked by MC riders who want me dead.

And from what I can see, they would kill Candi too. All except one man.

And he's the most dangerous of them all.

Chapter 18

Candice

Calem rides between me and Puck, and every time I turn my head, I'm sure I hear the rumble of bikes chasing us down.

But it's just my overactive imagination. The only thing chasing us is the wind at the sides of Puck's bike. Calem wears a kid-sized half helmet, and Puck always carries a spare. Leave it to him for preparedness.

Even though we have everything to keep us safe, there's something inherently unsafe about our passage, exposed and vulnerable, riding on a motorcycle with only the rush of air cushioning our bodies.

I know Puck will take us to his place.

Like me, he has two addresses. One for the Chaos bikers and one for just him. I know he's staged his "public" place for the bikers who hang out there.

For times like now, when we really need to have two residences, it's perfect, though we never could have dreamed of this particular contingency.

Plus, my private space is compromised because someone followed me, and I was clearly too shaken to notice.

Technically, I know where Puck lives—and we promised each other we'd quit the life, go somewhere quiet, and find significant others to share our lives with.

And the only way we can emotionally let go now is to see this handoff through, to get closer.

The precious cargo between us will have to be a part of it. The longer I have Calem, the less I want him to play a role, though I know he must for this loop to close.

And I'm the one to do it.

There's no doubt that I'm not at my best emotionally and, especially, physically. My chest feels like it's filled with broken glass every time I breathe, and a pleasant soreness has taken up residence where Viper's mouth and tongue were on my body just a few hours ago.

I can't think about that now. Can't think about Viper and what he might mean to me.

I feel like shit. Viper really put himself out on a limb for me even though he barely knows me. What he *does* know casts me in the worst possible light. And to make things so much worse, I allowed Viper *and* his brothers to think that I'm romantically taken by a rival rider.

Does he know Puck is a cop? I wonder. He certainly wouldn't know Puck's my brother.

We both use aliases, though my name has a grain of realness.

There's so many unanswered questions that I need to ask my brother.

But even if Viper did know Puck is undercover, Puck's conduct doesn't seem very *police*-like.

I couldn't have orchestrated a mess this bad, or the appearance of so many bad things, even if I'd planned it.

Calem's little hands circle Puck's waist, and I lean against him, wrapping my arms around him as Puck winds through the back roads of Kent then a once-rural Covington. Finally, somewhere on the outskirts of Fairwood, he slows the massive Harley.

We get to a barely-there gravel driveway off the main road, where a ribbon of grass disappears between dense trees that appear to close in on each side. They loom over the driveway, casting lacy emerald shadows on the rough drive.

As the bike crawls up the twisting driveway, the only noise is the crunch of gravel and intermittent birdsong. The trees grow denser still, as the driveway narrows. Then at the top, the trees thin and the forest ends abruptly.

In the center, on a knoll dead ahead, stands a dilapidated post-Depression-era farmhouse. Perfectly placed for maximum perspective. Instantly, I see why this is Puck's real home and not the addy that he fronts for Chaos.

The land is gorgeous. Off in the distance, the Cascade Range rises like emerald spires, piercing the low, dense halos of fog that give way to the cooler autumn temperatures of the changing season.

Puck rolls the bike to a stop and hits the kickstand. I tap his shoulder, and he steadies the bike as I dismount slowly, sucking in a painful breath.

No matter what I do, I can't move and not feel pain.

Like the Road Kill doctor said—three weeks. And that was probably minimum to not cringe every time I take a breath. Doc has no way of knowing all the things I did *after* it was injured, either. I probably lengthened the healing time by grim necessity.

I turn, and Calem is looking around at all that vivid green space with large eyes.

A huge maple tree stands to the left of the vintage farmhouse. It's starting to turn color, bright-lime leaves flaming to an orangey-red. A tire swing, weathered and beaten from years of decay, hangs from a fresh rope.

I look at my brother with some degree of suspicion. But I decide to quiz him on some of this later. Nest building isn't really his thing. Neither of us stay anywhere long enough to watch the proverbial oak tree grow. But some of the subtle exterior touches around the place speak to a different headspace than the one we've both shared for so long.

"Wow!" Calem squeals in clear delight, sliding off the bike with barely a hop, before racing straight for the tire swing.

"Hey!" I yell, though he ignores me.

Puck turns off the engine and twists his head around to look at me. "It's okay. Tire's solid. Replaced the rope not too long ago."

I feel the frown before I ask, "Why?"

Puck shrugs, throwing his leg over the seat and stretching like I've seen him do a thousand times. Like he'll touch the sky with his fingertips.

He turns, and we just stare at each other for a handful of seconds while Calem shrieks with happiness just a few yards away.

"Come here," Puck says, his voice thick with emotion.

I run the few paces to him and throw my arms around him, hissing through the pain in my chest. "Watch the ribs."

Carefully, my older brother closes his muscled arms around me, and I feel the warmth of his breath on the top of my head.

"You look older," I say.

"Yeah," he replies simply. "Because I am."

Silence thrums between us, then Puck asks, "What happened, Candi?"

"Road Kill MC happened." My voice is dry.

He releases me, and we have the beauty of just standing there, looking at each other for the first time in three years and not having to act, pretend, or cut our time short. Still, the job that lies before us hovers like a black cloud.

"Possible territory thing?" Puck glances at Calem.

I look too. Calem is twisting the tire around with him in it then letting himself spin out.

I return my attention to Puck. "Viper says that they became aware of the child trafficking ring not long ago. Wanted to snuff it out before it could get a foothold. Apparently, they're pretty adept at cleaning their territory." I suppress the eye roll I'm dying to give.

"Road Kill doesn't do what Chaos does."

My eyebrows shoot up. "Really?" I did my homework but still mentally lumped a lot of the MCs together into the same unsavory category.

"*Really*. Like you're probably aware, Chaos will do any criminal act. Nothing is too vile for them. Especially if money's involved." He squeezes my hand and lets it drop, staring off at the mountains. "I was there when they helped take down the sex trafficking two years ago. And from what I've heard, they chased the Bloods out and the mob since. There might be a ton of illegal shit going down outside of the southeastern part of the state, but not much goes on that they don't know about."

"The Road Kill rider who was there at the handoff wasn't just a biker. He was military. Had the feel."

Puck nods. "He is. Navy SEAL. Name's Noose. There's three in that club who are."

Ah. Love the name. The meaning's not lost on me.

Now it's my turn to look off into space. "So now what?"

"You know exactly what."

I do. "I'll have to talk to my contact. Make sure they know I'm closing in, that there was a breakdown with part one of the operation. I'll need backup for the sting." The other agents will take care of their end.

"You still have two hours until I would have been there, along with you and the Chaos Rider."

I shiver. "Yeah, Dagger. He's such a sleaze." He was the one who should have showed.

Puck nods and lifts a muscular shoulder as if to say, "Thems the breaks," then cocks his head. "What was all that emotional shit with Viper?"

Heat rises on my face, and Puck whistles, holding up a palm. "No judgement, but I really need to know who hurt you and what happened. I've got to know now, before we do this handoff and capture this insane pervert."

Strong fingers curl around my shoulders.

Our eyes lock.

"I slept with him," I say, tearing off the Band-Aid.

Puck's hands drop. "You're not a casual woman."

That's so true. And we both know why.

"No," I reply softly.

His Adam's apple does a sharp bob. "Okay. I'm listening."

So I tell him. Well, I recount the barest facts about sex with Viper. No matter how close a woman is with her brother, some topics that are just too awkward for words.

"So," Puck says after a full minute of contemplative silence, "you negotiated your body for freedom."

His words might sound as though he's insulting me, but Puck's dark eyes are lit from within by compassion. He, better than any human being, knows I do only what I wish to do. No more and no less.

"In a way, but like I mentioned"—I shove my dark-auburn hair back, and small tendrils curl around my fingers from the loose braid I fashioned as we were riding—"I wanted to," I finish in a low voice.

Puck's face shows the unspoken questions he has, but he skips over that part I admitted was more than consensual.

"So that big red-headed bull?"

"He fractured my rib. Got me when I was down."

He puts a palm over the sore rib, and his jaw locks. "But this Viper threw you against your wall? I'm trying, Candi, but I'm not going to lie. I sort of want to kill him."

I nod. *I get that.* "Yes, but in his defense, he thought I was the worst woman in the world—delivering children to pedophiles. In their minds, I would have deserved that and worse."

"Intellectually, I get it. But emotionally, I want to ride back there and beat everyone who touched you until their own mamas couldn't recognize their faces."

Stepping forward, he traces the vague mark from Viper's palm with his thumb. "He hurt you."

I take the deepest breath I can, wrapping my hand over the one that strokes the wound. "Yes, and then he healed me."

"How is that possible?"

Our hands drop.

I don't know. "If I knew, I'd tell you. But the whole thing was confusing as hell. And I know, Puck. Damn—do I know that I *just* met this guy. That he did bad things, chased by really wonderful things. But you know what?"

Puck folds his arms, and I know he's digging in his heels.

Ignoring his body language, I go on. "I feel like I've been looking for him my entire life, and there he was, all that time."

"Candi, you can't be serious."

"You saw him," I state in a low voice. "He claimed me when he shouldn't have. It wasn't a logical move. I never told him I was FBI, and he let whatever this thing that's begun between us guide him. He threw down for me." I fling my palms away from my body. "You know that means business in the MC."

I know Puck heard that, but after all the upheaval, the fact bears repeating.

He threads fingers through his wind-blasted hair. "Yeah, don't have a ready explanation for that one. Word on the street is Viper doesn't do relationships. Not since his old lady died a while back."

"Oh," I say, feeling kind of sick. "I didn't know I was competing with a ghost."

"Candi."

My face snaps to Puck.

"I love you."

"And I love you," I say instantly.

"We need to feed Calem and deliver him to the rendezvous. Your love life—or whatever this fucked-up timing and this thing is with the RK prez—will have to wait. And then I think I'm going to kick Viper's ass." Puck's quiet for a handful of heartbeats then adds, "And if he lives, then I'll let you date him."

I smile. Can't help it.

At nearly thirty-eight, Puck still thinks he can vet the guys I like.

I guess, after a father like ours, he can't see another perspective.

"Deal?" he asks. There's deeper questions in his gaze than the one-word question portrays.

I'll answer those later, if I can. Right now, we have a last handoff to make.

I don't say it. I hug him instead and whisper against his chest, "Deal."

In less than an hour, we'll be meeting the devil.

And my brother and I will send him directly to hell.

Chapter 19

Viper

Feel like somebody just fed me my balls and I tried to swallow the whole thing down.

I'm choking while I sit at the head of the table and stare at the wood grain.

Not a brother speaks.

The deafening and accusatory silence surrounds me like the inside of a mausoleum.

I'm *this close* to calling Mover and finding out what the fuck is going on. *Why would Puck, a cop, decide to come in here with the double barrels, shoot a brother, and take Candice?*

Her eyes. I shut mine, blocking out the silence of my men so that the only image I see is those golden eyes telling me to forget her.

Like I could.

Then she'd thanked me, as though no one had ever done something worthwhile enough to voice gratefulness.

Thank you for what? Fucking her? Beating her?

Letting her go?

She fucked me over by admitting she's with Puck. No small thing, considering Chaos Riders are Road Kill's number-one enemy.

But Puck's a cop, deep undercover, and only four men know that. I wanted to unveil that small detail when he was here, holding his guns and taking my woman.

Even though every fiber of my being wanted to, I couldn't endanger a cop who did right by us and innocents a couple years back. Besides, I don't have a clue how to explain it. Or how I would have stopped Candice from going with him. From going anywhere but away from me.

"Viper," Noose says from my right.

"Yes." Swiping a tired hand over my face, I finally look up from my brooding thoughts.

"This is beyond fucked up." He spreads his arms as if to say, *right?*

"Give us something, Viper. Anything," Snare says.

Murmurings of assent rise like vapor around me.

"You fuck this chick and throw down for her within practically the same day," Wring says in his steady way. "Hell, I *knotted* her."

My next words sound lame, but they're the truth. "Candice is not what she seems."

Lariat shakes his head, rocking back in his chair. "A Chaos fuck comes in here and shoots a brother then takes the woman you want to make property." He slaps his denim-clad thighs as if the facts are simple, and the front legs of his chair bark as they hit the floor.

He's so right.

Candice went with Puck.

And I didn't get the feeling she was afraid of him. I almost got the sense that she was relieved to see him.

Does she know Puck? My mind supplies the memory of the tender kiss he placed on her head once she was in his embrace.

"I'm calling church," I say suddenly, a murky thought rising to the surface of my brain like an oil slick on water.

Rider stands. "We don't have dick figured out, Prez." He swings an arm so tatted, there's no flesh visible. "It's what the knot boys just said. Arlington left with that guy—a rival rider—and she told you. She *rejected* your kingly ass."

That brings a tired smile to my face. "Candice Arlington's got something she has to finish, and she's not willing to tell me or anyone else."

"Could've persuaded that along," Wring admits darkly.

I look at him. "We did enough of that already."

We stare, and his face fills with all the things he would like to say but won't.

I am still the president of Road Kill MC, even though my conduct of the last twenty-four hours has been under heavy question.

Wring's stare hardens. "Puck could've killed Shannon and Duke."

I shake my head, giving Wring the weight of everything I won't say in front of the uninformed. "He wouldn't, and for the record, your property's shook up, but safe?" My eyebrows rise, letting the question hang between us.

I know his family is safe.

Wring gives a terse nod. "Yeah. But the thought of another man touching my family makes my balls crawl up my ass."

Noose snorts.

I stand and lean forward, spreading my fingertips on the tabletop. Taking a sucking inhale, I restate everything. "Candice can reject me, but mark me on this—I will have her."

"She's a dangerous woman—a woman we don't know enough about," Noose reiterates.

Can't dispute that.

I look over the men for an entire minute. "I'm sorry. I said I'd do the job and just ended up screwing the pooch and selling the pups."

No one says anything, so I fill the silence with the next thing. "I need to talk to Wring, Snare, and Noose—no one else. I'll figure this out. The kiddie ring will stop. You have my word."

Lariat asks in a quiet voice, "What about Candice Arlington?"

"She's off-limits." My eyes sweep the men. "No matter how dirty she looks, no matter that she rejected me in front of everyone, or that she might be with Puck." I say his name like the swear word I now think of it as.

But if my speculation is accurate, this shitstorm just went sideways for everyone.

"Gotcha," Rider says, clapping Lariat on the back.

Lariat captures my eyes, and I give him the nod. The one asking him to trust me—even though I'm a dumbass and shook the foundation of the men's faith in me.

Hell, I shook my own.

The brothers file out.

When the last one leaves and shuts the door, I ask Wring, "How's Storm?"

Wring lifts his upper lip. "Surly."

"Good. Must be feeling right as rain."

Wring lifts his chin. "Doc's patching up his little flesh wound."

"I wouldn't go that far. But he's got a case of hate for Arlington that'll never fade." Wring's eye contact is steady.

That's a problem with Storm: he hates women. I tapped him to do this job with me, and when he tried to do what I needed, I blocked his efforts.

As if reading my mind, Noose says, "You kill-blocked him."

"Beat-blocked," Snare corrects, crossing his arms and leaning against the wall.

My attention lands on these three men I've been through a few tough spots with. "Puck's a cop."

"Yup," Noose says, lifting a finger in the air, "but that doesn't help us, boss. It only deepens the mystery of his involvement. We've been informed, in fucking bald terms, that the police are taking a vacation of Road Kill MC being on cop radar until Puck's out of the undercover gig in Chaos." He shrugs his linebacker shoulders.

"Yeah." Wring shakes his head. "Him coming in here like a Clint Eastwood doppelgänger is weird as fuck," Wring says slowly, cupping his chin.

Snare's face snaps to mine, studying my face. "You've made a connection."

I nod reluctantly, but the answer more logical than anything I could have put together. "I have. It's so insane that I don't want to verbalize it." I graze a hand over my short hair. "But the hell with it."

They're silent, waiting for my next bomb to drop.

"What if she's also a cop, but serving in another capacity?"

Noose gives a hoarse laugh. "Fuck me runnin'. I feel like a buffoon."

Wring snorts. "Yeah, so what's new?"

Noose socks him in the arm, and Wring glares.

"Ladies," Snare begins in a droll voice, his scar stretching at his upper lip with the smirk. "Fucking please, stay on topic."

"What I was saying before Wring stepped on my dick, is that she smelled all wrong when I was digging around. Holes in the history. No record. Seemed too clean to be used as a mule. No juvey priors, either. Whistle clean. Stunk to high heaven."

"She's no cop," Wring says coolly, giving Noose a sidelong look of veiled triumph.

"Agreed," Noose says, shooting Wring a glance saying, *I got it, asshole.*

I shrug. "She's some *thing.*"

"Beside your future property?" Noose asks, a ghost of a smile hovering over his lips.

My brows drop. "Exactly."

"No chick that's law is going to be the property of a club prez." Snare's dark blue eyes are flat. Certain.

Wasn't thinking about failure when I threw down for Candice. Of course, I hadn't thought about Candice being any form of law enforcement, either. It occurs to me that I don't give a shit. It's about the woman, not what capacity she serves in.

"CIA?" Noose suggests.

Wring shakes his head. "Not sure that feels right. But this pedophile ring might be a helluva lot larger than we knew. Cop's in on it, and the staties don't work with government entities—that's the bottom line with those two. There might be a lot of jagups with their finger in the pie."

Noose grins. "I was just looking in the wrong bakery section."

"I want to know who she really is." I look at him. *Gives new meaning to sleeping with the enemy.*

"You mean you want to protect her?" Wring asks.

I plow my fingers through my flattop. "I already did her wrong. So wrong." I evade the question.

"You didn't. None of us suspected she was anything but a fucked-up bitch," Snare says. "And she didn't tell us different. None of us want to hurt females. But any human being that fucks up the defenseless gets what they get. I think that kind of shit falls under 'gender neutral.'"

Noose and Wring nod.

"Depending on what branch of our lovely government she's with, Arlington would die before she'd give them up. Especially a woman," Wring says. "If that's even the case." He lifts a dismissive shoulder.

"You're not wrong," Noose says. "Damn... *damn.*"

I ask the men, "Do I contact Mover? Do I drag his ass into this?"

"He's FBI," Noose says in a contemplative tone. "Probably, we should have told him we knew about these perv douches. Because you can bank on Mover knowing. Might be working on it himself." His dark-blond brows shoot up. "But letting them know we know is showing our hand. Getting their full attention on the club."

I nod, but Mover and I haven't worked out our shit. All we've managed to do is maintain an uneasy alliance that only the two of us know about. On the surface, we share a vague, mutual hatred that men often have and never fix.

So he and Puck took down Ned together, but they didn't know about each other's parts in the play until the very end. Their undercover roles within Chaos were locked down, and the four men who knew who and what they really were said nothing. We held our breath, hoping the two of them would get done, forget Road Kill, and split up Chaos for good. That had been the appeasements made by the FBI and cops when we were given our options. There weren't many.

Doesn't look like that's happening.

"Feds, cops—who else is going to jump out of the cake?" I mutter.

"Without tassels on the titties," Wring adds with a chuckle.

Noose claps his hands. "My knee feels like it was put through a meat grinder because of Little Miss Judo, so I'm no fucking good." He grabs the smokes out of the interior pocket of his cut. "Throbs like a rotten tooth."

"Don't light up, you fucker. Making the entire building stink." I give him my best glare.

Noose sighs, shooting me a classic stink eye right back.

He can be such an unrelenting prick.

Hard men are built like that. From the ground up, steel fasteners screw the skeleton together, covered with muscle meant to flex, defend, and protect. A hard head covers a sharp mind, and hearts too tender for the bodies are encased inside.

A fucked-up combination.

One that most of us have.

Snare, Wring, and Noose follow me out to my cabin. Prospects are crawling all over the club, except Old Gimp Foot. He's out. Puck's prediction of that was spot-on.

My gut is telling me that something's going down soon.

At least I can offer protection to the club I tied down to railroad tracks, for a woman I met and claimed inside of twenty-four hours.

Fuck, I'm freaked out, wanting to know where Candice is. It doesn't make me feel one iota better that Puck has her.

He might *have her* all right.

I don't look at the basement door. It fucking haunts me. Our time. The hurt I put on a female I assumed the worst of.

The touch I used to beg her forgiveness through my body, my mouth, and my cock.

Noose jars me out of my thoughts. "Just because Arlington knocked my dick in the dirt, doesn't mean my head doesn't work." Noose taps his forehead. "After our little chat, got my military contact to dig deep, in a very narrow, deliberate area." Noose appears smug, letting the moment lengthen, and I want to punch him.

"What is she?" I bark.

"Spook." His curt answer is sure.

His eyes hood.

"CIA?" I ask.

Noose barely lifts a shoulder. "Her languages were government-given. My contact couldn't give me what branch, but she's undercover something—so deep he couldn't even find what flavor."

"So we kidnapped a mystery law enforcement agent, and I knocked her unconscious with a knot?" Wring asks. "Jesus"—he puts a palm over his eyes—"that is beyond fucked up."

"If this is what we think it is, she probably was closing in on the fucker behind all this trafficking."

I nod. "Yup. Her comments make sense now. Everything fits." The concern for the boy. Her asking a near-perfect stranger to take him to the cops.

But what the fuck is her connection to Puck? "Do you think Puck is dirty now?" I ask suddenly, drilling hard toward intuition chased by a streak of logic.

Noose shakes his head. "Hard tellin'." His face scrunches in thought. "Been in the life a long time not to be living some of it."

"He's been deep MC for almost three years. Has to be hard to know your place anymore." Snare agrees, tipping his head back to stare at my old wooden beadboard ceiling, hands clasped and hanging between his knees.

"If he's dirty, do you think he's made Candice?" I ask slowly, spinning the believability of the tale in my mind like a slow-motion horror flick. "Fuck!" I yell, jumping off my beaten La-Z-Boy recliner.

I let them walk. Thought Puck was a cop, still undercover. Now he might be turning her over to the peddlers too. Not like Calem.

But like a vendetta.

Cops don't work with government, and like Mover, Puck might not know she's working the same angle he is.

"Hang on, Vince," Noose says, grabbing my arm, which I immediately rip out of his grip.

I grit my teeth, lips pulled back. "He's going to fuck her."

Wisely, the brothers say nothing about a literal translation of my words.

"I can't allow that."

"Fuck, you're so gone on her already," Wring says.

I turn to him. "You believe in second chances?"

He shakes his head. The sun coming in through the warped glass of a small window on the west side of the cabin bleaches his platinum hair to white. "No."

I stare at each one of the men. "Well, Colleen's gone," I admit for the first time ever, my voice choked as the back of my eyelids come on fire just from saying her name aloud, "and there's never been another woman for me. Just getting my dick wet in a willing hole. And you know the difference, boys."

They say nothing. *Answer enough.*

"I'm not a poet, but Candice moves me." I touch my hand to my heart. "And I've been a numb fucking shell since Colleen passed." I face them square. "Counting the days instead of living them, boys."

It's all the explanation I got. The only one I can give.

"And now you've got this woman—" Snare says.

Noose's smile is a twitch of lips. "That is fucking with you."

"In the best way," Wring says.

The worst way. Every way. My shoulders fall. "Yes," I breathe out, so fucking grateful they understand that if I don't see this through, I'll always wonder what could have been.

And I don't think my shredded heart can lose another woman.

Another chance.

Noose grips my shoulders. "We're here, Vince. You stubborn fuck."

I grin, and it keeps me from crying like a fucking girl.

We leave.

Our plan is to find Puck, because where he is, Candice will be, along with the fuckers responsible for the mess, and for me and Candice ever meeting in the first place.

Fate's a bitch.

Chapter 20

Candice

"W hat about your clothes?" Puck looks me over, and I realize I can't go to the meet with what I'm wearing. I have to dress the part. But there's no time to return to the house and grab slut gear—and maybe encounter another biker ambush.

I search through a guest bedroom drawer. "For a guy, you sure have your bases covered." I paw through what seems to be an assortment of Band-Aids posing as garments.

"So insulting." Puck smirks. "I grabbed some clothes from the club. There's plenty of women's shit hanging around all the time."

I bet.

Hmm. I grab a shirt—I guess it's a shirt—and hold it up for his perusal. "This is *not* clothing."

Puck grins. "Depends on your definition of *coverage*." He starts a tuneless whistle, and I smack him on the arm.

"Ow! You pack a wallop, sister."

"Oh please." I unbunch the shirt and snap it open. It has a double cross of fabric both front and back in a loose X. I assumed that when wearing it, one would cover my boobs, and the other would go over my back, leaving my midriff bare. *Prostitute chic. Wonderful.* "I'm not sure I can wear a bra with this." I bite my lip, eyes roaming over the front of the "top."

"Grabbed what I liked," Puck explains.

I roll my eyes. "I suppose you took your undercover work seriously."

His grin widens, if that's even possible, then he tries a serious expression, which he ruins by laughing. "Yes."

"Dick."

Puck laughs harder.

I roll my eyes and begin scanning the room I'll be staying in. Clearly, it's been professionally cleaned, as Puck is a closet slob, hence the batch of clothes unceremoniously tossed in the closest drawer I just rummaged through. "I think I like it," I finally comment when my eyes finish their restless travel.

I walk over to the sole window and gaze outside.

"The house?" he asks, coming to stand beside me.

I hate to see his smile fade, but commenting on where we live and for how long always brings a touch of sadness.

My reply is soft. "Yeah."

The worn draperies are a sheer, gauzy antique white covering the windows. A tension rod holds the fabric within the window, but the molding is painted a warm cream. Deep grooves define a profile within the wood casing, and big, square bull's-eyes frame the corners at the tops of the windows.

"It's beat-up, but she's a good old gal," Puck says, squeezing my shoulder.

He pushes the curtain aside as we stare out.

"Good view of the Cascades," I say.

He nods. "Good view of nobody at all."

That gets a smile on my face. "There's that."

I move away from the view, which is both arresting and somehow sad, and move back to where a clear tote rests on a small guest bed with a patchwork quilt thrown over it. Searching through the remainder of the clothing not in the dresser drawer, I spread some pieces over the bed.

I hold up the horrible top again. It's the part of the job I hate the most. The costumes.

"No Jimmy Buffet t-shirts." Puck's grin is back.

I glare at him, but then I think about the shared memory. "That was a helluva concert," I admit quietly.

"Yup," he says before adding in a quiet voice, "Just leave Jimmy here. That way, the next time you come over, you'll have something to wear."

I turn to him quickly, my eyes sharp on his face. "Is there going to be a next time, Puck?"

His expression bleeds to solemn. "I promised."

I turn around, slowly surveying the old house, and my gaze lands at the window we just stood at, and the surreal view of an outside that seems to go on forever—peopleless. My inhale hurts, ribs singing. "We leave. After this case is over," I state.

Puck hugs me, resting his chin on my head. The cheap outfit's squeezed between us. "Why do you think I got this place?"

I pull a face, craning my neck to look up at him because he's a foot taller than me. "I'm not going to live with you."

"I know. I've got twenty acres here." He waggles his brows.

Ah, a fam compound. I could get used to that. At least, with the family I love. The breath wheezes out of me, and tears soon follow. "Oh, Puck."

His eyes have a shine. "It's the best I could do. 'Bout busted the piggybank. I love the house, and it needs a shit ton of work, but the land *and* the house? Couldn't say no. And everything costs an arm and a leg around here now. Especially land."

My gaze wanders to the view again.

I wouldn't have been able to say no, either.

"Miss Candi?" a small voice calls from the bottom of the stairs.

Puck and I walk out of the small guest bedroom and down the hall to the top of the staircase, my hands still clutching the outfit for the meet. The handoff I don't want to do but desperately have to.

"Yes, Calem?"

He shows me his empty plate. Puck's a hobbyist cook and happened to have leftovers of pasta with homemade pesto.

A weird combo for a six-year-old. But when a kid's hungry and meals aren't a sure thing, he learns to eat what's available.

Hard truths.

Puck and I were raised wealthy, but we were poor in all the ways that mattered.

"I ate all my food." His shy smile is the sweetest thing I've seen all week, his missing two front teeth adorably obvious.

I laugh. "I see that. Do you want more? We have enough time."

Slowly, he shakes his head and says, "We're going to meet the bad men."

An appetite suck.

"Yes," Puck says, putting his hands on my shoulders and briefly squeezing them before letting them drop.

"I can't stay here?" His voice is quiet. Resigned. With just a thread of hope.

Oh baby, I wish you could. But the best I can do is state the truth, without even a hint of potential for anything else, "You'll be safe." That's all I can offer.

"I never am." His voice turns hopeless, forlorn.

I walk down the stairs with Puck close behind me, my hand gliding over the handrail. From what I can see, it's the only bit of unpainted wood in the house. Worn smooth from over a hundred years of people doing the same thing I am in that precise moment.

I get to the last step, and Calem puts his plate down on the beaten wood floor and wraps his little arms around my legs, pressing his face against my belly.

"Oh, Calem," I say softly.

"I'm scared."

Me too. I put my hand on his head, stroking the silky warm strands. "It'll be okay."

I only hope the words aren't a lie.

"This gun chafes my thighs."

Puck opens his mouth.

I hold up a wagging finger. "Don't make *one* comment about my eating habits."

My sweet tooth is legend.

His lips purse, then he talks anyway. "You're too thin. I was just going to say that the outfit makes hiding a weapon difficult."

Yes. I look down at my bare legs, where goosebumps dance over my flesh that's chilled from all the exposure.

Puck's crappy choice of attire is all I have, and if I'm perfectly honest, it was about what I would have had to wear anyway. I could have gotten away with looking a little classier for the first part of the handoff with a Chaos Rider, but when it comes time to meet with the actual perps, I'll have to be deep in character. After all, what reputable woman would ever turn kids over?

The stupid top cups my boobs perfectly and is so snug, the crisscross at the back actually keeps everything in place. I have to wear flip-flops because that's all Puck had, and they're slightly on the big side. All my really cool spy gear is back at the townhouse that's compromised to hell, and I'm not going back there in case Viper's men make an appearance, thinking they'll just ignore his stake on me.

I won't lie to myself: throwing down for me, in biker's terms, is *big*. I don't have enough real estate inside my brain to deal with what that means right now.

The car ride to the rendezvous point is quiet. I can almost feel the physical dread from Calem.

Or maybe that's just my own.

I can't save all the children who fall into the trafficking net. But I'll save who I can. Steeling myself, I carefully slide out of the car and turn to Puck.

"Man, am I not liking this." His eyes rake the stupid outfit as he goes all big brother on me.

"It'll help to just think of it like a costume. That's what I do."

Puck gives a quick chin dip. "But I know how all the men will be thinking when they look at you."

"And you know what I'm capable of."

Our eyes lock. "I do," he finally says, "but I don't have to like it."

"You brought the clothes home…" I raise an eyebrow.

His face turns a little sheepish. "Didn't have you in mind."

I shift my weight, feeling the press and dig of the snub nose .38 against my inner thigh. I hate having to carry, but I'd miss it if I needed it. And I just might.

Standing, I do a slow spin. "Can you see it?"

Puck studies me. "No, but it's a near thing. I know you like exterior, but the skirt shows all because of the silky fabric."

Yeah, no kidding. It's technically a mini, but it's actually lower mid-thigh. The material is what's sexy—not the length.

I open the back passenger-side door. Calem's big brown eyes look up at me.

He takes my hand, sliding out, and hops to the ground. He doesn't notice the outfit because he's seen lots of women dressed like this.

I'm not sure what it is about this boy—could be I know it's my last handoff—but I don't want to leave him. I don't care that he'll be placed in a loving home. There's just some indefinable *something* that makes me want to be with him always.

But I turn in the direction I have to go, tugging him along with me.

We're not at Gasworks park this time. We're at Scenic Hill park in Kent.

This is the second drop-off as per the arrangement I've had with these goons since the beginning. The first was supposed to be an intermediary, but it's this second part that's critical.

Now that I'm here, my heart's in my throat.

I've done a dozen of these in three years, and all of them were awful. They felt like a reward after Puck called me and said the children had been placed, and the ring of criminals was shrinking as we pick off player by player.

My unease has increased with each handoff, my instincts spot-on. Maybe my disquiet is because of what happened between me and Viper. Or my fractured rib. Or the mess with the first part of the handoff. *Or all of the above.*

"Miss Candi," Calem whispers from my side.

But I'm in character and don't answer, tugging his small hand from the far reaches of the parking lot where Puck dropped me to the place where that path begins that I scouted last week.

The metal grip of my gun has grown warm against my flesh and digs into my thighs as I walk. The whore's makeup I applied feels heavy on my face. Cool air drifts against me, biting against all that skin I leave on display, looking like the mule I play.

Worn out and rode hard.

I see him first and don't react. Sharpness means a lot of things to people like them. And when I phoned my Bureau contact, he said the place would be surrounded with feds. Today is the day the ringmaster will be here.

Finally, I can be done.

No more acting the part of dumb slut. No more taking kids to be transferred from bad to good.

Just no more.

A sharp image of Puck's house on the knoll rises hard in the front of my mind, making my vision of the evil person walking toward us waver like water poured over glass.

For a moment, I *am* the role I play, and the effort of being this person I am not has never been more daunting.

The man stops ten feet from where I stand. He's nondescript, around six feet tall, with brown hair so washed out that it's almost blond. I can't tell the colors of his eyes across the few yards that separate us. He could be anybody, and I never meet the same person twice.

The leader is smoke because his people keep getting taken. My handoffs were every two months then every four. This year, I haven't done one in six months—Calem is only the second.

The leader of this sick ring has every reason to be cautious. Holes in his organization mean one thing: getting caught eventually. And this isn't the only branch of his tree of crime. I can't stand to think about all the other kids who are taken and don't fall under our purview.

I can't save them all.

The man sinks to his haunches. "Hey, Calem."

Calem doesn't say anything. The man wears the typical clothes of the region: jeans and a loose T-shirt.

I know he's carrying.

His eyes flick to mine, gaze cruising down my outfit. "Bring him here, slut." He cocks his head back. "Why isn't Dagger here?"

"Ran into something complicated," I say. *More complicated than you know.*

I saunter over to where he squats beside Calem, making my hips sway, but careful not to reveal the gun under my skirt.

Calem drags behind me, not wanting to go near this guy.

I don't want him to, either.

Finally, he stands. "Nice little Chaos whore to give us the merchandise." He laughs at my expense and eye-rapes me again. Then his gaze narrows. "You think you're too good to talk to me?"

I know I am. "I don't have nothin' to say." I have four languages under my belt, and aside from that, I intensely study the dialect of my chosen region and the socio-economic phrasing I will be masquerading within. I must blend in, though Puck says I have the eyes of a police officer.

Hard to shroud the windows of your soul.

"Fine," he huffs, "but I want a taste of what you got."

No way. "Never had to before," I hedge, though I'm not usually a part of this stage of the handoff.

"Miss Candi," Calem says, panic rising in his voice.

"Are you sweet… *Candi?*"

He has no idea. I smile, and whatever he sees in my expression has his shit-eating grin wilting at the edges.

"No."

Stuffing his hands into his pockets, he says, "Wasted enough time. Boss man is waiting."

The man jerks his chin toward a distant point in the park.

A dense, shaded canopy of trees sways in the wind, lining a narrow asphalt path that winds into the deepest part of the woods then disappears from view. I shiver in the breeze. At late September, the slut gear isn't cutting it for warmth.

I've perused old blueprints of the park from when it was installed in the 1970s, back when a park-crazy mayor got ahold of Kent and transformed every spare patch of land into a park.

But I don't remember where that path leads.

And I don't like not having a clear visual geography of the map inside my head.

"Always just pass the kid off, then go," I say, thinking about my defense options and not liking being between two high points. I look at the 1950s houses perched on a steep embankment to my right and the slope of Kent-Kangley to my left.

The guy shakes his head. "Not this time, sweetheart. Boss man wants to see you, in person. Non-negotiable."

I've got a gun. I can take care of myself. They are obviously after Calem. I mean less than nothing in the big equation.

They'll protect the package, which is the seven-year-old boy at my side.

Maybe if I get closer, I can make the arrest myself. Of course, other agents will move in. They're everywhere. And Puck's fellow cops are too.

So why do I feel like the Lone Ranger?

"Don't got all day," he prompts, and turning, he starts walking toward the dark path.

I follow.

Chapter 21

Puck

I set my binoculars down with a thunk on the dash. *What the fuck are you doing, Candi?*

She knows better than to walk off with one of those fuckers.

I get out of the car, slam the door, stride around to the trunk, and pop the lid. Yanking out my Kevlar vest, I shrug it on.

Things could get saucy—fast.

Picking up my dangling mouthpiece, I say, "This is Hockey. Do you copy?"

"Copy, Hockey."

"Target is moving east on designated pathway. Copy."

"Copy, Hockey. Sending players."

I'm as anxious as fuck, but I want Candi protected. When she used my secure line to phone in for backup, they were leery because the first part of the handoff was botched, though she'd called that in too.

Candi is very by the book and only showed up for the second part of the handoff because the first was compromised.

Hate the feebs. If everything doesn't go as planned, they act like we might as well just throw up our hands and call it quits—after three years of chasing the same dog.

Not so for cops. For us, it's personal. We want this bastard.

And even though Candi has proven herself capable, I'm still protective. Too much, I guess. Doesn't matter. Can't take that out of the fabric of who I am.

My backup is closing in, and they don't know that the feds are involved. Thankfully, only Candi and I know about each other. As far as the other cops are concerned, she's part of the trafficking operation. They'll want her alive so they can question her. In a strange way, she's almost more protected this way than she would be if they knew she was a fed.

I follow, trying not to look like a cop, sloughing off that wary, hyper-aware manner that so many of us gain as we go along on the job.

My Glock 22 is tucked along the waistband of my jeans, and I know I hold myself different because of it. Making a conscious effort to stride more casually, I try to ignore how hot the Kevlar is, though it's making me sweat. My gun slides along the slick skin.

When I get to the pathway, I keep going, knowing I've got the team right there on either side of a valley formed by two hills. Houses built in the mid-twentieth century line one side, and the other is filled with four lanes running up a steep hill toward the east hill of Kent.

Deciduous trees line the path, casting everything in deep shadow. A smallish creek that probably held spawning salmon back in the day runs swiftly to my left. It's a trickling memory now.

The park is nearly soundless. It's midday in early autumn, and kids are in school.

Except Calem.

Up ahead, I hear scuffling noises and something muffled.

I go on alert, my heartbeats piling up like stacked boxes, jamming into my throat.

But I hold steady, wishing I didn't have to do without my earpiece and mic. I'm flying blind and don't like it. Of course, who does?

I round the corner and duck behind a tree, drawing my weapon.

The man who was talking to Candi earlier is on the ground. Bleeding.

Another man is talking to her, and Calem's tucked behind her protectively.

A thrill of fear zings through me. The man's back is to me and I can't see his face. Something's gone south. I'm sure Candi incapacitated the perp. *But why? Why screw our covers?*

Then the man turns, as if sensing my presence.

I nearly drop my gun at the sight of him. My knees go weak. I feel like I just got shot back in time about twenty years.

"Come out from behind that tree, William. And toss the weapon."

The sound of his voice sews a thread of terror through my body with a poisonous needle.

With his left hand, he shows me the gun he's trained on my sister.

With his right, he beckons.

I have no choice. I walk toward my father.

Viper

"Where *is* Puck?" I say, gritting my teeth.

Mover lifts a shoulder casually. "I implied he'd find the woman at your club. An educated guess. No more." He adjusts the sleeves of his suit jacket, and a wave of pure hate warms me to my core.

His eyes stare into mine. Dark like a raven's wing. They used to match his hair, before it began to silver at the temples.

Not unlike my own.

"Was I correct in that assumption?"

I nod. "Sure were. He came in there like a gunslinger and shot one of the brothers and took Candice Arlington."

Mover gives another shrug that simultaneously says everything and nothing.

"She's the bitch that's feeding kids to that trafficking ring that sprouted up the instant Ned was permanently put out of commission," Noose expounds at my back.

"Candice Arlington is one of ours," Mover admits reluctantly. "But we have bigger problems."

Goosebumps roll over my bare skin, my deeds piling up inside my mind. Mover confirms my suspicions in one verbal fell swoop. His admission is almost too easy. That, in turn, causes suspicion to take root. Candice is FBI. *Okay, one mystery solved.*

"Like most of our operations, we have distinctive roles and serve in only those capacities. And in this case, we both have the same Bureau contact—only one—who choreographs everything."

"We thought Candice was a trafficking liaison. A mule," I say.

"She's meant to appear that way. Unfortunately, the cop, Puck, he is determined to see his part through—as we are. He knows my role, but I was unable to reveal Candice to him."

"Why?"

"Because it would compromise the last, critical detail that by a fluke of circumstance will go perfectly well if uninterrupted."

"He took her!" I yell, and Noose straightens, as does a man with a clear case of scarring from a bout of teen acne.

They face off, eyes only for each other.

Tension is high, and every bit of rivalry that's ever been there between Road Kill and Chaos Riders is stuffed in the space we share.

My voice drops to a dangerous roar. "He doesn't know she's a fed. He might hurt her."

Mover smiles. "Candice Arlington is a capable agent. Puck doesn't have the skill set to stop her. She will see the handoff through."

Mover doesn't have a stake in Candice. He sees her as a small pawn on the Bureau's large chessboard.

I close the three-stride distance between him and me. I'm so close, he's somewhat out of focus. "Tell me where they're meeting."

"I can't do that."

I spin, shouting my fury into the room, feeling the cords of my neck rise with my rage.

"Why is this so important, Vince?" Mover uses my real name for the first time in twenty years.

Slowly, I turn to face him, leaning forward, I hold my fist against my chest. "Because I threw down for Candice. She's mine."

A surprised shout of laughter bursts out of him. "You're kidding?"

I step into his space, both my hands in fists. "Do I look like anything is remotely funny?"

Mover stands as well, and we face each other, staring each other down for a moment.

Then he says, "Let me get a clearer understanding. Road Kill MC thought they'd collapse the debauched child trafficking ring, without knowing two different law entities were involved. Then you grab a deep undercover FBI agent, rough her up—"

"We didn't know. Thought she was a mule."

Mover nods at Noose's insertion. "Nevertheless, she is a federal agent, and this was the final sting." His hand raises and he makes a fist, giving it an abbreviated pump of triumph. "The final piece to capture the one who's behind this."

"And now Puck has your agent and… what?" I ask.

"Now we wait until the handoff is complete. Then our team comes in and handles things the way we handled Ned."

"Well, Snare's not here because of the way you *handled* Sara," Noose says in a voice gone low with barely contained menace.

Mover's dark eyes narrow like a shadow on Noose. "Not everything I've done, I'm proud of."

"No shit," Noose states with a heavy dose of sarcasm.

Mover gives him a withering stare then says, "Dagger."

Dagger, the guy with the acne scars, moves forward out of the shadows.

"Debrief Vince about our other problem."

Dagger slides his attention to Noose for a moment then returns it to me. His entire demeanor changes. Standing up straighter, he clasps big hands behind his back.

Gone is the typical rider surliness. Instead, his eyes sharpen on me. "We have an agent within your ranks, and he's gone rogue. The timing couldn't be worse. We were in no position to go after him. We're at a critical junction in the apprehension of the man responsible for this pedophile trafficking ring. We could not go in and take him. Even now, he believes everything is a go."

"What 'go'?"

"He is working with myself and Mover—Thom—to see this last handoff through, but he was not aware that Arlington was an agent, either. He was vetted too early. There are some things in his past that make him too volatile for the role he's been assigned, but there wasn't anyone else we thought would be a believable enough fit."

Dagger shrugs.

"Fucking Storm," Noose guesses, pushing away from the wall he was leaning against, a grimace twisting his lips. "Don't you boys do some bigtime psyche profiling? *Pfft.*"

Yeah. Fucking Storm. All the pieces of the puzzle are fitting together beautifully.

"He fractured her rib," I say almost to myself.

"And you allowed that." Mover's eyes glitter at me from the short distance that separates us.

I whirl to face him. "*No*. Didn't know what he was going to do fast enough. I'm not a fucking mind reader."

"So we have an injured agent, courtesy of Road Kill MC, a rogue agent who thinks his role within this case is progressive, and the entire thing hinges on Arlington making the meet and handing over Calem Oscar."

"I want to be there."

Mover folds his arms and gives a chuckle. "Now that's rich." He cocks his perfectly groomed head to the left, studying me. "Did you hear me? This is an *FBI case.* The police are also involved, and their key player believes Arlington is a mule and in no way suspects her real status. Putting you in the mix is out of the question. Look at how you handled it when you got ahold of her." His eyes go razor sharp on me in condemnation. "What happened between the two of you to make you decide she was going to be your property? You haven't cared for a female since Colleen."

My body tenses. "You don't deserve to say her name."

"Me saying her name doesn't kill her twice, Vince."

Our chests touch now—my Slipknot T-shirt and his thousand-dollar suit. "Shut the fuck up, Thom."

He lifts his hands, palms out in a sign of surrender. "Fine. I am telling you to stay out of this. Let agent Arlington do her job. I told you more than I should, Vince—more than I needed to. And if you still want to pursue her after this is through"—he leans against their version of a church table and claps his hands on his thighs—"be my guest."

I can tell by his expression he thinks a lasting thing between an agent and me is a long shot.

Well, fuck him.

"Let's go," Noose says. And the intensity of his comment has me looking at him.

I sharpen right up on his subtle tell and turn to Mover. "Fine. But just so you know—this isn't over. We're not over." I fling an index finger between us.

Mover stands and extends his hand, ignoring my threat. "I would do anything to take back the wrongs I vested upon you, Vince."

I would too.

Hard to erase our history. But I can't keep blaming him for Colleen's death—or our missed time. Someday, I'll have to learn to forgive.

That will have to be later, though. I've got property to find, protect, and claim. Whether Candice knows it or not.

I don't drop something that is important to me. Ever. No shirking of duty. No ignoring a second chance. No matter how remote.

And haven't I heard that tune somewhere before? Colleen wasn't easy. But she was the best complication of love I've ever known.

Easy doesn't mean real.

Noose and I cruise out of there like our asses are on fire.

He claps my shoulder as I'm getting on my ride and we've made distance from the Chaos club's door.

"What is it?" I ask. I know he has something. I saw it back when we were having the little convo with Dagger and Thom.

He grins like that cat that just swallowed an obese canary. "Got trackers on every brother's bike."

It's a safety thing. If someone tries to fuck up one of our own, we can locate them. Nothing more.

Until now.

Of course, it's part of Noose's job within Road Kill to secure just that exact flavor of shit. And it takes about four point two seconds for me to put together that he knows where Storm is.

That means we know where Candice and Calem are too. Storm must have been tailing her.

The relief is so powerful, I almost feel like I'm going to puke. A wave of lightheadedness sweeps through me.

"You okay? Kinda paled-out there, hoss," Noose says, a frown forming between his eyes.

"No," I admit in a rough exhale. "I just thought we were fucked, that there was no hope of finding her. Felt like my guts were scooped out."

"Maybe she's okay," Noose says.

I shake my head. "Too many variables. Fucking Puck. Storm, for shit's sake. They don't know what Candice is, and she'll die keeping the secret. She almost did with us. Hell, she might become a mule for real."

"We can't have that," Noose says, lighting up while his free hand digs around in the small gear bag hanging between his handlebars. Extracting a black device that's about the size of a half-sandwich, he flicks on a small stem, and lights flicker on.

Shooting out a smoke ring, he points his cigarette at the flashing lights on the device. "Active cruisers." He points to ones that are lit but not flashing. "Inactive."

Five are blinking.

I scrub my palm over my face. "Who's fucking who's?"

"Settle, chief." Noose runs down the flashers and stops on the very last light. "Got 'em in order of patch in. Keeps it straight for me."

"Do you know where he is?" I ask in clipped monosyllables.

"Unforgettable. Know that fucking place anywhere." He taps the top of his head, and a long ash falls like gray snow to the ground between us.

I feel one eyebrow shoot up. I'll explode if he doesn't tell me before my next breath.

"Scenic Park."

My breath wheezes out of me. Guess that makes sense. They always handoff in parks. First Gasworks. Now Scenic.

"Let's ride," I say, whipping my leg over the seat and starting it with a roar and kick of throttle.

Noose tosses the device into his satchel and hops on his ride. Then we ride out of Chaos territory like a couple of bats out of hell.

Chapter 22

Viper

Noose pulls into the parking lot of a park I've been to maybe twice.

Growing up in Kent, a kid could actually bike to this spot and not get creamed. Hell, my much-older brother rode his bike down Benson on the east hill and would hardly *see* a car in those days.

That was back when, though.

When kids drank out of the garden hose and rode in the backs of pickups and Moms relied solely on their own arms stretched across the front seat as seatbelts. Shit's changed.

Sliding off my bike, I drop the short distance to the ground and take in the surroundings.

Noose turns off his engine and gimps over, grabbing a cig. He crams it into his craw and lights it in one practiced motion.

"Fucking Storm is FBI," I say.

"Yup."

Smoke curls around his head, giving him the appearance of having horns before it floats away.

"Thought you were supposed to vet that shit?"

Noose smirks. "Never saw it." He shoots a ring into the late-day sunlight. "Never thought to look for it, either. Knock my ass over with a feather. That fucking handy revelation sucked."

"He's fucking crazy too and a woman hater."

"Bad combo," Noose agrees and holds up the transmitter with his free hand, showing a blinking light.

The light snuffs out as I look. "Got lucky that he was still firing off a signal until we got here."

Surveying the landscape, I don't see a soul. My eyes take in the nearly empty parking lot. No cars are around.

Where the fuck is Candice?

"You packing?" I ask Noose without taking my eyes off the environment. I expect the worst and hope for the best. That phrase my old man taught me is the truest fucking thing I've ever heard.

"Ropes."

I roll my eyes. I have a gun and a knife.

"It's all I need at the moment, and you, hoss—you've got hardware?"

I nod. *We're covered.* "Where do we start?" I swipe a hand over my hair. "Fuck, this is frustrating."

"For starters, let's get the fuck outta the open. You know this, but your head is so far up your ass you can't think it through."

"Asshole." I stab a finger in his direction. "That's why *you're* here."

I scan the park again.

"Ah-huh," Noose grunts.

I swing my head back to face him.

He shrugs. "Let's go." He jerks his jaw toward where a narrow asphalt running path begins, meandering through a dense copse of trees.

I don't like it. Of course, I'm not much for being out here in the middle of everything. Too much open space. Just like Noose said—anyone could fucking nail us.

And the place is supposedly lousy with cops and feds.

"Hate being out in the open," Noose comments again, echoing my thoughts like telepathy.

"Yeah."

We get to the path, Noose having a slight limp that keeps him slower. "As long as we don't do anything, the feds can't get us for anything."

Noose cocks his head, giving me a sideways look through a veil of smoke. "We're here to observe, chief?"

"Depends."

He chuckles. "That's what I figured. Damn, it's hard to be right all the time."

"How's your knee?" I ask him as he does the stiff limp beside me.

"Fucked up. But…" He takes a last drag on his smoke and tosses it on the ground, where it smolders until he crushes it with his uninjured leg, twisting his boot on the dying ember. "It's not my clutch leg."

"Lucky break."

His face smooths to neutral. "I can still knot somebody."

We exchange a somber look.

"Yeah," I agree softly. "Yeah, you can."

We continue down the path, hoping for a needle in a haystack. A hot, mysterious, damsel-in-distress needle.

A low, throaty shout sounds just beyond our location.

Noose tenses.

I run toward that sound, adrenaline pouring through me like an open faucet.

Candice.

It sounds so much like the noises she made when we were sexing each other up. I would know it anywhere. But this one is filled with fear instead of heat.

Weird how the two sounds are so similar.

A sharp whistle from behind me lets me know Noose can't run.

Wants me to hold on.

Can't.

I round the corner. A large tree swoops in a twist, reaching across the path, the leaves appear like green fingers extended toward me.

Dappled light filters across the dark path, jumping as the figures come into view, and I skid to a stop.

A man about ten years older than me, dressed in a suit, holds a gun at Candice with this left hand, arm extended, while Calem cowers behind her.

What the fuck is this?

Puck walks toward the guy holding the gun as another man writhes on the ground, moaning and bleeding.

Fuck this. I walk straight for Candice.

The guy with the gun flicks his eyes to me. "Stay where you are, or I blow her head off."

Puck and I stop our forward momentum.

Candice's eyes are on me, silently pleading for me to go, telling me she doesn't need saving. It's like she's speaking to me without a word crossing her lips.

Telepathy again, but this time it's painful, etching itself into my brain.

Her need. Her fear.

Noose comes up behind me, smelling of engine oil, cigarettes, and the indefinable smell I associate with him.

"Prick," he mutters at me.

"William, Candice, and the boy are coming with me." The man's eyes are the same color as Candice's, glowing like soft twin suns in the murky gloom of the deep woods.

That's when I know.

He's got to be her dad—looks just like her, and the age is right.

So why is Dear Old Dad holding a gun on his daughter? Why is there some guy on the ground who just got his clock cleaned?

And where is the fucking law?

Lots of unanswered questions. But I don't need the answers now. I just need Candice. Away from here and protected.

"I don't care about him." I fling a thumb at Puck. He took Candice, so maybe he's turned bad. He can be out of the immediate equation. I'm fine with that.

Then there's Storm lurking around somewhere. My eyes find Candice again. She's worth it. "I want Candice and the kid."

The man smiles, and the ghost of Candice haunts his face. It's fucking eerie. "Have you *had* her?" His voice carries but the question is asked in a low tone.

Not enough. I could have her every day for the rest of my life, and it would never be enough.

His eyes hold mine. "My *sweet* Candi," he adds.

What. The. Fuck? My head whips in her direction.

Large tears roll down her cheeks. Guilt, terror, and rage trail down her face like wet traffic to leak off her jaw. Her knuckles bleed white where she grips Calem's T-shirt.

Slowly, I turn back to the dad. "Why don't you fuck off," I tell the guy. "Give me the girl and the kid, and we'll be out of here."

He keeps me and Puck in his sights, but the smug smile that climbs his face is all for me. "I take what's mine, biker dredge."

"Sounds like somebody needs an attitude adjustment," Noose says.

"Be that as it may," he returns instantly, "I am the one with my weapon trained on my whore of a daughter."

Candice flinches at "whore."

And… he just admitted what their connection is.

I know whores. Hell, I've fucked enough. Candice Arlington is a lot of things, but whore wouldn't be anything I'd connect with her.

"Candi, come, or I'll shoot this derelict who seems so intent on taking you from your daddy."

"Keep your fucking hands off her." Puck speaks up for the first time, hands fisting at his sides.

He never even looked my way when I showed up. His eyes were on the man with the weapon.

With the power.

"Oh, I don't think so, William. Candi and I will be getting deliciously reacquainted."

Candice mewls, fear and loathing racing over every inch of her body.

"Where are the feds and cops?" Noose asks for my ears only.

Yes, exactly. I give a small shake of my head.

Candice begins walking toward him, and each step she takes is filled with reluctant dread.

"Don't go to him," I say in low command.

She shakes her head. "He'll kill you."

I step forward.

Her father clicks the hammer back. "If I can't have tasty Candi, no one can." His smile is lecherous. "Come to Daddy, precious."

Candice makes a sound out of her throat, so soft I strain to hear it.

Whimpering.

Calem follows as if in the middle of a nightmare, face pale, both hands wrapped around Candi's. But Candice lets go of his small hands when she gets within range of her father.

He points the gun at her chest.

"Get down on your knees."

No.

"Fuck," Noose whispers in revulsion.

"No," she answers, voice filled with fury.

He turns the gun from her to Calem.

Puck takes a step.

"Don't," he says, giving the weapon a boost, and it nods at the boy.

Noose and I inch forward. It's damn hard to keep this many people at bay with one weapon. He's only got two eyes.

Without warning, Candice steps into the weapon's line of fire, slapping her hand into the barrel, and it goes skyward as she plunges the knuckles of her other hand into the man's throat.

A ragged cough escapes as he collapses to his knees, surprise widening those striking eyes.

Then Puck is there, taking him down, and Candice kicks the gun away as Calem starts crying.

Puck starts to beat the father.

Leaving him to it, I jog to where Candice stands. Ignoring the bleeding guy on the ground and Puck, I grab her carefully and draw her against me. "Thought I'd lost you," I say against her temple.

My heart beats heavy in my chest, like it weighs a thousand pounds.

Then Candice slides her arms around my waist, and she hangs on.

Feels right. *Perfect.*

Right now, everything I just went through has been worth it for this moment in her arms.

"Step away from Arlington."

Storm.

We turn. Storm stands there, wearing SWAT-type gear, just like the two obvious feds alongside him.

I can't believe I never saw it before. Saw the crazy but never saw the law.

His eyes move to Candice, face somber. "I'm sorry about the rib."

Candice takes a shaky breath, eyes widening at the sight of Storm in law enforcement gear with two agents by his side; apparently putting together his involvement for the first time. "It's okay. I lived."

I take a step back from her. "You know Storm?"

She shakes her head. "Don't say anything more, Viper—please." Her eyes move to Puck.

When we turn to look at him, he's still beating the fuck out of her dad.

"No!" Candice screams, tearing out of my grip and running to Puck. "Don't! We finally have him, Puck!"

Noose drawls, "You're not gonna have much. He's tenderized meat at this stage."

Blood drips from Puck's knuckles as he stands, and Candice launches herself at him, nearly tipping him over. "Don't. I love you, but don't. Let justice be served."

Puck steadies, then hugs her tight against him. "He's never touching you again."

She nods against his chest. "I know."

Never touching her again.

His words echo inside my skull.

I look at the man lying on the ground, practically taking a dirt nap, and want to stomp him into the ground myself.

I must make some move toward him because Noose has suddenly captured my arm.

"Don't." His gray eyes clash with mine. "She's with *Puck*." His eyebrows slowly rise. "Didn't you hear her?"

I did. Just don't want to listen. *Puck.* Something tears inside me. For a woman I've known for less than two days.

I sort of stagger backward, taking in the scene of Puck and Candice embracing over a father who apparently molested her when she should have been protected instead.

A man who wanted her again. The man responsible for the kiddie ring?

Storm moves in, giving hand signals to the other feds, and a group of suits suddenly appear, swarming the barely breathing sack-of-shit dad.

When they have him trussed like a turkey, along with the other guy who someone beat to fuck, Candice walks over to me, Calem close by her side.

Puck watches her movements with an expression I can't quite read. There's possession in his eyes, along with something else.

I stop looking at him and look at Candice. Randomly, I notice she's got sweet butt clothes on. They don't look like her.

I swallow some fucked-up emotion like it's a ball gag.

"So now you know," she says softly.

Not just that she's a fed, but the other childhood horrors. And that she was playing me. She was with Puck all along.

I don't understand her angle, but the destruction of me—that's real—thorough.

I had a normal childhood filled with home-cooked meals, an American flag that flew from the front porch, and a dad that kicked my ass only when I needed it.

I have no frame of reference for being a helpless girl fighting off her father.

I look at her worthless dad again, half-conscious and in cuffs. And I have the same urge again to do what Puck did—and more.

She glances at Noose, and he puts his palms up, limping back a few paces, giving us the illusion of privacy.

"I know," I concede. There's so much more I want to say, but don't. Too much audience.

Too much pride.

"Thank you, Viper."

For what? For hurting her? Fucking her?

I shut my eyes so I can't see her anymore.

Is she thanking me for maybe loving her? Because that's what a rider does when he throws down for a female. It's not just about fucking.

It's not simple.

Like I always told the crew, real pussy is a complicated thing.

And it seems like complicated pussy is the only thing a man wants for the long term. Figures.

"How did you find me?"

Opening my eyes, I glance at Storm, who's in the middle of working out the kinks of lassoing the prick that was the head of the trafficking.

At least, that's how it looks like from my end. "Noose had a tracker on Storm's bike. Safety protocol. But where he was…"

"You figured I'd be."

Hoped. I nod.

Then an idea forms in my head. A bad one. "Mover told us where you might be. Him and Dagger said Storm had gone rogue."

Candice frowns. "No. That can't possibly be true."

She turns, her hand warm as it cups my side. "Puck!"

By this time, cops have shown up, and he's in the middle of a huddle. His eyes rise and meet hers.

He jogs over. "You okay?"

Her eyes tighten, and she shakes her head. "Not really, but I can pretend until I can get out of this place."

Puck takes her free hand, his other is gripping Calem.

A thin veil of red blocks my vision, and I want to strangle Puck.

The facts are glaring.

Candice screwed *me* when she was with *him*. I guess it was all just negotiation, after all.

Whoever says men don't feel never had their hearts dragged from their body cavity and summarily shredded by a woman.

I breathe deeply, taking hold of my emotions with an iron fist. Candice just faced her molester. I'm not going to jump her shit.

Or beat down Puck.

Yet.

Candice tells Puck what I said.

"Mover," Puck grates. "*Knew it.*"

I shake my head, picking up on the undercurrent. "Thom isn't involved. He *led* us to you."

She frowns up at me. "There's no agent involved named Dagger posing within Chaos."

Shit.

I take ahold of her shoulders. "Then why was Mover telling us where to find you?"

Puck and she exchange a glance.

"To put us here at the scene," Candice states in an empty voice.

Storm walks up, casting a look over us all.

"Viper." He nods then looks to Candice. "What happened here? The perp is claiming police brutality." He shoots a cool look at Puck.

I openly stare at Storm. He's not the same guy. At all.

Noose rubs a hand over his nape, his expression as incredulous as mine.

Puck's face suffuses with color. "He's Candi's dad."

Storm's deep red eyebrow shoots up. "Yeah? Well that's an interesting coincidence. And he has a permit to carry concealed. And he doesn't know the other guy that someone took care of." His light-hazel eyes flick to Candice then away.

Candice just keeps looking more sick as Storm's words flow.

I can predict where this is going, and it's not good.

"He's gonna walk," Noose comments slowly. "This whole thing was very smooth on their parts."

"He's dirty," Candice states.

"Yes, but we still don't have him," Storm says. "And you're both... well—" Storm rocks back on his heels, looking at Puck like he's a worm. "I can't speak for him, but Arlington"—Storm looks at her—"they're going to nail you to the wall for showing up here, and the handoff didn't happen first before you defended." His eyes move to me. "You'll be signing non-disclosures up the ass, just in case you're wondering."

My lips twist at the irony. "Actually, I wasn't."

He moves his attention back to her. "Then your *dad* gets beaten up by a cop who just happens to be here horning in on our investigation. How was he right here at the right time?"

Storm and Puck glare at each other. I expect them to whip out their dicks at any moment and compare sizes.

I have this. Puck's fucking Candice, so there's pillow talk, and he shows up here because they're both on the same case, just different law enforcement. *Nice*. Way to fuck up a career. But since I'm a one percenter, I don't care about all that.

I guess oil and water don't mix after all.

Maybe if Candice wasn't involved with another man and married to the FBI, there might've been something between us.

More than something.

Walking away from her feels like being an old-growth tree torn out of its century-old forest by the roots.

But that's what I need to do.

I back up, never taking my eyes from her. Because if I do, maybe she'll just disappear.

Candice turns away from Storm, sees me leaving.

"Wait, Viper—" she says, dropping the two hands she holds and running after me.

I pivot, showing her my back as Noose and I stride out of there.

"Viper!" she yells.

I half-turn. She grabs me around my neck with a firm hand and draws my face down to hers, practically hanging off me like a monkey.

Kisses me.

Wet. Deep. Long. Every bit of what we did comes back with ferocious clarity.

The scent of her body. The softness. The taste.

Tactile overload unfolds in a kind of slow-motion, erotic pulse that threads between our bodies, and it's the hardest thing I've ever done not to crush that small body against mine and leave here with Candice on the back of my bike and never look back.

Instead, I break the contact, our chests both heaving, and gently put her away from me.

Looking over her shoulder, I see Puck, Storm, and Calem.

That's enough.

Then I walk away with the taste of her on my lips, the scent of her filling my nose, the feel of her body perfectly fitted to mine.

Chapter 23

Candice

I watch him walk away, and it feels like Viper used an ice pick on my heart, taking a chunk he didn't think I needed.

But I do need it.

This man who didn't ask for anything and went to the ends of the earth to find me.

A despised woman. A woman deserving of everything his men had planned on doing.

I need to make this right with Viper. With me.

But first, my father will have to be dealt with. Reluctantly, I turn away from him and walk back to my brother and Calem.

Agent Ren Stanwood—aka Storm— is right. I'll need to face the firing squad, and it won't be pretty.

"Administrative leave?" I nearly yell at my supervisor, and his pale-green eyes tighten at the loudness of my voice.

"I've been on this case for *three* years, Ted. We *have* the one responsible."

My fucking father, *of course,* of all the life ironies—it has to be him. The pinnacle of Murphy's Law, staring us all right in the face.

"Candice," Ted begins, scraping a tired hand over his face before dumping his chin into his palm. "Listen, Thom is MIA, and Samuel Jerstad, has no criminal record, and is a *pillar* of the community."

I grit my teeth. "He was my rapist, Ted."

Ted hangs his head, eyes downcast. "I know that he is your biological father and…" He looks at me with clear expectation.

"Puck's father."

"There's so much disregard here, Candi. The fact that you and William were working in tandem, against law enforcement policy for both police and Bureau entities. That Puck ruthlessly beat up a civilian—regardless of blood relation. This guy is our man. But now, with everything that went down, we can't charge him."

"Jerstad *said* he would do things to me again. Ted—he held me at gunpoint."

"I believe you, Candi—God knows. But there are no witnesses who corroborate it. Puck's testimony is negated because he took matters into his own hands. Calem Oscar is too young, and the guy who was your mark for the meet, you beat down because he tried to grope you."

A scream of frustration lodges in my throat. I've been made as FBI, Mover has flown the coop, and my own perverted father is *absofuckinglutely* involved in this operation. But because of his clever wording and Puck's fists, he *will* get bail. Even if he did have a record, Samuel Jerstad has more money than God.

"The statute of limitations on your abuse has run out, Candi. We couldn't nail your father for his crimes against you now even if we wanted to." His eyes land on me, brimming with compassion. "And man, do I want to."

It all makes horrible sense to me—that's why the perverted fucker is spearheading the minor trafficking. I knew he had a taste for young flesh because I was his first victim. Or maybe not. That epiphany makes me even sicker.

"*I* want to." I breathe my anger out in a flush of heat.

Ted leans forward, resting both hands on his thighs. "Right now, the best I can do is hold him for twenty-four hours. Then he's free."

Our gazes lock. Ted, who's been my direct supervisor for ten years, is my rock. He's not Puck, but he's a good man, and a great human being to have my back. "I can't help you this time, Candi. You're one of our best agents, but there were too many variables that broke the rules. And now we'll have to wait and see if we can flesh them out again. From a new angle."

"They're like cockroaches. They've scuttled away to find another dark hole to crawl into and hide. Meanwhile, you know they're not going to stop taking children." My eyes plead. My words beg.

Ted clasps his hands, leaning his butt against the massive wood desk again, and gives a curt nod. "Understood. A helluva lot of manhours were lost on this. We can tag Jerstad with surveillance until we're blue in the face, but you and I both know that the chief doesn't do squat, but he's got plenty of Indians who will."

I give a sad laugh. "That's not very politically correct, Ted."

"Just my age showing," he says, weaving blunt fingers through his short silvering crop of hair. And I realize with a pang that at almost sixty, Ted won't be here much longer. His absence will leave a void.

His grin comes out lopsided. "I still want to say what comes to mind without constantly worrying about fear of offending whatever—*whoever*." Ted's weary exhale is the only sound for a handful of seconds.

"Yeah." My answer is soft, my heart heavy.

"It's a month, Candi. Not the end of the world."

"Maybe the end of *my* world." *Because I never built another.* There was no other contingency for me not being a fed, except the dream Puck and I have clung to.

"I wasn't going to bring it up before, but… this would be the best time in the world for you to retire."

I snap my face to Ted, meeting his light grass-green eyes. "You think I can't hack it?" I put my palm on my chest, unable to stop the hurt and insult saturating my voice.

"I *know* you can." He pulls his pantleg at the knee and crosses one leg over the other. "You were my most gifted agent."

The beginnings of a bright headache begin behind my eyes.

"Then what is it?"

"I feel that natural gift has been… exploited, used, and warped. I want you to seriously consider retirement." He adds, "You were in the early program for trainees?"

I give a numb nod. I was in a special program the Bureau had in the early 90s to entice more women field agents.

I was smitten. I could start my FBI clock ticking. All my training began right out of high school. I attended college while training to be an agent, so technically, I will have my twenty years satisfied in just a few months. Government math doesn't always add up, and I've never taken a sick day.

"Between your unspent sick days, vacation, and leave time—you could retire tomorrow."

He's right, and his restating of the facts frightens me.

"I'm not ready to stop working, Ted. Even now, I'm wondering what happened to Mover. *When* Jerstad will be nailed to the wall?" Biting my lip, I don't allow myself to entertain that bastard not paying for his sins against me and Puck—against untold minors.

My mind finally settles on Calem. "And where Calem Oscar will finally land."

"Somewhere safe," Ted answers. "I'm just telling you to seriously consider the idea, Candi."

After a full minute, I answer, "Okay."

"About Samuel Jerstad."

My gut tightens when I hear his name.

"You didn't know where he was or hadn't seen him?"

I shake my head. "Puck and I took off as soon as I graduated, and I never looked back."

"Why didn't you press charges against him then, Candi?"

I don't have a good answer, but I start with the truth. "I was ashamed. I sound like all the other cliché women out there." My eyes meet his. "But we're *not* clichés, Ted. The real truth is, we're human beings who desperately want to trust men. And the man I was supposed to believe in and trust the most hurt me in the most despicable way."

Ted takes my hand. "I hate that fucker."

I lift my chin. "Not more than Puck and I do." I look away, staring out all the glass that runs the entire length of his wall in the inconspicuous high-rise building that hides my region's Bureau headquarters. "And that's the other thing. Puck was running interference back then. He'd help me when he could—then our dad would hurt him too. So it was like a double wound to me. I'd be molested, then he'd hurt my brother for interfering with the abuse."

Ted lets my hand drop and gives a low whistle.

"So you both went into law."

I turn away from the window and stare at him.

"Doesn't take a psychiatrist to figure out why," he adds.

I softly shake my head. "No, like a lot of abused people, we wanted to make a difference."

"Candi, you did."

I cover my mouth, trying not to weep, because if I let my despair escape, it might never stop.

His eyes run over my face. "Take the thirty days to think about what I said."

I stand, nodding quickly, holding my eyes wide so the tears don't fall. "Thanks, Ted."

"Call me if you need *anything*. To talk, whatever."

I don't turn around. I keep walking, focused on that door that leads out of his office and out of the Bureau.

I feel lighter without my gun and badge.

But not better.

He's not left my head in the week since the failed sting went down.

Viper.

Just thinking about him brings all that wonderful lust and butterflies back to life in the center of my being. The wings of excitement and the potential for happiness flutter against my tender insides.

Not doing what I want has been agonizing. But keeping a low profile was necessary after Puck and I got the same slap on the wrist.

Though I feel like Puck's got broken. They didn't tell him to contemplate retiring—they told him to do it.

Like me, Puck has a lot of unspent time off, and when he added it all up, he had his twenty and a hefty buyout for the remainder. He'll realize his dream of leaving behind the merciless lifestyle of undercover stress and a vast nothingness.

I feel set adrift, though.

It's wonderful to finally claim a normal relationship with my brother. To see him anytime I want. To sleep in for once.

The first few days off, I slept in like I was in a coma.

I didn't sleep, though, on the day they released Samuel Jerstad. *Insufficient evidence*, the court cited.

Jerstad didn't press charges against Puck.

I would think not; Jerstad wouldn't want anything *unsavory* coming to light.

And Ted was right. The statute of limitations for the crimes against me is long gone. But not the one for my soul.

That statute has no end.

There was one thing I wanted to do, a loop I needed to close, even if it hurt me to do it. But I've been biding my time.

I back my Scion out of my garage for the last time. My car only has two large duffels and four totes—the last of my life in six pieces. I leave the scene of my own kidnapping, knowing I won't be back. The busted walls and blood over the carpet will mean losing my deposit.

My lips quirk with black humor. *The Bureau can pick up that tab.*

I'm staying in the small guest bedroom at Puck's now, and he's been cooking for me—a lighter man now. I've moved my things to his place. He and I have been walking the land around his old farmhouse, picking out potential building sites.

My rib feels better, though it's not even been two weeks. I'm a fast healer, I guess. I keep remembering Viper's perfect place, and sadness overwhelms me until I put it on a mental shelf with the other boxes I never inspect.

I drive from between the shoulder blades of Renton and Kent and travel east.

Toward Viper.

And maybe, absolution.

Viper

Doing restoration work is funny. Ninety percent gets done, and that nagging ten percent lingers.

Well, no longer.

Candice Arlington saw to that.

Having her fuck me up was like putting diesel in a gas engine. I needed to work that shit out.

She walked out of my life, and now the void she left is a whirlpool. Slowly sucking me down.

Down.

Didn't matter that Storm came and apologized for how he had to act. "In character," he said and muttered words like, "deep undercover" and "role playing." *For the better good.*

Candice hadn't even known. Talk about the left hand not talking to the right.

I guess Storm wasn't too bad. Maybe he even believed in the MC "role" more than he let on. He told the powers that be he hadn't seen or heard anything that would lead him to believe we were a *criminal* biker club. We'd committed crimes, though, and he knew it. Storm, whose real name is Ren Stanwood, was a brother in the end, and maybe not the best pick for a fed.

Like there's a clean MC? What a joke.

I signed all the non-disclosures he wanted. Second time around on that one. Hell, I feel like I should be on FBI retainer or something.

I'm not fooled, the feds' eyes *had* to be sharp on our club. We've been close to way too much illegal shit in the last few years. Where there's smoke, there's fire.

So I agreed not to talk about any of the proceedings or what I'd witnessed.

Like Candice's father saying he wanted to do those sick things to her again.

Or the look of relief on her face when she realized I'd ridden in like the cavalry. The pleasure was so transparent, so naked, that I knew in that instant no one ever saved her before. Not in that exact way.

I would never tell anyone how good that slut outfit looked on her or how much better I knew she looked naked. That would remain our secret. Our pleasure.

That knowledge all slid through my brain in a heartbeat's pause of time.

Standing, I press my palm into my lower back and groan. Been on my fucking hands and knees all day, getting the finishing touches done upstairs.

Basement's perfect. One hundred percent done. A damn miracle of epic proportions.

Now my floor is up top too.

After dumping my toolbelt on the wide stone hearth of the fireplace, I stomp downstairs and to my bathroom. I crank on my fancy-pants shower and strip my shit before gliding under the hot water.

It's almost worth an orgasm to have this hot goodness after putting myself through the paces of sore knees and swabbing clear lacquer between baseboard and flooring.

Love this old place. I tip my head back, letting the hot spray run over my face, and shake my hair out, flinging water droplets. Resting my palm against the cold tile, I hang my head, letting the water run between my shoulder blades.

Candice springs up inside my head again. That bitch is relentless. At least, the memory of her is. If I spend too much time thinking about her, I'll have to jerk off. Already half-hard as it is.

Not doing that bullshit.

I finish up fast then get out, yanking a towel off a solid chrome towel hook.

Drying off, I cast a lustful glance up the stairs to where I know there's a beer waiting with my name on it.

The hell with carbs, I think, trudging up the stairs. I get to the top and hear gravel crunching.

I still, cocking my head and trying to identify a vehicle—bike—whatever. *What the fuck?*

Riders are riding, banging club whores, or getting tossed at the club.

I wanted some peace, and nobody better be fucking with my pie slice of quiet.

Tucking the towel into itself at my hip, I open the door and peer out.

Don't know the car, so I shut the door and walk to an old chest on the mantel above the river-rock hearth running the length of the wall. Opening the lid, I extract the gun then stalk back to the door.

Flipping the latch again, I jerk the thing wide, wearing nothing but my towel, and a piece in my hand.

Candice is standing there with her hand raised. Poised to knock, I think.

Slowly, her hand drops as she takes in my state of undress and the gun.

We stare at each other for a solid minute, and my dick comes to life again.

Swell.

"Are you going to shoot me?" she asks softly, pure golden eyes melting me like molten fire.

No. But I want to fuck her. My cock's *all* about that. "No," I croak, clear my throat, and try again. "What do you want, Candice? Thought you made things clear that we weren't doing this."

"It wasn't clear to me," she says, and with one hand, she jerks the towel from my hips.

Boner goes full tilt.

I pull her into the house and kick the door shut.

Chapter 24

Candice

I meant to talk. I really, really did. Then I saw him there with only a towel and a gun in one hand, water dripping down his muscular body.

My hungry eyes eat up Viper's form. Mature, deadly, tender. He's all the stuff a man should be.

All the man I want him to be.

He's nothing like the horror show of an example from my childhood, but he's all that I dreamed could possibly exist.

The president of an MC has me in the palm of his hand like a fragile dove.

Will he release me… or keep me close?

I would have liked to sort those questions out and do the rational thing—close the "loops" as I intended. Instead, that bitch instalust has me by the clit, and with a shameless, throbbing intensity, she won't let go.

And I don't want her to.

The mistress of my libido carries me away as I strip Viper of his towel, and he stands, legs planted wide, wearing a giant erection and nothing else.

He grabs my hand and hauls me inside, kicking the door shut.

Viper's intense aqua gaze holds me hostage. "What are you fucking doing here, Candice?"

I'm breathless but manage, "Hopefully, everything."

"Dammit," Viper sets the gun on the windowsill next to the door and moves me against the solid wood with a press of hips.

His body flattens mine, heavy arms caging my head, and my breasts smoosh against his chest.

"Do you want this?"

I nod. *God help me, I do.* "I thought we'd talk," I say vaguely, heart in my throat and panties damp with anticipation.

"You fucked that idea at hello," he growls.

"Yeah." My voice is breathy.

"We can talk later." Dipping his head, he slides his hands from the wood of the door to cradle my face.

The intensity in his eyes makes me think he'll bruise my lips, but Viper doesn't. His feather-light kiss is like a delicate promise to plunder. Sipping, pecking, Viper finally licks the seam, and I open my mouth. Our tongues twine as my hands find his short hair. Grabbing what I can of the short strands, I pull down hard, and his head jerks back, looking down at me.

"You like it rough?"

My fingers tighten inside the blunt strands. "Only with you."

He sighs, pressing his forehead against mine as my fingers stay buried in his thick hair.

"You spur a man on with your actions, Candice."

"I trust you. That's why I can. Why I'm free."

Viper opens his eyes, and a trick of low light, or not enough, makes the irises so translucent, they could be any color or none.

"I told you…"

He kisses me, and my breath stops.

"I'm fucked up."

Viper kisses me again and again. Heat and lust collide, but I have the last word before there's none left.

"But I think we're the same."

He shakes his head. "That's where you're wrong. I'm just the brand of fucked up you need—to be with me."

Viper gets me. Gets us. What we need to be to each other.

I gasp when his hands cup my ass and lift. He splits me between my legs with his cock, our eyes intimately level.

"Rib?" he asks, going back to licking and pecking my neck.

"Better." I suck in a breath when he nips the tender skin between my earlobe and collarbone.

My head falls back, gently tapping the door. With a sigh, I grant him better access as he sucks my throat. Pain and pleasure mix with perfect synchronicity, and when I think I can't stand another moment—and want even more of the same exquisite torture—Viper releases the suction, staring into my eyes from inches away. I like a man that asks permission when my body is already screaming yes, which he silently does so well.

"Yes," I whisper.

Opening his thighs, he rests me on them, and with both hands, he grasps my button-up blouse. With a mighty jerk, he tears the cloth apart, yanking my body and sending buttons flying. I cry out.

His eyes fly to my face. "Tell me I didn't hurt you."

I shake my head, so excited, I can't speak. *Breathe.*

"Good." My short skirt gets hiked.

I'm wearing only a G-string, and when he notices, Viper says in a hoarse voice, "Christ, Candice."

My pussy floods with moisture.

He slides down my body, spreading and pinning my thighs wide against the door.

The heat of his breath bathes my entrance.

"Oh my God!" I say, grabbing onto his hair as his deft finger moves the tiny string aside.

Then Viper's at my center, digging in.

"Ah!" I shout as his tongue finds my heat, lapping and stroking.

I'm helpless but not vulnerable.

His hands are gentle on my flesh as his tongue lashes my clit, circling my labia relentlessly over and over again, pausing only to suck my clit then moving again.

"Close," I breathe the word.

His pale-blue eyes roll to mine.

Shifting his weight, Viper plants a shoulder under one of my thighs, prying me even wider while supporting my weight.

"What?" I look down in a daze, hands loose on the top of his head.

One blue eye looks up at me, tongue hovering over my spread entrance.

Letting me slide down so that one of my legs rests against his propped knee, he moves his free hand between my legs.

Holding my gaze, Viper slowly puts two fingers inside me, sliding deep into my wetness. At the same time, he flattens his tongue on my clit.

My body seizes, and a deep warning pulse clenches inside my pussy right before I blow apart with a hoarse shout.

The sound is half pain, half shock, with pleasure in there somewhere.

Viper doesn't slow, but when the pulses of my channel subside, he lays off the pressure with his tongue, slowing the pump of his thick fingers deep inside me.

I sigh as an aftershock ripples through my core, and my thighs quiver.

"Oh my God," I whisper, my fingers falling away from his head.

He withdraws from me, and while I watch, he looks up at me, licking my juices from his fingers. "Like that?"

"Huh?" I asked, firmly in stupor-afterglow territory. I've never been with a man who goes down on me like Viper.

He begins to rise, pulling me with him, and my legs fall together as my knees buckle.

Viper chuckles, swinging me up into his arms. "Feeling good?"

I give a languid nod. "Oh yeah." *So, so good.*

He walks, and I go along for the ride. Down familiar stairs. But I won't be tortured this time.

Unless multiple orgasms are considered torture.

"No cuffs this time?" The ghost of a smile crosses his face, but I find I'm pretty distracted with the rest of the view.

"I'll go without for now," I reply softly, looking up at him from where he laid me down on the bed.

Looking down at me, Viper grasps my bare ankle and slowly spreads my legs. "But maybe some time."

A thrill shoots through me. "Yeah."

His cock stands at attention, bobbing as he knee-walks between my legs.

I roll over, placing my face against the soft sheets. My ass rises as I present myself to him like an offering, whispering "Please."

His hand is warm as his fingers travel my spine, caressing each bone. Then he grasps my shoulder, and I feel the head of him at my soaked entrance.

Wet from his attention and my orgasms.

I remember how Viper filled me before, and now he does again. He noses into my tightness that first inch then pulls back. Soon Viper is fucking the first third of me, always a sensitive part of my anatomy.

I feel every ripple as my pussy sucks at his cock.

"Oh God," I groan, and he grabs my forearms, moving to the end of me. My face is pressed against the sheets without support, and Viper pulls me backward by my arms, using the leverage to fuck me.

"Harder," I say, and it comes out slightly muffled.

But Viper does something different. Letting go of my arms, he takes my cheeks and puts them on his thighs, drawing me backward until I'm upright, with my back against his chest.

Bowing me.

My rib gives a twinge, but I ignore it.

Taming me with his dick deeply impaled, Viper arches his back and presses upward at the same time with his cock. One arm crossed against by breasts, pinning me against him, he rolls my nipple underneath his fingertips.

Another orgasm washes through my body like a tidal wave of pleasure, and I yell, involuntarily bucking against him as wave after wave of deep pulses wrack me.

But his arm is steel against my body, holding me tight like he'll never let me go.

And somewhere deep down inside of me—where I never go, never examine, and never look—I want him to keep me pinned against him in a forever embrace.

His pumping begins to speed. "Can't last with your tight cunt milking me," he rasps.

I feel him hardening subtly right before hot, wet seed fills me like a soothing balm.

Connecting me to him.

I might have just destroyed myself, or I might have found redemption, but as the fire of our mutual orgasm marries our bodies, I've never felt more entangled in my life.

In the best way possible.

From the ashes of the worst of circumstances.

Viper spoons me protectively, finger combing my hair away from my face and tucking it between our bodies.

"That was perfect," he says then lightly kisses the shell of my ear, making me shiver. "And I want to do it about another fifty-two times today." He pauses for a moment, and I laugh softly. "But we have to talk."

My good humor fades a little. "Yeah."

His voice is somber. "Nothing's funny, Candice."

I turn, only showing him half my face because of how we're wrapped up in each other. "I laughed because I can't believe what happened when all I wanted was to tell you…" I roll over a little more, and his hand stops its ceaseless affection.

Spreading his fingers across my bare stomach, he brands me with his warmth, and our eyes meet. "Shit," he says, voice shaky. "You affect me. And I shouldn't tell a woman that. There's probably a rule about that somewhere"

I put my fingers over his lips. "It's okay. I feel exactly the same about you. There's *definitely* a rule about that."

Relief sweeps his face and is gone so quickly, I'm not entirely sure I saw it.

"I wanted to explain things," I say, finishing my earlier thought.

"Like how you're fucking Puck—*and* me."

Viper rolls away from me onto his back, the absence of his touch is a cold void from my flesh.

He stares at the ceiling.

"*What*?" I nearly scream, sitting up and turning to him in one motion.

Viper's brow calmly ascends.

"Puck's not—*God*!" Then I think about it. Looking back on our interaction, I guess our affection could have been misconstrued. I never actually told him what Puck was to me. It was so clear to me who he was.

Viper sits up on an elbow. "What do you mean 'what'? It's fucking obvious."

I laugh.

His expression moves to instant thunder. "Okay, now you're starting to piss me off."

I push his shoulders down on the bed and quickly throw a leg over him, straddling his torso.

"That's not going to work," he says, but he's already got a half-hard-on.

"Puck's my *brother*."

His eyebrows shoot up, and his lips stretch into an awkward smile. "No shit?"

I nod. "No shit."

"That's why he was so… *violent* with that fucker."

I suck in a raw inhale. "Our father." My voice is devoid of emotion.

Viper puts his hands on my upper arms and spins me in one move until I'm on my back and he's above me.

I can't stop the tears when I see his eyes. They're filled with his emotions.

All for me.

He's allowing me to see him. Really see him.

And what I see is Viper's rage at the injustices against me.

"Well, I like Puck a helluva lot more now."

I smile through my tears, and he thumbs them away. "I couldn't tell you that I was FBI."

"I know," he says with a frustrated exhale. "I would've gone to the grave with the knowledge, though. And—the important fact that Puck was a brother—not a lover. *Christ*."

"I didn't know that then. I thought you were going to torture me."

Viper places a soft kiss on my lips then puts a hand between my bare breasts. "I couldn't do it, Candice. When I saw that picture of you that Noose had, I sort of knew then—just couldn't admit it to myself. When I met you and had to touch you in violence."

He sits up, creating distance between us. "Hardest fucking thing I've ever done." Viper's eyes touch on me briefly. "And I've done a lot."

I touch the cheek where he slapped me, and with a low curse, his eyes shift away, but not before I notice the shine in them. "I'd do anything to take that back. Anything." His voice is rough, mournful.

My heartbeats thump as I spread my legs, his back to me. "Prove it."

His head snaps back, eyes moving to what I so obviously offer.

A single tear slides down his face.

I hold out my hand.

He takes it, sinking between my legs and doing the kind of worship to a woman's body only a man who loves her is capable of.

Viper hasn't told me he loves me yet.

He doesn't need to.

Chapter 25

Puck

W hat are you saying, Perry?" Perry was my partner before I spent three years undercover.

"You're out, Puck. Well, not technically. The assload of unspent sick days, vacation, and just general, pain-in-my-ass stubbornness has kept you within the department just a little longer."

"Roughly three weeks."

Perry frowns, setting his half-drank beer on my scarred kitchen table. "So why do you care about this perp?"

"You mean my fucked up bio-dad? Who actually can't be held for trafficking minors? *That* perp?"

Perry has the grace to look embarrassed. "Okay, dumb question. Of course I know *why* you've got vested interest here, bud—and I'm not saying he's innocent. Not buying that for a hot minute. But let it go, let justice be served. Jerstad's going down, partner. You're looking at retirement at not even thirty-eight. Unheard of, Johnstone." Perry shrugs, swinging long hair behind his shoulder.

"I want him dead."

One of Perry's thick brown brows climbs high. "Really?" He snorts. "Would've never guessed. He almost was—ya beat him half to death."

My head swings to him. "You know what he did to Candi."

Not many do, but there's only so much time two partners can spend together before dark secrets see the light of conversation.

Perry nods, eyes serious. "I do. But, pal, that was a couple of *decades* ago. Candi's a fed. She's moved on. You should too."

I don't believe that's true. "I don't like the possibility of Jerstad making bail, and those type always do. Just tell me what you know, what his address of record is."

Perry whistles low, and since he's been undercover on another case, his hair's grown to epic proportions. When he shakes his head, a mass of thick shoulder-length spiral curls bounce around with the movement. "No can do. Yeah, so perfect. Then you can go over there and kill him, get your ass booted to the can, and I can't mooch microbrews off you on the weekend anymore. That doesn't suit my needs very well. It's all about me." He smirks, looking like he just sucked a raw lemon. "No fucking way, pal. I'm into the full-mooch situation, not a partial mooch. It's all the way or nothing."

I roll my eyes. "You're lucky I like you, or I'd kick your ass."

He mock-shoots me. "You'd try." His smirk widens into a grin.

Grunting, I admit, "I want to tag Jerstad's ass so he doesn't go after Candi."

"*Jesus*. He's *not* going after your sister. She's a federal agent and damned dangerous. And if he's half as smart as you say, he'd know that means incriminating himself. He won't commit to that. Even for his sick vendetta."

I snort, narrowing my eyes at Perry, and change subjects. "You know, Candi wouldn't have put you in that headlock if you didn't come on to her with one of your lame lines."

His face goes sullen, brown eyes hard. "It was a brilliant line."

"Nope." I fold my arms.

Perry frowns, saying nothing for a few seconds. "Fine." Crossing his arms over his muscular chest, he continues, "I guess I could have been more original."

"Any reference to her name being sweet or any bullshittery like that is an instant guillotine for romance."

"Right," Perry says, glum.

I get back on task. "Don't play me. I know you've got a bead on Dear Old Fucking Dad."

His smile is wicked. "Yup."

"I don't want either of us to hide, but I want Candi safe."

"Puck—God, that girl can take care of herself."

I know this, but every time I look at my sister, I see the helpless girl getting raped by Samuel Jerstad. As far as I'm concerned, she'll never be safe enough. "Humor me. Just keep surveillance on him for twenty-four hours, Perry. Give me enough time to get a semi-permanent plan for Candi."

She probably has all kinds of plans.

"And the kid?" Perry asks.

"Calem's in protective custody, waiting for placement." My exhale is rough.

Perry notices. He frowns. "What?"

"Candi wants him."

His brows jump "What? That's crazy," he says with an expression of surprise mixed with doubt.

"Not so crazy, really. I mean, she's been having to hand over these kids for three years. I think Candi just wants a happy ever after. And there is no husband and kids in her future."

Except an MC prez. I put that thought out of my head. "And Calem's special," she had told me.

"Okay," Perry stands, pushing away from my kitchen table, where he had only one beer. A record. "I'll get a guy on it. But I'm telling you, Samuel Jerstad would be a class-A moron to try to do anything to Candi—or you. He's a suspect, even if he's crying like a bitch about police brutality."

I *was* pretty brutal. But he's still breathing, so it wasn't brutal enough. I glance at my knuckles. The skin had been torn clean off my right hand, scabbed over hard now.

Jerstad is no moron, but he *is* determined and cruel, and as far as I remember, he's all about holding a grudge.

"I fucked things," I admit, still unrepentant. Nothing felt sweeter in that moment than crushing the man who hurt us without mercy.

Perry shrugs. "Jerstad was *still* at the scene when Candi was attempting a handoff. Doesn't matter that the other guy she put in the hospital had a record that was clean as a whistle. The boy corroborates some of it—"

"You know we can't use Calem's testimony."

"Points a damn steady finger that they were there for any reason other than taking in the sights. We *all* know they're guilty. We just have to find that shred of evidence that underscores what we already know."

I want to kick something. "So much fucking work down the drain." The only reason I don't feel like I just wasted three years of my life in the MC is we managed to save kids through it all. That's it. Though if I were honest, I'd say the MC life was more to my liking than I thought it would be.

The freedom and the ride had some appeal. But the bad elements of Chaos, like hurting women, was never my thing. I'd been expert at getting out of those details.

And I never thought I would say it, but easy pussy gets old. Maybe I'm just tired, but I want something more. Same shit everybody ends up wanting in the end.

"And that fuck Dagger telling the Road Kill chumps to tag the FBI agent," Perry says out of the blue.

Dagger. That prick. "Storm?"

Perry nods. "Loved that biz." He rolls his eyes. "And *of course*, Mover *and* Dagger are MIA. That's not suspect *at all*."

"Troubling-as-fuck."

"Yup." Perry starts walking toward the door. "Lots of loopholes and no closure. But that's the feebies' problem." He turns, half-facing me with a big hand on the old glass doorknob of my front door. "I know you want to protect your sister, Puck. But we've got a guy impersonating FBI."

"If Dagger's an FBI agent, I have a uterus."

Perry's lips twitch. "That's what I'm saying, circling uterus territory."

"Fuck off."

He grins. "Anyways, then we have Mover, handing out free advice to civilians and then disappearing."

Perry's right. That's the feds' problem, but where it impacts my sister, it becomes mine. And goddammit, I always had a feeling about Mover. I had three years to observe him as the Chaos Riders' president. Anyone who isn't a fucking moron would get a sense of a man after all that time.

"And my sister is dating the Road Kill MC president," I break the news as gently as a bull blasting through a china shop.

Perry leans against the door as though the wind just got knocked out of him. His muscled arm bulges as the doorknob creaks under his grip. "What in the blue fuck?"

I give a sage nod. "Yeah. She's insane. But they have some…" I whip my palm around. "Connection."

Perry gives a short laugh, but not like it's funny. "I suppose you're quoting her."

"Basically. It's my attempt at girlspeak in a nutshell."

Perry groans, mock-banging his head on the front door. "Candi couldn't have picked anyone worse."

"Yeah, but it's her life, and I'm not the boss of it."

Perry meets my eyes. "Even for her own good?"

I pause for a second then concede, "Even that. Besides, Viper is a good guy where it counts. Navy vet. Did two tours in the Gulf. Overall, they're not bad men—Road Kill MC. Have a moral code. Might not be the same one as most, but they're consistent as death."

His face turns thoughtful. "What kind of men are they, Puck?"

Fuck. The men I'd like to be a part of. But that part's not verbally consumable at the moment. "The kind of men who don't abuse women," I finally say, though I know shit went down Candi's not being totally up front about.

"Except the fed that hurt Candi."

"Yeah. That fucker, Storm. Too enthusiastic with the roleplay."

Our gazes meet, and an unspoken assent passes between us. No one who's legit has to go that hard to convince others they are.

"Got your hands full," I tell Perry.

"No." He shakes his head, his good humor returning. "The feds do. This is their mess. Got Mover missing. Have the other dickhead playing agent. Candi's been ousted."

"Technically, no. But Ted did put the seed in her ear about retiring."

Perry chuckles. "They are so not having your fisticuffs ass back." He snickers.

"Fuck off."

"You're getting repetitive."

I point at the door, and Perry opens it. "Go watch Jerstad," I tell him.

Perry's all serious now, brows dumped low over eyes a perfect shade of root beer. "If he's there, I'll have my eyes on him."

Guys don't hug, but my gratitude is palatable, and Perry's no fool, so he reads the emotion easily.

"This doesn't mean we're taking long showers together, Johnstone." I smile. He does too.

Then he's gone, and I'm staring at my beat-up wood door. The glass knob winks in the dying afternoon light slanting in from the back-door window, and dust motes float through the air. The windowpanes in the doors mirror each other perfectly.

I think about Candi being with Viper. He's too fucking old for her. Candi's too fragile to be with a man who's that hard. I dump my head into my hand. Wanting to pray. Not knowing who to ask. Or even what to ask for.

Viper

I wrap my arms around Candice, loving the feel of her soft small body against me. She erases my old pain, and in my own way—in the only way I know how—I try to ease hers.

I know pain. Gave it out. Took it. Seen things. Done worse. But this slip of a woman has filled the hole in my heart with a precision so neat, it terrifies my old ass.

"Thanks for using a condom," she says sarcastically.

Shit.

Hate the feel of a woman with a condom. Grim necessity within the club. Mainly because the sweet butts have been with everyone.

Raincoats shall be worn by anyone with a cock. Which is everyone. Candice was different. Can't get enough of kissing her. Don't kiss the club whores. Too intimate.

Reminds me of Colleen and the million kisses I gave her. Every one of them straight from my heart. Gave that woman every piece of me. Surprised I have any left.

I trail a hand along Candice's side, pausing at the injured rib. Sitting up, I still her slight movement with my hand when she would do the same. Bending over the injury, I kiss the deep-purple bruise close to her sternum, and nuzzle my face against the silky skin of her breasts.

Her bright-gold eyes look at mine. Tiny lightning strikes of green catch the light as silence stretches between us like taffy. Grasping her face as gently as a hollow egg, I turn her to the side of the cheek I slapped. There is no mark on her skin. Only the one in my memory.

With one arm, I swim over her body and kiss that cheek. Not lightly, but deeply, moving my lips over every bit of skin. I start at the corner of her eye and move downward on a diagonal, missing her lips by a centimeter.

Candice opens her mouth to speak, I think, but I don't allow it. Instead, I kiss her lips, and her tongue sinks between mine.

She groans. "I taste myself."

I laugh against her skin. "Hell—you should. I've eaten a banquet of your pussy lately."

She grabs the sides of my face, kissing me more deeply. Spreading her legs, I cup her ass and sort of toss her legs around my waist.

Candice hugs me to her tightly. "You're great at it," she purrs between pants.

"I'm like fine wine, babe. I just get better at all that shit with age."

Softly, she shakes her head. "Never had a man do what you do, make me feel like I do when you do it."

"Love pussy."

"I think you like saying the word." Candice's lips quirk, but not like she's especially amused.

"Yeah, I do. I don't mean it like a dis. I'm a worshiper—long-term worshiper of the Vagina."

She laughs, and I kiss her nose then her mouth. "Love the way women smell, how soft they are, the noises they make." I slide a hand between us, cupping her mound and sinking a finger inside her wetness.

She does a half-sigh, half-groan, eyelids fluttering.

"Like that," I whisper.

"You didn't wear a condom," she says again, but not like she's really mad.

I spread her legs wider, caging her face with my hands. She's so tiny, my fingers span from her chin to temple. "You're special." I kiss her again. "Special to me." Hurts to say it, though it's the unflinching truth.

Her eyes open all the way, sharpening, though making a woman have that many orgasms is something I work hard at. Love seeing Candice have pleasure. By my hand, my body, my cock. "Are we going to talk now?" I ask.

Usually that's the woman's line, but when said woman has your balls in one hand and your heart in the other—a man finds he gives a shit.

Candice nods. "You didn't leave me alone."

I couldn't be more surprised by her words. Shaking my head, I touch the space on my chest above where my heart lies. It's sappy but the truth. "Felt something besides the numb. Wanted to exhaust this."

"Even if I told you no." Her face is neutral, tough to read.

I'm still talking about the truth here. "*Especially* if you told me no." My eyes hold hers. "Nothing good is easy. That's been my experience."

Candice wraps her hands around my neck and whispers, "Thank you."

I lean away. "No, it's me that's thankful. After I lost Colleen, a part of me died with her."

She doesn't ask me who Colleen was. Probably knows just from how I said her name or because she's a fed and they have an inside track. Either way, I keep on confessing. "I was just going through the motions of shit. Not really living, just existing."

"That's *not* living," Candice agrees.

"Yeah."

Her hands slide down my bare arms, trailing over the contours of my muscles. "I know because that's what *I* was doing."

My heart beats a little faster. I'm killer at reading innuendo. "Was?"

Her sudden smile is happy. My answering one is hopeful. I don't have to see my face to know it. I feel the emotion deep inside myself. A fracture. But not like a break. More like heat, seeking the source of all the small cracks of grief and emptiness and fusing them together to become whole again.

"Not anymore. I think I've never felt more alive than I do right now."

I can't stand it anymore. I have to know. "Because of me?" I ask in a voice so quiet, part of me hopes Candice didn't hear me.

"No." Before my stomach drops like a rock, she finishes, lacing our hands together, "Because of us."

I'm brave enough to believe.

Chapter 26

Candice

I'm going to have to take one of those day-after-sex abortion pills. That's *my* name for it. It's not really called that. It's more along the lines of "egg implantation disruption," or some other feel-good verbiage like that.

My mindset sounds cavalier, but the truth is, I've been irresponsible with Viper. The first time, I could forgive myself because of the unimaginable circumstances. But the multiple times afterward? *No.*

What I've allowed has been deliberate, like all my sexual encounters are—how often I want and with who I want. But I've mostly kept men and companionship on the contemplative mental backburner.

Women work through childhood sexual trauma differently. Every experience is unique. Every transgression has shades of difference.

My father raped me. Other women have been raped by the one man they thought would be their protector. Most shy away from sex after the experience, getting triggers at the thought of actual recurrence.

Not me. I always knew whatever man I was with—
was not *him*. I never choose men like my father and
always put myself in control of *me*. I was not
unconsciously drawn to repeat the events that scarred
me. But the horror of what Samuel Jerstad did doesn't
fade. It's on a shelf, seldom dusted, carefully tucked
away inside the confines of my mind. I can't take the
trauma out of the fabric of the human being I became.

Being with Viper, a man I thought would be my
torturer but ended with him giving me the most
tender, mind-blowing sex I ever experienced, was the
single greatest unexpected event of my life. Having
feelings for him crushes me. Because sex is easy.
Feeling is devastating.

The only man I ever allowed myself to feel anything
for was Puck. And that's my blood. Not corrupt blood
like the man who raised us, but pure blood. Loyal.
True. Kind. All the things my father never was. And
now, I feel like Viper offers all those traits, and more.

"A piggybank for your thoughts," Viper says,
brushing the loose strands of hair from my forehead.

I close my eyes to avoid his penetrating stare.
"Thinking about my father."

Eyes darkening with emotion, he says, "I'd kill that
fucker if he was here in front of me now."

I see the emotion. His face is suffused with the same
intensity that drew me to him. Genuineness that a
person can't fake. At least, not to someone as jaded as
me.

"I know," I whisper. "I don't understand how we've
come to this point so fast."

He lifts a muscular shoulder then lets it drop. "But here we are. Can't take back shit that happens like this, Candice."

I trail a fingertip along his strong jaw, feeling the bristle of day-old stubble. "We're such different people."

Viper nods, and I thread my fingers through his hair, thick and short. I love the butchered strands beneath my skin.

"Colleen was my wife."

I don't acknowledge I knew. But seeing facts in a file are dead words on a computer screen. Here's the flesh-and-blood man before me. Different.

"Died of breast cancer. Couldn't have kids." His eyes are dry. Probably cried all the tears he ever would. Ever could. "Promised myself I'd have fun with women, that somehow I'd be tarnishing her memory by taking another old lady. Not that there'd ever be anyone who could fill her stilettos." His smile is so small, it's hardly there.

I remain silent, letting him speak.

Viper's eyes move to mine. "Then you came along." He's still propped on an elbow, and his free hand goes to my long hair, fisting the deep-auburn strands. "I meant to hurt you. Get a hold of whatever fuck was hurting kids and clean up my MC's backyard. That was *it*."

He tightens his grip just shy of pain. "But I couldn't do anything but adore your body, Candice. It's all I am capable of." Viper draws my face to his and kisses my lips softly. "It's like I've got a guardian angel, and all this time, his hands were tied. And the minute he was free, he put you here in front of me."

My lips curl into a smile. "Maybe it's a girl angel?"

"Maybe," he says softly. "But I wasn't convinced there was a heaven."

"And now?"

His blue eyes hold my gold ones. "Might be a convert."

Candice

"You sure cook for me a lot."

I gobble fried eggs and sausage. All the sex has made me ravenous. I sit on a stool at an ancient kitchen counter and swing my legs restlessly.

I wipe the entire yoke and remnants of crumbled meat with a half slice of sourdough bread then fold the toast. Taking a huge bite, I moan at the taste.

"I do like your sounds, Candice."

"That's not my real name. Not really."

Viper sighs. "Well, my name is Vince Morgan."

"I know, and I love the sound of that," I say thoughtfully. "Two first names together always sound great. But Viper is stuck in my brain."

"Why tell me your alias now?"

I've thought about it and made the decision. "Because I'm going to take early retirement."

Viper snaps his face to mine. "Why?"

"I'm done." I turn my fork over and under, under and over, tapping the tines lightly on the edge of the plate. "Burnout comes fast to agents who work on these sex-trafficking rings. And the children." I can't meet his eyes. Too much grief.

"Good."

My chin lifts. Finally, my gaze meets his.

"You didn't have any more of a life than me."

True. "Yeah. But I have to say, if this thing between us—"

"Our relationship?" His eyes razor down on me.

I don't miss a beat. "Yes. I guess that's what this is."

"You're damn right it is. I threw down for you." He pierces me with his gaze.

"Then I have to tell you, I come with baggage."

Viper's brows rise. "Short of you saying you have a hidden husband somewhere, there are no fucks given."

I laugh, remembering his T-shirt. I do care about him. And the depth and speed of that care scares the shit out of me. "I'm adopting Calem Oscar."

"The kid?" Surprised, he sets down his half cup of black coffee.

I nod slowly, figuring this will be the deal breaker, and I steel my heart for the words that sever the delicate bond that's been forming like a tether of titanium.

Viper comes around the counter and plants an elbow right beside my plate, leaning in close. He gently takes my chin in his hand, staring deeply into my eyes. I notice flecks of silver within the pale blue, adding to the illusion of icy paleness, like sapphire snow. "Colleen and I wanted kids." He kisses the tip of my nose and pulls far enough away to recapture my eyes. "You're not going to scare me with that."

My relief is so powerful, it causes me to be vaguely lightheaded. "Good," I manage.

He dips and kisses my mouth, his warm breath bathing the surface of my skin. "I might even want some of my own. Even though I'm a geriatric." He winks as tears fill my eyes.

I shake my head within the loose grasp of his fingers. "I don't think I can have any."

My gaze falls. Shame I shouldn't own filling me.

"From what that bastard did to you?" he growls.

I nod. "I've been told it's possible, but unlikely."

"You don't have to talk about it if you don't want to."

Covering my eyes with my hands, I remember. And I don't want to. The footsteps. The smell. The pounding of an organ inside me like an invader. Hot, stale breath in my ear.

I shudder. "Puck saved me."

Large warm hands cover mine. "Not every time."

Our eyes meet. "No," I say in hoarse confirmation, "not every time."

Viper pushes my legs apart and moves in between them, wrapping his arms around me. "Some men are demons, flesh-wrapped as humans, but they don't possess a shred of humanity, Candice."

Tipping my head back with a finger, he brushes a kiss on my lips and finds my tears instead.

"He broke my ribs if my body didn't respond how he wanted it to," I confess in a whisper.

"God—Candice." Gently, he pulls me tight against his chest. "And Storm hurt you too."

"That wasn't Ren's intent. Just went too far, didn't even know I was an agent."

"Don't care. I want to kick *his* ass too."

"Get in line. He's not a real popular agent."

"What else did your father break?" Viper asks me with clear disgust coating his words.

I place my hand on the upper left part of my chest. "My heart."

Viper takes my hand in both of his. "I will never do that. Never," he says fiercely.

"How do I know for sure?" I cry softly, weeping out every broken piece of myself that I've kept together for twenty years.

"Because I know how it feels," he says simply. Then Viper tucks me in against his body, lifting me from the stool, and carries me to an old couch.

A fire is lit, and the entire scene is romantic. I'd like to say we made love for the fourth time. But that would be a lie. It was better than that. Viper held me like he'd never let me go.

And I let him.

"I have to go. Puck will worry."

"Puck will worry? I'm with you." He thumbs his chest.

"Pfft—that's why he's going to worry, Viper."

He grins, and the little boy he must have been peeks out at the edges.

I bet he kept his parents hopping. *Speaking of.* "Are your parents still alive?"

He nods. "Barely. Old man's too stubborn to die. Mom takes too good of care of him to quit." He shrugs. "Works."

"Did you have a normal childhood?" I ask, holding my breath.

"Normal's a setting on the dryer... but yeah. Folks were good to me." His laser-blue stare holds me captive. "They'd like you, Candice." He cocks his head. "What's your real name?"

"Actually..." I look down for a couple of seconds then meet his eyes. Though twilight makes it hard to see much more than shapes, light from the front porch illuminates Viper. "We took my mom's maiden name—Johnstone. Arlington's just a fake name."

"And Candice?"

"That's a little bit real."

Viper's eyebrows rise.

"It's my middle name. Never went by my first anyway." With slow reluctance, I confess my dreaded first name. "Beatrice."

"Beatrice Candice?" Viper starts to laugh from his belly. "That's truly awful."

"Thanks," I grumble. "Apparently, nobody had a sense of how two similar names sound awful together."

"Or that Beatrice just sucks by itself." Viper snorts, and I laugh. "Your Mom—did she pick that name?"

"Oh," I say, and his amusement fades, probably because of the expression on my face.

"What happened?"

"I know it never happens nowadays, but she died... having me."

"Candice—shit, I'm sorry." He wraps me in his arms as we stand just a few feet away from my Scion.

"You didn't know. My mother had a great aunt where she came from in England, and I guess she wanted to honor her somehow."

I feel him shaking and pull back.

"Sorry, babe, but *Beatrice*?"

I roll my eyes. "I don't go by the name, but it's on my birth certificate."

"Candice *is* better."

I make a sour face at him. "Yeah, duh."

"Listen, didn't mean to laugh at your unfortunate name." Viper's face grows serious, and he forces me to look at him with a finger to my chin. "I'm sorry your mom wasn't there, Candice."

I gulp back the deep hurt the void has made in my life. "Thank you," I whisper.

"And I don't like you going home at night."

"I'm staying at Puck's. Nobody knows where I live but him."

His eyes take in the dark landscape that surrounds his small cabin. "Don't have a good feeling."

"You worry too much. I'm dangerous, remember?"

"Hey, babe, don't discount my instincts. I've lived a helluva long time by gut alone."

"There is no threat. I'm on admin leave, and I'm taking Ted up on his suggestion of retiring."

"I am dating an old broad," Viper says with mirth.

"Oh, shut up."

He hugs me tenderly, pressing my back to his front, and my head easily fits under his chin. Kissing the top of my head, he says, "Don't go back to that townhome. Don't stop until you get to Puck's. Call me the instant you arrive."

"God, you're bossy. And I can text, you know."

"Hate the fucking tech." He frowns.

"Your age is showing."

I turn in his arms.

"I don't care. Want to hear your voice, not get your words on a screen."

My lower lip trembles at his concern. His care.

"Hey," he says softly, "just let me give a shit."

"Why do you, Viper?"

He doesn't answer right away, just shakes his head. But finally, when his words reach me, I cry. And when I leave, I know I'll be coming back. Forever.

Because those words will keep a woman tied to a man.

"I give a shit because you're the last woman I'll love, Candice."

Chapter 27

Puck

*O*n *my way.* The text makes me breathe easier. Knowing Candi is safe, even if I'm not with her.

Kk.

My answering text is too abbreviated. But I just need to acknowledge. Not lecture. Not worry.

But until I hear from Perry that he's outside bio-dad's door and that fucker's contained therein, I'm not going to rest easy. It doesn't matter that my sister and I don't have recourse about the events that happened over two decades ago. Candi and I both heard his threats. It wasn't just Calem Oscar that Jerstad wanted. He wanted my sister too.

Candi and I both heard his threats. How arrogant does a man have to be to swoop in and try for his adult daughter? Who just happens to be an FBI agent. Even better than that—who could kick his ass.

She would be happy to. Candi would be in line *right* after me. I want to hand out the violence again. There could never be enough of all he deserves. Just knowing that fucker is alive is a daily abrasion on my brain. Like bleach. I could ignore the memories when Candi and I were busy, cleaning up where we could. But now Jerstad is in our face.

I'm not surprised he was trafficking kids. Not since he was raping my sister when she wasn't even a teenager. Just a girl. An innocent, trusting girl.

My fists clench. I wasn't old enough to protect her when she needed me most. I got old fast. Got strong fast. Got *hard* fast. All the "fasts" were installed because of the sickness spreading in our home like a rampaging plague.

But just because Candi and I can't nail Samuel Jerstad for his crimes against his own children doesn't mean we can't work our damnedest to see he gets put away for trying to harm everyone else's.

My phone vibrates, and I set down my second beer to check it out.

Perry: *Not here.*

I stand, the chair scraping across the floor with a shriek.

Me: *WTF?*

Perry: *Settle. Doesn't mean he's after our girl.*

Me: *Doesn't mean he's not.*

Instantly, I send out a text to Candi. *ETA?*

Okay, so Candi's driving. I got that. She's cautious about texting and driving. Not because it's the law, but because that's just who she is. But she's not cruel. She would hear or see the text and not get right back. *She told me Viper lives somewhere in Ravensdale*, I remember. Any way the crow flies, she would be less than twenty-five minutes out.

Scrolling minutely upward with my thumb, I read that our communication is only ten minutes old.

Shit. Don't panic, Puck. Yeah right, I'm so type B that way.

Fucking panicking. My thoughts briefly touch on Viper—he was the last one to actually see her. *Fuck it.*

I tap his number on my glass-encased screen.

He answers on the second ring. "Yeah." That one word. Cautiously wary.

"It's Puck."

A few seconds of silence pound away, then he asks, "Something wrong?"

"I don't know."

I can almost feel him sharpen across the cell line. "Candi just left here 'bout fifteen minutes ago."

My heart starts racing for no reason. Intellectually, I understand she's still a possible ten minutes out or so.

I turn my cell to face me. *No message.* Putting the phone against my ear, I breathe but don't talk. Thinking. Sweating shit out.

"I know you're her brother," Viper says into the silence.

"Yeah," I answer, vaguely surprised she told him.

"Makes things different."

Yeah. "For me too. I don't want her dating you, but this isn't the time to discuss it."

His unimpressed snort comes across like a rung bell. "What do you want to discuss, Puck?"

"Our father's out on bail, and my partner says he's not at his residence."

Viper puts shit together fast—I'll give him that. Probably why he's the president for the reigning MC of the quad-state region. "Think he's going to make a move for her?" His voice is low, careful—part question, part statement. But I hear the menace in it.

"Candi can take care of herself," I say automatically. I state the facts, attempting to convince myself.

"Then why are you calling me, spinning my shit up like a top?"

Why am I? "Because Samuel Jerstad is diabolical in the extreme. Smart, perverted, loaded—hell, those things don't dial down with age. They just get more."

Viper grunts. "Yeah, I know that."

"Can you spare a few of your men to follow where you think she might have gone—her route?"

"I threw down for her. Want her as property. I can spare every fucking man I got."

I can't contain my next words. "Candi's not anybody's property."

"That's what she said." His amusement carries over the line.

"Fuck you, Viper."

"Later. Right now, my woman's out there with a possible agenda from her father."

341

"Yes." I'm glad that he sees the need for paranoia. We have that much in common. "You don't seem too worried."

"Not. As soon as shit got real, I had Noose take care of all the problems with knowing where Candice is."

My mind whirls, and the pieces of the puzzle coalesce. "You had her car tagged."

"Yes."

I feel my face tighten. "Don't you fucking trust her?"

"I don't trust anyone else."

Fuck. "Then get your guy to find out where she's at."

A few silent seconds grind by.

"I already know. She's at your place, Puck."

Spinning, I glance at the front door, and my stomach drops to my feet.

There stands our biological father, face beaten, one eye partially swollen shut from the fist love I gave him. It's been over a week, but my efforts still hold to his flesh in a rainbow of violet, chartreuse and sickly green. Not that the beating appears to have slowed him down.

"End the call, William," my father says softly, a gun stuck against Candi's head. He shoves the barrel hard for emphasis, and her head jerks forward with the movement. "And don't let on there's a problem, or I will forgo the pleasure of tasting your sister again and kill you both now."

Adrenaline singes my extremities, my fingertips and toes numbing out. "Yeah, she's at my place," I mimic robotically in answer to Viper while Candi's terror-filled eyes lock with mine.

A heartbeat of time drums between us, and Viper asks slowly, "What the fuck is your problem?" Clearly misinterpreting my hesitation. "We're both after the same thing for Candice—her protection. Don't be a dick."

"I'm not being a dick," I say.

Silence on the other end.

Jerstad looks at me expectantly. "End it. *Now*."

"What's wrong, Puck?" Anxiety fills his gravelly voice where irritation reigned before.

"We'll talk later. I need to go."

"Something's wrong."

I pause for a nanosecond then answer, "Yeah. We'll talk *soon*." I swipe my thumb across the word *end*.

"Who was that?" Jerstad asks.

Hope Viper got my message. "Road Kill MC president," I answer truthfully, but my eyes move to Candi's.

He's got her zip-tied. Needed to get her lethal hands bound.

Jerstad shoves Candi forward, and without the balance of free hands, she stumbles. I catch her.

The gun swings to me. Candi and I stare down the dark hole at the end of the gun together.

"Puck," she says.

"I'm here."

Still holding the gun, Jerstad reaches his free hand into his pocket, grabs another pair of zip ties, and tosses them to me. Automatically, I catch them midair.

"Put them on and use your teeth."

"No."

Without hesitation, he points the gun, firing directly over our heads. Plaster explodes, raining down in a puff of white like a split bag of flour.

Ears ringing, I do as he says. *Maybe I can keep him talking.* "How'd you get to Candi?"

Candi wheezes an exhale.

His grin is malicious, the same one he wore when he hurt us. "Children are a great distraction to our sweet Candi."

"I'm not yours," she says.

His eyes, so like Candi's, shift to her for a moment. "Oh, but you are. I spawned you, and I've fucked you."

Candi flinches.

"I'd say that makes you mine."

"What the fuck is wrong with you?" I yell.

"There is a child, hogtied and ready for abuse on your front steps. Candi didn't think about her own safety, of course, or why a child would be bound thus and deposited like a gift." He smirks at her. "She just rushed in to get to the kiddo. The *bait*."

Jerstad chortles at his self-perceived brilliance, eyes sparkling like captured suns.

"You used a kid to incapacitate your own."

"Excellent deduction, William. And my associate will take the child, while I close this loop with you and Candice."

"What *loop,* you miserable bastard!" Candi screams in his direction before her voice drops. "Just leave us alone. You'll never get away with any of this. I'm FBI, and Puck's a cop. There's no *disappearing* us."

"Who said anything about that? No, *no*. It's a family reunion. I will have my sport with you, and Brother shall watch."

"Fuck that," I spit at him. "I'll *never* watch you hurt Candi again."

"Strong words, William, but ones that are meaningless." He indicates my bound hands with a flick of his chin. "March," he commands, cocking his head in the direction of the stairs. "And if you so much as *think* about taking me, I'll splatter the wall with sister's brains."

"I'd rather die," Candi says in a voice filled with dread.

Jerstad smiles, and the ghost of Candi's expression rides his fucking face. "I don't think fucking to death qualifies."

Candi shudders. But we move up the stairs, our father at a safe distance behind us.

Viper

"Noose."

"Yeah."

I'm holding my cell so tightly, it creaks. "Mobilize everyone."

After a second-long pause, he answers, "Affirmative, hoss."

"It's come to my attention that Candice's lunatic father is at Puck's place."

"That would be bad."

I think about the things I know—and all the things Candice didn't tell me. Goosebumps sweep over my flesh. Fate is giving me a last-chance warning, almost as if to say: "Here's the one woman for you. Don't blow it. Don't let her father dismantle her soul."

That's not happening.

We started out so wrong, and now we're so right. How can this perverted fucker from the past come back to haunt her at the exact moment that we were coming together? Because that's just the fucked-up way life works—that's why. "I'm going in."

"Viper…" Noose begins in a cautionary tone.

"No—fucking shut up. Candice is mine. *Mine*." I bite that last word off with my teeth.

Noose hears it. "None of us are present to have your back right now."

"I can take care of this."

"We don't know if Jerstad has backup. Who's involved."

Doesn't matter. "Meet me there with the brothers."

"We'll be there, even if you're not thinkin' shit through."

Pressing *end*, I shove the cell in my handlebar bag and adjust my weight. I get the bike balanced and roll out of there, taking a glance at the Garmin when I get to the end of my long driveway.

I shoot out to the north like the devil's after me. Or maybe I am the devil, ready to put that bastard at hell's front door.

Chapter 28

Candice

I knew I couldn't have the freedom to live my life. Samuel Jerstad came back, just as I've always known deep down that he would. Moving out of state and trying to let the dust settle on our horrific past didn't work.

Ignoring what happened didn't work. Staying busy, making a difference for children who were like us, didn't work.

And here we are, right where we began. Another child is at risk because of my reactions. Why did I just charge in? I should've known that something was terribly wrong. Why would a child be tied up like that on Puck's porch?

They wouldn't. But all I could see was *me*. And what I would have wanted if anyone besides Puck had noticed and tried to help me.

They didn't see… didn't notice.

However, I can. So I holstered my weapon and jogged to the broad, beat-up front steps, hand to my side as my rib let me know it was still healing.

The little girl's eyes got wide just as I mounted the second step, my hair beginning to stand up on end at my nape. A shaft of moonlight hit her small face, and a dark shape broke the ray, shadowing it perfectly.

I whirled. And a fist smashed into my unprotected jaw. Mover, the missing fed.

My consciousness trembled, but my body remembered its training, deftly catching his nuts with my instep as I fell backward against the steps, barely arresting my fall by slapping my palms on the rough wood.

I heard the child's whimpers behind the gag.

Clutching his balls, Mover sank to his knees, beginning to list to the side, but before I could do more, Samuel Jerstad plowed his gun into my face below my eye. Hard. So hard that the flesh of my cheek lifted, exposing my gums to the cool night air.

"At this range, they won't even be able to identify you through dentals."

Our eyes met. And I knew what Jerstad meant to do.

If there was a way to do it, I would kill myself before I let him have me again. I'm no defenseless twelve-year-old girl. But a force to be reckoned with.

Slowly, he pulled the gun away, too far for me to reach it with a well-aimed blow.

My eyes caressed his damaged face. "Love how Puck rearranged your face."

His smile was my only warning before he planted his foot in my crotch and shoved. I howled.

He ground a foot against my most delicate part. "Fucking lippy whore!" Jerstad said in a hoarse voice of derision mixed with lust. "Lippy!" he cackled as I moaned, trying to scoot up a step. Anything to get away from the abuse.

Mover was stirring on the ground behind us when another face appeared. The fake agent—*Dagger*—I presumed. The pockmarks of his face skew the moonlight, acting like shadowed measles.

"Nice," he said with deep satisfaction as my father buried his foot in my crotch.

A woman might not have balls, but a shoe in lady parts is no picnic. I realized it was just part of his idea of foreplay. Prepping me for future torture.

"Grab her."

Dagger moved around me cautiously, Jerstad pinning me with his foot. Scooping me under my armpits, he dragged me up in one motion. He was a good foot taller than me, Puck's size.

His rank breath bathed the side of my face as he said, "He's promised me a piece of pussy pudding after he's done." He gave the side of my face a long lick with his foul tongue.

I'm sorry Viper. I really thought there might be a life with you.

Dropping my head, I jumped, and at the same time, I swung back into his skull. *Hard.*

The blow to both my chin and head was too much, and I dropped. Partly because Dagger was staggering backward and couldn't hold my sudden weight and partly because I'd just rung my own bell.

Jerstad came forward and took ahold of my long hair, fisting it hard and yanking me around. I cried out, vision tripling at the abrupt movement. Blindly, I reached behind me, searching for soft eyeballs to tear, and found his gun pressed against my head.

"I will kill you."

I said on the exhale, "Kill me then."

"Not until William can witness."

I let my weight fall, and he followed me down. Then Mover was there, breathing hard. He sank a hit into my solar plexus, and I screamed.

His hand covered my mouth. I sucked in air around the edges and bit down with everything I had. Mover slapped me, and my head rocketed against my father's chest.

The gun got repositioned.

"Will you cooperate? Because there's things I can do to your brother. And I will."

My body stilled. *I can't have Puck hurt. Won't.*

"Then I'll start working on that worthless man you're fucking."

I said nothing. My face hurt, and my head hurt worse, my rib a constant throbbing nightmare in the background.

"Yes, dear Candice—I know about Vince Morgan."

Heartbeats piled up in neat stacks inside me, and I couldn't breathe. The rib, the strike—the abuse was so well-rounded, I could barely stand upright. Somehow, I did.

We passed the bound, helpless little girl whose eyes pleaded with me for help. But I couldn't even help myself. Mover and Dagger closed in around her like vultures after carrion.

"He'll die too," Jerstad confirmed.

Not Viper, I had time to think before he herded me through the front door to face my unsuspecting brother.

Viper

I want to tear in there and raise hell. But I didn't get this old eating stupid as a regular diet. On occasion, I've been known to be as dumb as a box of rocks.

Not tonight.

I identify Dagger and Mover easily as they haul what looks to be a young girl away.

Dragging a hand over my camo-ed face, I shake my head at the sight. *Fuck me.*

I want to take care of those two. Especially Mover. Unreal to think he's mixed up in something like this.

But I have to stay on task.

Get to Candice, dumb fuck. Don't play hero for everyone.

I parked in bum-fucked Egypt then moved as quickly and quietly as I could through thick woods and underbrush, homing in on the signal of the spare tracker tech gizmo Noose gave me.

As long as a man still breathes, he remembers combat, and the things a man has to do to survive. Getting to Candice takes precedence even over my own safety. And I'm ashamed to admit my brothers's safety too.

All of them will risk everything to wade in here and make sure I get my property. God help whoever thinks to hurt her.

Ren

I've got a fucking unmitigated disaster of a case.

Fucking Road Kill. The brotherhood the FBI never was. Now I have Viper, who's been more like a father than my own ever was—albeit a criminal one—putting himself directly in harm's way.

Gotta love that fucking noise.

Lifting my binoculars, I spot Thom and chuckle. Nicely played, if I do say so myself.

He's managed to wrangle that fucking rich perp into the most compromising position of his wretched existence *and* grab that fuck Dagger along for the ride.

Excellent.

Though on closer inspection, it looks like he's got a pronounced limp. Arlington got to him.

My lips curl in amusement. She's got some hands and feet. I adjust my balls. About neutered my ass.

I grimace. Feel really bad about her rib. Thought I had better finesse than that. In my own defense, I didn't find out until after she was another agent. I'll have to make a proper apology later.

I watch as Thom and Dagger take a young girl with them for safekeeping. Dagger thinks he'll be part of a big financial score once they hand off the girl. Thom allows him to believe it.

When Jerstad drags Candi inside Detective Johnstone's house, I move closer and crouch within a group of trees so dense that even the light of the full moon can't penetrate the woven evergreen canopy.

That fucker won't ever touch Arlington again. But he will get to know the inside of a prison cell for the rest of his miserable existence. My lips press against the sensitive mic to issue a final command.

Viper

Dagger and Mover are busy with placing the girl in the back of an unmarked black SUV, and I look away in disgust.

I'm almost to the door and hit the back porch.

Being familiar with how old homes work, I don't travel the center of the steps, but instead move up the sides, where foot traffic hasn't made them soft from the passage of time and use.

Making a wide berth of the back door I try the knob.

Fuck. Locked.

Flattening my hand on the glass of a double-hung window, I pray the sash isn't locked. As I press upward on the glass, the window shifts up silently. I duck through the opening slowly, scraping my back slightly on the bottom of the wood.

Dropping low, I extract my knife. Slightly hooked on the tip, the blade is serrated on one side.

Standing, I'm careful to remain at the edges of the beat-up floor and lean against a doorjamb that clearly leads to the hallway and beyond.

A scream pierces the air and shivers through my tense body like an electrical shock.

Candice.

Clutching my knife in my fist, I swing my head, flinging drops of sweat, clearing my vision.

I proceed into the hall, and my eyes meet Storm's. My upper lip lifts, and I bare my teeth at him.

"Arlington," he whispers then jerks his jaw toward the upstairs. "You can't go after her. This is a federal case."

A second scream shatters the silence.

We both tense.

"I'm fucking going, Storm—Ren—whatever the fuck your name is."

"Fuck—Viper!" he hisses.

I shoulder past him, his gun gleaming like an ebony sword as I slide by.

"Don't do this," Storm says from behind me. I ignore him, hearing his soft curse.

Moving to the steps, I pivot fast, facing Storm who is up my ass. "Go along the sides."

He's not going to blow my cover like a herd of elephants.

His red eyebrows hike.

Using my tiptoes and feeling as awkward as fuck, I keep my feet as close to the row of chunky wood balusters and handrail as possible, hauling myself up with slow precision.

Storm must understand, because I hear nothing behind me. Finally, I make it to the top and whisper-hiss back at Storm, "Outside edges."

I hear the slap of flesh ahead and move toward the sound, crashing through the last door on the right a few seconds later and stop dead at the sight.

Jerstad is naked, an obscene erection poised above... *Puck*, who is splayed out on a guest bed, a red handprint on his naked ass. Pants to his ankles, Jerstad is on his knees between Puck's legs, pressing a gun to the back of Puck's skull.

Shock ripples through me, and my hand spasms around the hilt of my knife. *That* was the flesh that was struck.

My eyes search her out. Candice is restrained with zip ties against an old-fashioned radiator. Red lines mark her arms; some have broken the skin, and she's bleeding. Tears of impotent rage streak her face.

"Save him," she mouths.

My head snaps back to the two men.

I move toward Puck's would-be rapist with smooth strides, raising the knife, and at the last moment, the skin of his neck ripples as his head twists and sights in on my approach.

"Viper! *Stop*," Storm roars.

Too late. I've already moved the knife up in a shallow arc along the lower region of Jerstad's back, piercing the kidney neatly.

A bloodless mouth of a wound opens to pure white then begins to fill in with the blackness of organ blood. I twist the blade.

I expected Jerstad to scream—or move. He doesn't. Instead, he bucks, arching his back, his cock precariously close to touching Puck's naked buttocks. Puck rolls from underneath his father as the gun falls loose from Jerstad's grasp.

Then my shoulder is gripped roughly, and I'm shoved out of the way. The knife makes a dark stain of scarlet in the shape of a question mark as it clatters to the floor.

"Call a medic!" Storm shouts, a mouthpiece dangling from around his neck, one earbud in, the other out.

"Viper," Candice cries, pressed against the ornately embossed metal.

Puck stands, slowly drawing his pants up and holding them with one hand. Our eyes meet. Shame and horror mingle in that dark-brown gaze.

Tearing my eyes away, I go to his sister and bend down, extracting my everyday utility knife from my front jeans pocket to cut away the zip ties.

"He was going to—" Candice begins, voice coming out like a raw hiccup.

"I know, baby."

Puck walks over. Candice and he exchange a long look.

"Now you know," he says quietly.

Tears pour out of her eyes, and blindly, she holds out an abused hand to each of us. Carefully, I avoid the lacerations to her wrists. We each take a hand, lifting her together, and Puck puts one arm around her.

"I thought it was only me," she says mournfully.

Puck places a gentle kiss on her forehead. "No."

We walk out of there, my hand laced through hers, Puck against her side as they support each other.

Medics rush in. But there's no saving Jerstad.

He's earned his spot in hell.

Chapter 29

Ren

2 weeks later

"I pulled every string I didn't have to get your ass out of hock."

"I don't think the FBI has hock," Viper says, crossing his strong arms across his chest.

I smirk. "No, but since there's been no proof of wrongdoing from Road Kill MC, and each time you've been about ready to get nailed, we've been able to establish self-defense or one of the other contingencies."

"Doesn't hurt that Samuel Jerstad was a child-molesting sick fuck that had abused a FBI agent."

We're quiet for a second.

"Or the brother, a cop."

"Yeah," Viper says, looking vaguely ill. "That fucked-up scene I walked in on." He shakes his head, running a palm over his crew cut.

I agree. Some people should not breed. But they do, and we're left with their sick urges and ruined kids. But not in the case of Candice and William Johnstone. They used the twisted trauma of their childhood abuse to make a difference.

I tell Viper, "Looks like a leave of absence as president won't hurt. Fly under the radar until we're done looking into your corrupt ass."

"I'm not *that* corrupt."

We stare at each other, sitting opposite on the seat of our rides. Standard protocol."

"Even I'm being investigated," I say. "Standard protocol."

"Noose can see to things for a while."

"Good," I answer then hesitate.

"What?" Viper asks.

"Candice Johnstone, aka Arlington. Dagger's in prison, and Thom is on admin leave just like me. The little girl Dagger brought in as 'bait' is safe."

"I am beyond fucking relieved that Mover was not hurting kids—and the one they used to lure Candice is okay. I couldn't make that connection of him and child trafficking agree in my head." Viper lightly taps his temple.

"He was playing a role, like me."

"Well, if you ever want to touch Candice in violence again, the only role you'll be playing is hurt. Same goes for him. You FBI fuckers beat the shit out of your own agents, women."

Viper's just put me on notice. "Fair enough. I know you want her for your property."

"Maybe more," Viper admits. "If she'll have me."

"You haven't seen her in—what?"

"Two weeks."

I whistle.

Viper raises his forearm from his folded position and flips me the bird. "Said she needed time."

"She at Puck's?"

Viper nods. "Yeah. Heading over there right now." He frowns.

I wait for him to tell me what the issue might be.

"Said she has something important to tell me."

I grab my chin, finger-combing the mess of my beard. After the hard ride over here, it's blasted to hell.

"I guess this means goodbye, Ren."

My head snaps to Viper's. "Probably, but I don't know what the final ruling will be. Not a lot of agents knew about my undercover status, and the criminals are dead or in jail."

"I'm lucky not to be."

I incline my head. But with me, Candice and Puck all vouching for Viper's motivation and having the same story, we saved his ass.

Viper's not perfect, but he's about as real and decent as I've ever met. Of course, I never really had a dad, and the foster system doesn't breed good ones. Just greedy fuckers with an agenda for everything that's wrong in this world.

Can't help my upbringing. Parents were killed when I was a baby. Never knew them. But I learned the hard lessons of life early.

"Yeah, you're lucky not to be in jail," I finally answer.

Viper's lips quirk. "Love all you law folks, coming up with a story to save my ass."

I scowl. "Wouldn't have done it unless I knew you were trying to achieve the same thing as us."

"Very unprofessional, very unlawful," Viper insists with a sardonic twist of lips.

He's right, but sometimes, doing the right thing means breaking rules to see it through. For the greater good.

Viper stares at me for a full minute. "If I didn't know better, I'd say you're a better brother than an agent for the FBI."

He's insightful. I'll give him that.

"I can't answer that, but I know that being with you and the brothers felt natural, almost meant to be."

"I also know that the hate front you had toward women was honest."

Too insightful. "I didn't mean to hurt Candi that badly. Didn't know she was one of ours until I'd already fucked things."

He stands, coming off the seat of his bike. I do as well.

"Appreciate what you did for me, Storm. And maybe what you did to Candice was excessive to appear genuine, but there's a part of me that doesn't believe it. The sweet butts don't lie."

I shift my weight. I do like topping the women. It's consensual.

Barely.

I only want to take. It's the only way I can get off. And I'm not going to analyze the *why*. Not dredging up pain. Not that kind.

Don't have an ounce of tenderness for females. Can't remember having any. One gave birth to me, obviously. A woman I can't remember because she died the day I was born. All the other females who came after were just assistants to the predators of my fucked-up childhood.

I shove the train of thought away before it leads somewhere I'm not willing to give the mental real estate to.

"I won't ever hurt her again. And Candi knows I fucked up. I already apologized." I lift two fingers. *Twice.*

Viper's stare narrows. "It'll take a while to earn my trust."

Because you're pussy-whipped. And I never thought I'd see the day when that happened. "It's between me and Candice, Viper."

His arms drop, hands fisting. "Depends on how you look at it. You patched in, undercover or not. You know what females mean to riders."

I know. I fucking identify with the lifestyle of a MC rider a hell of a lot more than an FBI agent. "That's why we're one percenters. Because we protect what's ours."

"Regardless of the cost," Viper finishes my thought neatly.

"There will never be a female that fills that space for me," I say, tapping my chest where my heart lies.

"Never say never."

I look down, regulating my breathing. I don't want to argue with one of the few men I've ever respected. After a few seconds, I look up. "Lay low. I'm saying this from the capacity of a federal agent."

Viper smirks. "Like I said, Noose can run the helm for a time. I've got a woman to claim."

"Claim?"

Viper gives a decisive nod. "Yeah, if she'll have me."

Candice is a wild card . I don't blame her or Puck for bowing out of their respective law-enforcement positions. Their lives were even more fucked up than mine, if that's possible.

Viper puts out a hand, and I shake it.

"You going to be here when I get back?"

I want to be. "Don't know. See what the Bureau decides for me."

Our grip holds a fraction of a second longer than necessary.

Viper drops my hand and turns, swinging a jean-clad leg over the saddle. I watch him drive slowly away from the club until he's a speck in the distance, swallowed by trees that sequester our way of life.

Candice

He's coming. My heart picks up beats as I think about seeing him—what I have to tell him.

I'm not sure how he'll take the news. I'm not sure how I feel about the news that's nothing short of a miracle.

Puck comes into the kitchen. "Viper's coming over?"

I nod, setting my coffee down. "I'm nervous."

My brother walks over, placing both palms on my shoulders. "Don't be. No guy turns himself inside out and stabs our father to rescue us without having some strong feelings."

I laugh. "I don't know. He didn't declare his undying love or anything."

"Did you?" Puck asks quietly.

God, no. "No."

"Well, maybe you should. You've been keeping him at arm's length since this mess happened."

I stand, and his hands fall away. Tears in my eyes, I turn to face him. I can't erase the ugly memory of our father attempting to rape Puck.

"Why did he hate us so much?" I ask for the tenth—hell, the hundredth—time.

Puck shakes his head. "I don't try to even come up with an answer."

I grip his hands in my own. "He raped you too."

Puck is silent. "It was a punishment when I interrupted his abuse of you."

"Oh my God." My forehead taps his chest.

He cups the back of my skull. "I'd do it again. I hated him hurting you. And remember, we know better than most, rape isn't sexual. It's control—it's rage. He didn't care about gender. He just wanted to use himself as a weapon of manipulation."

I know this. Intellectually, I'm very well versed in the why of rape. But being violated is always more than the sum of the words. It's a part of your soul they've stolen, that you can't get back.

We turn toward the sound of gravel crunching.

"He's here." I pull away from Puck and run a nervous hand over my hair.

"Don't worry, if he doesn't want to make it work after all this, I'm a horrible judge of character."

He's not.

"I'm going to make myself scarce."

Puck walks off, and my eyes trail him, wishing that he could find someone to share his life with. To heal the hurts that we share with each other.

Having someone who didn't live through the trauma, but can shoulder the burden, is a gift. A rare one.

Slowly, I walk to the front door and open it. Viper dismounts, setting a black half-helmet on the seat, and turns. Tight jeans with a button-fly crotch hug every place that's hard and narrow. The inverted V of his hips top out at his broad shoulders. A hard face, chiseled by time and experience rounds out his pale-blue eyes, appearing almost white in the late-afternoon sunlight. Hair I know is a soft black color beginning to silver at the temples glows faintly, appearing darker than it is.

He catches sight of me behind the screen, and his expression changes. Some slight tightness around his eyes relaxes. His cut hugs his chest as he walks the short distance to the front steps of my brother's farmhouse. "Candice."

I swallow hard, wanting him so bad, I can taste it on my tongue even as my nose picks up the faint smell of soap, bike, and the unique male smell that is Viper.

Something's happened to change my perspective. A milestone bigger than all others.

Viper doesn't spur me on, his expression neutral. I move around the screen, letting it snap shut. Viper comes up the steps, and I don't wait or play it cool. I run the few steps to him and throw my arms around him, sucking in a sob that feels like a torn piece of my heart.

"Hey, babe," he says, snapping his arms around me and lifting me gently. "I'm here."

"I know. I wasn't sure—" I choke back the flood of my emotions. "That you'd come, that you'd want to."

Viper leans his face back, a slight smile curling his lips. His thumb sweeps my tears, and he sets me on his boots, my bare feet on tiptoe so I can gaze into those glacial-blue eyes. "I'm not ever going anywhere," Viper says. "I meant what I said before."

"You might not feel that way when I tell you what I have to."

His eyebrow sweeps up. "Doubt it. Have my heart set on you."

Heat rises to my face. "I'll show you instead."

Curiosity sweeps his features, but he laces his fingers with mine. "Lead on, babe."

I tug him behind me, feeling the warmth of our connected hands, the hope thundering away in my racing heart.

We walk to the kitchen, where I've left the proof.

Viper lets go of my hand, watching my face take in the only object setting on the center of the table.

A white stick.

He picks it up. Looks at the two pink lines.

"Holy fuck." He does a slow blink. "Does this mean what I think it means?" His body twists, two fingers holding the pregnancy test between us.

I nod slowly. Terrified. Hopeful.

Viper carefully sets it back on the table then steps forward, grabbing me by the waist and hiking me up so that my head is slightly higher than his. "Why didn't you tell me?"

"I just did."

"God, Candice."

"Does this mean…?" I can't finish. Instead, I hold my breath, his hands low and warm on my body.

"It means that I have two people to love instead of one."

I feel my face screw up in a frown. "You love me?"

Viper slowly slides me down the front of his body, cradling my face with his big hands. "I loved you the minute I saw your picture." He tucks my loose hair behind my ears, kissing my forehead and ducking to press his lips against mine.

I kiss him back. Hungry. Ravenous.

His mouth gives back everything I take.

Chapter 30

Puck

Six months later

The organic smell of freshly churned earth has always given me a good case of the feels. Not much does nowadays.

Candi's found her happily ever after, the Bureau is a dim memory of forced slavery, and having Samuel Jerstad dead brings a certain kind of closure.

Neither one of us could run from the past. It caught us. But my sister and the handful of people who are now aware of my once-hidden shame are too many. I can't move past their knowledge of my abuse.

Candi's encouraged me to get counseling.

Yeah right. I've been a part of Chaos Riders for long enough that the only therapy I can stomach is killing road. So I'm on my bike.

A lot.

There's some pleasure in watching her and Viper's house come together on my land—ours now. I had enough acreage, and Viper had been willing, the lovesick bastard, to have a brand-new place just for him and Candi with her brother only a stone's throw away. So I'd divided the land and given them a five acre chunk.

Now there are two good men protecting her, and the worst one is gone forever. But I still like keeping her close.

She'll be marrying a criminal. How's that for irony? But I'd rather have her with Viper than a man who looks good on the outside but is rotten within.

Viper is walking toward me slowly. My sister isn't as nimble as she once was. The baby makes her more careful.

A future nephew or niece. They're both waiting to find out the sex until after the baby is born sometime in early June.

I grin even through the morbid turmoil of my brain. Candi having a baby, and Viper is making an honest woman of her. That's all it takes to chase the shit back for a time.

"Hey, Puck," Candi says as she moves up to where I stand. She only pants a little.

Viper tucks her head under his chin and draws her in close against his body, wrapping his arms beneath her breasts but above where her stomach bulges with their child.

I don't reply to the greeting, and her expression turns from neutral to worried. Staving that off at the pass, I say, "Just admiring the ground getting torn up."

We all look at where the foundation will go.

"I'm so excited," she says with a thread of breathlessness in her voice.

Viper's quiet. I've found that's his way. As is mine. Chatty men make me wary. I mean, what the fuck is wrong with them just *being*? Do they have to talk all the time? Agitating as fuck.

Candi seems to sense my irritation and cocks a dark auburn brow. "Are you grumpy?"

Grumpy. *No*. Lost. Yes. And that pisses me off on principle.

I want to have a purpose. Something *worth*. But I can't find it. And my shame haunts me. Always has. But now that there are some who know, my sense of shame has deepened.

Candi takes my hand, and I let her. "It'll be okay, Puck."

I nod silently.

She doesn't know that I don't want to die, but I don't exactly want to live, either. Didn't think the end of my career and having freedom would make me suddenly become introspective.

Looking down at Candi's engagement ring, I think of the weird turn our lives have taken. A single large rectangular diamond winks back in the mid-spring light. Set in white gold, the silver tone of the slim band complements her fair skin. Simple, like Candi wanted it.

Viper and Candi live at his small homesteaders cabin out in Ravensdale until their home here is complete. Nice place. But Viper says he's ready for something brand-new. "A fresh start," he said.

I completely understand. After all, he probably doesn't want to marry Candi and live down in the basement where he'd planned to torture her.

I feel my lips twist. Got to get my mind in gear. *Perry said I can do consulting work*, I think, and like a telepath, Candi breaks into my thoughts, "Did you get back with Perry on that consulting biz?"

I shake my head. Perry doesn't call that much anymore. Probably because I never get back.

"Sounds like it'd be up your alley, Puck." Viper gives me a look over my sister's head.

What he doesn't say is: it would keep me out of my head until I can stand to be in it. He's probably right. Maybe I will. I make a mental note to call Perry.

But I don't want to jump from the frying pan straight into the fire. Perry knows my talent lies in saving the indefensible. The question is, do I want to get in the game again? Am I even solid enough to take on that role? Might be too fucked up to save anyone. Can't even save myself.

"Let's go see what magic I've accomplished in your house, Puck."

Candi's been throwing herself into decorating all the rooms that are finished enough to decorate. She began with the one Jerstad tried to rape me in.

I like seeing things altered. It's not the constant reminder it was. I'm not giving up this house because of my father trying to defile me in it. Jerstad wasn't successful. He died. I lived. Period.

We walk to the front porch, hiking up the brand-new steps. They're soundless, solid. A new front door mimics an antique, but with built-in security.

Opening the door, we walk through the threshold, and the smell of new paint and drywall assaults me. Large sheets of recycled brown paper are taped off on the refinished floors, and it crinkles underneath our feet as we make our way to the back of the house.

A small half-bath has been installed where a useless closet used to be. Bright white fixtures fill the space and a tiny window set high, fitted with old-fashioned glass block, allows in light. My eyes take in the fart fan that Viper and I installed.

Candi thinks it's too loud. I told her it was better than the alternative. She rolled her eyes.

We keep strolling through the spaces, and Candi points out all the changes from four days ago. The last time I got the tour.

"Starting to look girly," I say.

She nods. "You'll thank me when you nab a serious chick."

Boiling shame rolls through me again. What woman is going to want a man who's been raped? By his own father, for fuck's sake.

Candi's told me about one hundred fifty-two times that Jerstad's attempted rape was a bid to do the most psychological damage possible. To both of us.

It's been successful. Too successful.

The insta-hard-on and twice-an-hour boner is gone. In its place is noodle dick. My libido is on a leave of absence.

Candi says the right girl will come along. Like the right guy came along for her.

What were her exact words? Oh yeah—"If I can fall in love with my potential murderer, anything's possible."

We laughed until she cried. Shedding all the tears I can't. The ones I won't.

One month later

"This third trimester is not fun." Candi puts a hand to her lower back and twists slowly, trying to get the kinks out. She's such a tiny thing that the baby doesn't have anywhere to go but out.

It's early May, and that's typically not a time for hot weather in the Pacific Northwest. But today has a cloudless blue sky of impending heat.

"It's so hot," she says, wiping sweat off her brow.

We're outside again. Her and Viper's house is framed and roofed. After drywalling is complete, it'll go fast.

"It looked so small when they poured the foundation," Candi says.

I nod. It always does.

It's not a huge house, but at two thousand square feet, it's perfect for a MC prez and his bride.

It's a miracle Candi can have a child at all. The news stunned Viper speechless.

When I came back in the house after Candi told him, he had a dazed expression. In fact, I think he wore it for the rest of the month.

Now Road Kill is over here a lot. Beer and BBQs. Feels good to have a full house. Distracting.

I've been ex-communicated from Chaos. Mover was legit and now retired. Dagger's in prison for impersonating a fed. The sting was more than child trafficking, but an integrate web of deceit with lots of players.

We reluctantly include Storm. And though Candi's forgiven him for his rough treatment—dismissing it as part of his role—Viper and I haven't totally gotten over it. A man who can be that violent toward a woman bears watching. Storm won't be staying a fed for long. That's what the MC does to a man: makes a tame man wild—or an already-wild man unable to be anything else.

In fact, the entire group will be here any minute. With a sideways glance at Candi, I ask, "Has he told anyone?"

She doesn't ask what I mean, proving the incident is still very much in the forward part of our brains. "He'd never tell anyone about your assault," she replies in a low voice, turning to face me. "Puck, it wasn't your fault." Tears bloom in her eyes like shiny translucent flowers. "Jerstad wanted to wreck us mentally before he did the physical. He tied me up so I'd be witness to your misery."

I can't meet her eyes.

"Hey," she says, "he didn't actually succeed in raping you, Puck."

"No," I answer, still looking away. "That time, he didn't, because he didn't have the time."

Candi's exhale is shaky, and the next moment, her arms are sliding around my waist.

"Shit"—her voice is irritated—"I can't give you a real hug."

We look between us at her bulging stomach.

I chuckle. "Nope." Our eyes hold. "How can you just go on?" *And I can't,* I think.

"Because a woman understands the potential to be raped. It's not an alien concept. The possibility is part of our consciousness."

"I never saw it coming when the rapes started. He always just beat me for interfering with hurting you."

Candi waits silently.

"Then one day, he knocked me out." Gooseflesh crawls over my bare arms, my body remembering ahead of my mind.

Candi leans forward, clutching me tighter as the sordid words float over her head.

"When I woke up… his cock was in my ass," I say in a voice so low, it's less than a whisper. The first hot tear slides down my face, soaking her hair, deepening my shame.

"Oh, Puck," Candi whispers.

I don't speak again.

Candi holds me while my eyes leak and my spirit aches. She's told me before that I'm one of the toughest males she's ever known. But the tender boy I was still lives inside, battered and fucked up.

I can't reach him, and I don't know who will.

Chapter 31

Candice

June

"I'm worried about Puck," I tell Shannon, Wring's old lady and now my close friend.

She hears me, but she's racing around after Duke. He's over two now and gets into everything.

I look down at my full-term belly and sigh. Not because I don't want the baby. Viper's. But because I do so much. Having a child was never something I allowed myself to wish for.

After the physical trauma of being assaulted at such a young age, there was a question about whether or not I would even be able to. The doctors erred on the side of caution, telling me the chances were slim.

"Don't worry about him!" Shannon says, exasperated. She finally gets to Duke and grabs him, settling him on a hip. She's about six months along—just behind me—and groans with the effort.

"This is your wedding day. Not a day to worry about Puck."

I can't help it. For so long, he was all I had. Having Viper has made all the difference in the world, but I haven't forgotten my brother. He doesn't look great. Puck's lost weight and has taken to working out in an unhealthy way. I know what he's doing, of course. If he can work himself to the point of exhaustion, he doesn't have to think. Remember.

But he did take the consulting job with Perry. I bite my lip, looking at the full-length mirror inside the borrowed room at the church.

"I guess it was some slice of insanity that I thought to get married when I'm about ready to pop."

Shannon smiles.

The other old ladies will be here soon. My eyes burn as I remember Calem. I won't find out until next week if the adoption went through. Being married should help that along, though.

But those are the only things. Filling in what Viper does for a living is… interesting. And adoption placement agencies aren't really crazy about the word "retirement" in the forms. Even with all that, I've got a good feeling.

Shannon smiles, tucking a loose strand of pale-blonde hair behind her ear. "Just concentrate on getting married, and everything else will work out."

I know it will, because the man I love is waiting out there for me.

Viper

I remember now why I hate ties.

"This fucking thing is like one of your knots," I tell Noose.

He's got shadows beneath his eyes. Doesn't get much sleep with the twins. I remember when he used to look like that after the all-nighters.

Not anymore. I smirk. Then my smirk fades as I think about Candi, ready to have our kid at any moment. I'm in for it.

My smirk morphs into a smile. Always wanted a kid—a family of my own. Feel like fate smiled on me.

'Bout damn time.

Aria looks up at me with big brown eyes like Rose's. "I think you look nice," she says very clearly at almost five years old.

Women start conversating pretty damn early.

Noose yawns so wide, I can see his tonsils. "Ties suck." His mouth snaps closed, and crossing his arms, he leans against a long table that's been shoved against the wall.

"Can't believe you're going to be a dad," Wrings says thoughtfully. "You're fucking ancient."

"Language," Noose says, giving Wring a sharp look.

Wring glances at Aria and mutters, "Sorry."

"I'm not fifty," I remind them.

"*Pfft*," Lariat sounds off. "I don't know if I could do the gig at your Geritol age."

Making sure Aria's not looking, I flip him the bird.

"I didn't think a chick could get that big," Trainer comments thoughtfully.

Why in the fuck are they in here, anyways? "Get out!" I wave a palm toward the door. "I've had enough encouragement to last forever."

"I didn't say nothin'," Snare says, dark-blue eyes glittering.

I point at him. "But you want to."

Snare snickers.

I jerk my thumb toward the door. They all file out and Puck stands at the entrance. He's my best man.

Moving through the threshold, he closes the door and walks to me. We bump fists.

"How's Candice?"

"Cranky."

We grin at each other. The last month has seen me tiptoeing around hormones like a full-fledged expert. I don't know how Puck's survived.

But damn does that woman like sex. Candice doesn't care that she's bigger than a house. And I'm happy to oblige.

"Ready?" he asks quietly.

I nod. My sadness for Colleen doesn't even stir. I figure she's up there in heaven, lifting a champagne glass and toasting us. After all, her dying words were "Find someone else who will love you."

I nodded through my tears, giving her that absolution, when all the fucking time I knew there'd never be another woman like her. But that's not what life's about. It wasn't about replacing Colleen or having someone else just like her. It was about living, and finding love. Candice gave me that.

In a minute or two, I find myself at the altar, waiting. Candice walks into the church where everyone's gathered, and I catch sight of her. Gorgeous. Like a floating cream dream.

Her dress is one of those that starts right under her tits and falls to her dainty feet. Her breasts are offered up in the low-cut neckline like ripe melons.

I don't think I'm supposed to get a hard-on right now. Not that my dick has ever cooperated once in my entire life. But damned if the vision of her as my bride with my child filling her belly isn't as sexy as fuck.

I can't swallow past the lump in my throat, the feeling of flat-out luck I have to be here right now, in this moment.

Candice walks down the aisle, my own father at her side. The sight squeezes the air from my throat.

She's showing the world that there's a man she trusts more than anyone.

It's a gift I can't wait to receive.

Charlotte

I knock at the front door of a *really* rural house. Beautifully done.

Looking down, I squeeze Calem's shoulder. He smiles back. I never get to see something like this through. It feels so great, I want to cry. Somehow, I hold back.

A built older guy answers, drying his hands on a wash towel. "Hi," he says then sees Calem. "Hey, pal!" He grabs Calem, spinning him around right in the foyer.

"Hi, Viper," Calem says.

A woman a little older than me comes out with a new baby in her arms. *This must be Candice Morgan.*

"Hi," I say to her as the man and boy reunite. "I'm Charlotte Temperance."

"Hi, Charlotte," Candice says, holding out her free hand. She has unusual coloring, deep-red hair and eyes that are a true gold with vibrant streaks of green. I don't stare. Instead, I set my eyes on the newborn.

"Oh," I say, not able to keep the delight out of my voice, "is this your new baby?"

She nods happily.

Vince Morgan draws her into his side protectively. "Ours."

They smile at each other, and I hold back a sigh. Sappy, but true. My news might make them even happier, which just makes my week.

"May I come in?" I ask.

"Oh, gosh, so rude of me," Candice says, sweeping her arm forward.

Calem rushes over to Candice and wraps his arms around her legs. "I'm so glad to be here, Miss Candi."

"Not to be discourteous," Vince begins, "but we've already been through all the hoops, rules and BS. Now the kid's ours, right?"

I slowly nod. "So why am I even here?" I guess for them.

He gives a mild shrug. "Bluntly—yeah."

"I have some great news—interesting news."

Candice frowns.

Just then, a huge guy comes walking in through the back door, even dirtier than Vince was. Covered in grease, with dirt creases between his heavily muscled body, I know just from looking he must be William Johnstone, Candice's brother. They look alike, though his eyes are deep pools of drowning brown.

"Hi," I say a little breathlessly, "I'm Charlotte Temperance."

His lips quirk. "That's quite a name."

Don't I know it. "Yes, there's no getting around it."

"No nickname?" Candice asks quickly.

I feel a slight flush of heat and know I'm blushing. "Temp."

"Temp?" Candice's eyes travel upward in contemplation. "You're too girly for that." Candice winks and begins walking toward the kitchen, Calem's hand in her free one.

William's eyes travel my form from head to toe. "Very girly," he says. Not with disrespect but more like he notices me. Really notices.

Okay, time to be professional. I clutch the paperwork closer and follow Candice. Vince and William fall in behind me.

I try to disregard the distinct scent cloud of motor, fresh earth, and soap that follows around William Johnstone. Harder than I thought.

"As you know," I begin, attempting to leave my flustered exterior behind, "I'm the social worker assigned to Calem. Normally, I work with adults, but in this case, adults were so involved and the circumstance so unusual, I was called in to facilitate."

William sticks out his hand. "I don't think we've been properly introduced."

I put my hand forward. "I know who you are, William."

His large hand folds around my much smaller one, and I gasp from the contact, biting my lip to hide it.

"Puck," he says, but his eyes tighten at my reaction.

I nod, dropping his hand as quickly as I can and still be polite.

What the hell was that? Felt like an electrical shock. I fight not to rub my hand on my skirt.

William "Puck" Johnstone is looking at me more intently than before. Maybe he felt it too.

"It's good to meet you," I say, voice slightly breathless as our eyes lock. Shifting my gaze away, I concentrate on sliding the manila folder away from me across the battered surface of an antique kitchen table and sit down.

Everyone settles. Calem sits next to Candice, letting his head fall against her shoulder.

The scene brings tears to my eyes, momentarily distracting me from the chemistry between me and Puck.

"I'll just spit it out, though there is plenty of paperwork to back my news."

Vince frowns.

I hold up a palm. "It's protocol now to DNA test all adoptees. Routine." My eyes meet all of theirs. "As a contingency against a blood relation out there that could gain custody. We don't like to separate families."

I don't miss the look that Puck and Candice exchange.

"Anyway," I continue, purposefully ignoring their silent communication, and tear off the Band-Aid, "Calem is actually your half-brother."

"What?" Candice leans forward.

Puck scowls. "That's not possible."

I nod. "It's very possible. And as such, the two of you are first-degree relatives, and the boy will inherit the estate of his deceased biological father, making you co-executers of his trust." That part doesn't really fall under my job description. But the attorney who handles anything wonky checked into everything and told me what I was allowed to say. Someone else will handle the estate details.

Candice gives the baby to her husband, who smoothly puts him over a shoulder, rubbing gentle circles on his back.

The silence is deafening, but I'm used to awkwardness. Nobody does the work I do without being used to dysfunctional dynamics.

"That's why he was doing the meet. Why Calem was so important." Candice appears shell-shocked.

"Who's the mother?" Puck asks.

I shake my head. "Her DNA was not in the database. But from what we understand through some preliminary research, she… " I don't finish my sentence right away then finally end with, "is no longer with us."

Drug user. Hooker. Then the aunt took over and dies under mysterious circumstances. A bus accident that might not have been all that accidental. Of course, they don't pay me for detective work.

Those events don't feel very mysterious anymore. I'm thoroughly versed on the events surrounding Samuel Jerstad, though there are blank spots I'm not privy too. His involvement in the child trafficking is well documented, as is his demise by law enforcement and the disbanding of said ring.

I tap the paperwork. "Here are all the documents, legal and otherwise, proving what I've said and giving you legal guardianship of Calem."

Reluctantly, I stand. This is always the hard part. I feel a personal responsibility to the boy, though in this case, the outcome seems sound.

I hesitate, and Candice's smile is kind. "It's okay. I know how you feel."

The tension in my shoulders eases. "It's so hard to leave them."

Candice nods. "I know."

"How long have you been in social services, Temperance?" Puck asks, his intense eyes pegging me like a moth to a board.

I swallow once, throat tight. "Not very long. Maybe three years?"

"It'll get easier," he says.

I think about how he was a cop and Candice was FBI.

"Or maybe not," I say, letting my eyes drift to Calem. I scoot the chair back and tell Calem goodbye, trying not to cry.

He trots around the solid wood table and hugs me. "Thank you for bringing me to..." Calem doesn't know what to call Candice.

"To your sister." My eyes seek Puck's, and his gaze is already on me. "And your brother."

"Candi," Calem tries the new name out. "I like that better than Miss Candi.

Candice's eyes fill with tears. "Me too, honey." She sweeps his long bangs out of his eyes and smiles at me through her tears. "Thank you," she mouths.

I nod and turn away before I break down. Quickly striding for the stairs, I feel a large hand wrap my elbow.

I turn and look up. Way up. Puck is a large man, an intimidating one.

"I'll walk you out."

"That's okay. It's not necessary," I say, wanting him to walk me out so badly, my mouth is dry.

"I know. I want to." He doesn't let go of my elbow. And I don't want him to.

Chapter 32

Puck

Charlotte Temperance is hot. *Temp.* Strangest name I've ever heard. Quirky. Fits her somehow.

I walk her down my new steps, hand still lightly gripping her elbow, and check her out surreptitiously.

She's taller than Candi, maybe five foot fourish. Thin but not bony, athletic and charged with emotion. I could read her face like a book in there. She ought to watch her expressions.

Frowning, I decide I'm not in the business of telling people what to do or protecting them anymore.

I'm doing better. It's been almost a year since Samuel Jerstad tried to put the icing on the ruin-Puck-and-Candi cake. The aftertaste still lingers.

Haven't been able to shake that, but time makes the coping easier. The distraction of Candi and Viper's house getting finished and the final stages of my own restoration haven't left me time to think.

Don't want too much retrospection. Instead, I fill my time with the consultation work I finally took Perry up on. Led to some arrests of deserving scumbags. Perry and I are hanging when we can, and I'm basically a Road Kill rider now. Feel more at home at that camp than any other I've ever been a part of.

The last year has been like living as a sleepwalker. Vaguely awake, but sleep drowning my feelings at the edges. It's not a perfect existence, but a content one.

Day by day, the numb continues to creep in like slow-moving quicksand. It doesn't worry me. It's better than feeling.

I have my sister, nephew, and now a half-brother to love. I'll throw Viper in there somewhere too. And now there's Temp here.

I know for a fact she noticed the liquid chemistry we have. My eyes run down her outfit, which hides everything that matters but shows me the potential.

Her hair is board straight and thick, running just past her shoulders. It's black like a raven's wing. Her jewel-like seawater-colored eyes are very slightly almond shaped. Exotic. Intoxicating. Wakes me right out of my brain fog. Not sure if that's a good thing.

"You don't have to hold my elbow the whole way. I'm fine, really." Black eyelashes sweep closed in a swift blink, briefly resting like ebony lace over fine cheekbones.

Usually, I go for cheap, easy, and bottle blond. Temp is refined, classy and dark.

Candi wants me to settle down. I just want to keep running my bike on the road, forget about the past, and bang a different woman every time. Simplicity.

Temp is staring up at me.

"Right." I lift my hand and check out her car. It's a thirteen-year-old Dodge mini-van.

"Sexy wheels," I say more for something to say to distract me from my own thoughts than anything.

She laughs, and the sound drives up my spine, making me wonder what other sounds she would make.

Boner goes quarter-tilt. *Fuck.* I shift my weight.

"Oh," she turns away, thank God, and surveys the ugly mini-van. "Yes. It's a requirement of the state. For us to transport children in certain types of vehicles."

"Ah." I tip my head back, checking out the sky. Stalling.

"My other car is awful too. My real car."

I look down at her, reassessing her size. She might be a bit taller than Candi, but she's as tiny as my sister, with curves in all the right places. *Built to fuck.*

"Yeah?"

Her voice lowers. "Yeah. It's a real hunk of shit."

She surprises a barking laugh out of me.

Temp grins at my amusement. "They don't pay social workers a lot, and well…" She spreads delicate hands wide. "I just keep using the same POS because it runs when I turn the key."

Great sense of humor. "You don't look like a cursing girl."

Shaking her head, she says, "I am. Any chance I get when there's not a child listening, I'll swear like a sailor."

"Kids around a lot?"

She bites her lip in a most distracting way, and I notice how deeply pink they are. "Yes." Then she seems to remember something. "Oh! I forgot to give this to Candice."

Her eyes meet mine, and that pull between sweeps back, engulfing the moment with weight, like an invisible bubble has captured us.

"Or you—I can… can give it to you, Puck." Reaching inside a slim black clutch purse, she extracts a small card.

Charlotte "Temp" Temperance

206-631-6312

I look up from the card, meeting her gaze.

"In case there's any issue. Legal, transitioning, whatever."

"Whatever?" I ask softly and step close to her.

Temp takes a step back, a soft pink blush tinting her face. Stroking the card between my fingers, I realize I want to have sex with this girl. Badly.

My eyes rove her again. Probably out of my league. Too sweet. Too perfect. So *not* for Puck.

Then her fingers brush mine as I sweep the card out of her hand, and that lick of heat flares. Eyes clashing, she backs away and slowly moves to the van.

She gets in the driver's side but peeks around the front of the dash windshield. "Nice to meet you, Puck."

Is it me, or is her voice a little breathless?

"Same here," I say. My eyes say a lot more than my words—if she's looking.

She pauses, hand wrapping the door window frame as she stares. Finally, Temp slips inside the vehicle and starts the engine. She pulls away, and I watch the disappearing van until there's nothing to watch.

I mean to give the card to Candice so she can file it somewhere in the house and forget about it. But as Charlotte Temperance pulls away, I stuff the card in my pocket instead.

I'm intrigued. And probably damned for it.

Epilogue

Viper

"God, babe, you feel amazing." I'm gentle. I treat Candice like something fragile, though she's taught me her temper, her pain, and her longing to be treated as an equal. But in this, I'm always tender.

I sink into her slowly, pull out slowly, and thrust in sure and steady. She arches her back, widening her legs, hips rising to meet mine.

Gabriel William Morgan is asleep in his cradle in the corner of our bedroom.

"Shhh." She kisses me on my jaw. "You might wake the young prince."

My lips quirk, and I slide in deep, holding still inside her. "You can nurse him."

She rolls her eyes, and I bend my head, capturing a nipple and kissing it. It tastes sweet, the smallest remnant of milk at its tip.

"Perv," she says.

"You got it." I lick the tip then kiss her on the mouth. Deeply, long and wet, like she likes it, pumping into her shallowly, and Candice moans, capturing my head and yanking it down for more kisses. My arms hold my body high so I don't crush her. Flatten her tits, and milk will leak. Does anyway when I make her come. Which I already did. Twice.

"Kiss me, Viper."

I do. "Whatever you wish is my command."

Impaling her deeply, I roll us so I'm on my back and thrust upward.

Candice groans.

"Ride me, baby." Rolling her hips, Candice moves with a fluid grace.

Palming her tits, I knead them gently, squeezing the fullness, loving the silky feel.

Candice's head tips back, and her palms land on my thighs, fingers biting into my flesh.

"Close," she whispers, eyelids low. Rising and falling on me, her wet heat engulfs my cock.

My favorite part. Seeing my woman blow.

Her pussy squeezes my cock once, then her body tenses. I reach between us, turning my thumb up, and slide it between her cleft.

Moving my thumb back and forward, I thrust deeply, and her knees come together, squeezing my hips. She gives a hoarse shout of pleasure, nipple tightening as her pussy starts pulsing around my cock.

Can't last. Not with the fine treatment of her body. My release follows her so closely, it's almost simultaneous. Grabbing her hips, I hold them still, shooting everything I got inside.

Releasing one hand, I slide it up to the small of her back and press forward. Candice drapes herself over my body as I soften inside her.

My other hand joins the first, and I hold her against my body as our heaving breaths slow to panting. Then we're breathing deeply.

"You were noisy," I say.

Candice pops her head off my chest. "Gabe didn't wake up."

I smirk. "Give it time."

Her smile is wistful. "I love you, Viper."

Can't talk for a second. Might cry like a girl. Didn't ever think something like this existed. Once. Maybe. But never twice. Got the whole thing. Beautiful wife. Healthy son.

I find her hand between our bodies and lift it. Admiring the rock I put on that tiny finger, I say, "Always."

Her eyebrow lifts. "Always?"

"All of it. For always." The love. The life. The everything.

Candice slides her arms around my neck and hugs me. I crush her to me.

The baby starts to fuss, and Candice's milk leaks against my chest. She slides out of bed to get Gabe, and I admire her as she tends to our son.

Luckiest man on the planet.

THE END

Never *miss a new release!* ***Subscribe:***

https://tinyurl.com/Subscribe2MarataEros

Love Road Kill MC? You might also enjoy the sample which follows, also by Marata Eros ....

Viper

CLUB ALPHA

A novel

New York Times BESTSELLING AUTHOR

MARATA EROS

Club Alpha** is a STANDALONE, PSYCHOLOGICAL DARK ROMANTIC SUSPENSE and contains scenes of graphic violence. *May contain triggers**

Viper

Synopsis

"Would you pay fifty million for your soul mate?"

Francisco "Paco" Castillo is a bilingual billionaire with unconventional ideas about love, sex and possession. He believes there is no other half to make him whole. Paco dreams of experimenting with a dangerous reality not of his own making. Club Alpha owner, Zaire Sebastian, can make Paco's vision a reality—for a price.

Greta Dahlem is an extreme sports executive whose ambition masks a terrible secret. When her mentor Gia Township, sponsors her as a player in Club Alpha, Greta's unsure she can survive the inherent risk of the game Zaire weaves. But in her heart, Greta yearns for a man who will complete her, and erase the brutal tragedy of two years ago.

As the fantasy progresses, Greta comes to realize she is the loose string in a plot of murder and deception that begins to unravel. Without knowing who to trust, Greta must decide between two men. When the three are thrown together, the lines of reality and fantasy blur.

Is there any way for her to know what is real?

PROLOGUE

Greta

Completion.

That's what it is to graduate with honors, and finally go after what I'll *be* in this life.

Marketing. International travel, stretching the bounds of the four languages I've mastered. Perfection.

Hot guys.

My eyebrows flick up. *Speaking of which.*

I track a handsome specimen right now.

A man moves across the room lithely, coming to stand at the exact opposite of the huge bar. His crystal tumbler full of amber liquid catches the light. His coloring suggests he's Latino or some exotic Spanish mix. At six feet two-ish, he's built to move, dance—and do other stuff.

My lips curl at the *other stuff* part of my internal monologue. I'm *so* wanting to find out what the sex fuss is all about. By all accounts, it's pretty life altering. It's beyond time.

My studies are through—it's Greta Time now.

His gaze locks with mine, and he smiles. A deep dimple winks at his cheek, and a cleft bisects a chiseled, square jaw.

Beautiful green eyes with thick black lashes rim the windows of his soul.

He pauses, and I say *yes* with my eyes.

Please approach me.

My breath catches like a trapped bird in my throat.

What a beautiful man.

My hand grips the smooth curved wood of the high-end bar I find myself in; the other holds a low ball of peach schnapps.

I take a sip, grimace slightly, and set down the drink.

People flow between us as we stare across the room, and I lose him momentarily as the moving scenery of bodies blocks my line of sight.

I crane my neck, swinging my head side to side, searching. I remind myself that I'm not here to meet a man. I'm here to meet my fellow graduates and celebrate our graduation from the most prestigious university in Washington state.

Someone sits down beside me but it's not *him*. I look around the other man.

Tall, dark and handsome has vanished.

I take another absent-minded sip then knock back the rest of my sweet drink. Disappointment burns alongside the alcohol inside my stomach. *Where'd he go?* I restrain myself from pouting.

I stand. Against my better judgement, I'm brazenly determined to seek him out, then a wave of dizziness hits me.

My hand flies out to the bar and latches on. Frantically, I look toward the entrance, hoping my friends will arrive. Though I'm known for being frighteningly punctual, none of them share that trait.

I lift my fingertips from the polished surface and touch my forehead. My hand comes away clammy and shaking.

Alarm sweeps through my system. *What's wrong with me?*

I forget the man with the deep-green eyes—and my drink and friends—as another wave of dizziness follows the first.

I stagger backward toward my seat, my knees hit the stool, and I sit down abruptly.

"Miss?" a low voice murmurs from my elbow.

I turn my head, but my neck feels loose, as though it's made of rubber.

A man's face wobbles in front of me, his features coming together and shattering in the field of my vision.

"Are you well?"

Well? No. I shake my head, and streamers of color flow across my eyes. I groan, feeling nauseated as the dizziness grows.

I feel pressure at my elbow then a grip. I'm walking?

"Is she—" a deep melodic baritone voice inquires.

"I have her." Curt. Final.

"Okay?"

"Fine," says the disembodied voice at my side.

I'm gliding. My head tips back against a warm chest.

Everything fades to black.

Paco

Standing at the edge of the bar. I sip the sparkling cider.

My bodyguard, Robert Tallinn, remains by the exit while eyeing the entrance.

Though I've attended school in the states for many years, I still believe America is the most aggressive country in all the world. I remain vigilant while traveling.

My jet is scheduled to leave for Costa Rica early in the morning, and that is why I partake only of the non-alcoholic beverage in my hand.

Tallinn fought my spontaneous urge to visit the lounge within the elite hotel we're staying in.

Coffee is *grande* in Seattle. Very. I am here to romance the local coffee barons for their money, in exchange for my beans—a perfect trade, in my estimation.

Tallinn hates the lack of protection the hotel offers. I told him it's his job to keep me safe.

His smile was tight at those words.

I raise my glass to him now, and he glowers.

I laugh then take a sip and set my glass on the smooth polished surface of the wooden bar.

That's when I see her, and my back goes ramrod straight.

The crowd is thick. Beautifully attired people mingle with others they consider to be of equal caliber.

But she stands out like an angel among demons.

Her head is tipped over a pale-amber drink. Her platinum hair is twisted into a loose bun at her nape. The size of the knot tells me its length—but not how it would feel in my hands.

Her graceful neck is bent as she studies nothing at all. She appears to be frozen in time. Waiting.

I stand, drink forgotten, and stare at the most beautiful woman I've ever beheld.

She lifts her face as though she has become instinctively aware of my gaze on her. Eyes like a late-summer sky fall into mine, and my chest grows tight. Light-pink color rises to her fair skin, and I feel myself harden inside my slacks at just a look. The attraction is beyond casual lust.

I feel as though gravity has asserted itself and I am being pulled into her orbit.

I must meet her.

As we continue to stare, people move between us, and another man sits beside her, large enough to block my view.

I set the tumbler at the edge of the bar and begin walking toward her.

I see her searching face for an instant as she appears to swing around the torso of the man who blocks our mutual appraisal.

I understand in a vague way that my approach isn't casual.

Someone steps in front of me.

"Oh, pardon me!" a woman says.

I go around her impatiently.

The angel stands. She appears to look shaken and unwell.

I stop.

The man beside her rises, his back facing me, and takes her elbow. She remains hidden behind him.

I vacillate, thinking of the connection, the electrifying chemistry from a glance. I begin walking again.

I intercept them, and the other man is half-carrying her, his arm locked around her narrow waist.

My eyes are for her, though, as I pose the question to the man, "Is she—"

"I have her," he says in a closed tone. Final.

"Okay?" I finish my question.

Her cheeks are flushed, and her head has fallen back against his shoulder. The blue eyes I so admired are hidden by closed eyelids. Dark-blond lashes fan against her high cheekbones.

He is clearly with her. I should drop it.

I cannot.

"What is wrong?" My eyes still rove the woman, not giving the man my full attention.

The man turns. "Drunk."

I look fully at him.

He winks; a deep sense of oddness surrounds the gesture.

Turning, he ushers her out. And I let them go.

Tallinn suddenly appears at my side. "What the fuck was that?"

I shake my head. "I am not sure."

Tallinn stares after them thoughtfully. After a full minute has elapsed he says, "I didn't like that dude."

Neither do I.

I stare at the empty space they had just occupied.

Greta

Brutal fingers grip my butt cheeks and pry me open. A hoarse cry escapes my cracked lips.

He plunges inside me again.

My muscles instantly tense around the intrusion, though my virginity is long gone.

Slick wetness covers my inner thighs to my knees.

Later I find out it is semen.

Sweat.

And blood.

His thrusting continues.

Silence is the only noise. The screams fill my head because my mouth is gagged.

Panting.

The only break in the quiet is the grunts of their ecstasy.

I'm unceremoniously flipped over onto my back. Four faces with masquerade masks loom above my warped vision.

"No," I say in muffled agony for the hundredth time, lifting my forearm to cover my battered face.

One of the men hits me, smashing my face into the stained mattress.

Another lands on top of me, stabbing inside my wounded vagina. "Yes," one of the assailants says as he uses me.

I slide back and forth on the mattress as he pounds into my unwilling body. Another pries my jaws apart, forcing my lips open. He jerks the gag out then thrusts his length inside my mouth.

Vile salty essence fills the space. My chin is jerked back and the hot liquid glides down my throat.

I choke.

He removes himself from my mouth and clamps it shut, pinching my nostrils together.

I have to swallow, or I won't be able to breathe. My throat convulses, and he releases my jaw.

I scream as I suck precious oxygen, gurgling through his semen. "No!"

The next blow slams my other cheek into the mattress as my hips are lifted and a new man assaults me. His stabbing penis tears and burns where no one has ever been.

I can't live through this, I think.

But I do.

CHAPTER ONE

Paco

Two Years Later - Present Day

September 29

Francisco Emmanuel Lewis Castillo.

I set the pen down and lean back, regarding my good friend and co-conspirator.

It is *terminado.*

I've signed my soul over to the devil. He no longer chases me from the dark corners of my mind. This particular demon stands in the sunlight, taunting no more.

Zaire chuckles, running a hand through hair a shade of blond so dark that it flirts with being brown. He sets his ten-gallon cowboy hat on top of all that shaggy hair.

Clear hazel eyes regard me with amusement.

I say nothing.

Zaire Sebastian has been after me for the five years he's run the enterprise I finally succumb to.

Club Alpha.

He flat-palms the paper, spinning the sheets until they face him. His eyes flick down, and a fingertip stabs my signature.

"Careful, you might cause it to bleed, *amigo*," I note softly.

Zaire laughs. "Always so cryptic, Paco." He makes a low sound of chastisement in the back of his throat. "How long have I known you?"

Forever.

He reads my expression and nods. "It's just now I find out you have a hundred names?"

I dip my chin. "Just four."

He grunts his answer and I'm struck by how different Zaire and I are.

He perpetuates fantasy.

I manufacture exotic coffee for exotic tastes, my own not excepted.

It is the taste for the very fine and my need for something extreme—a thing not within my control—that has finally driven me to Mr. Sebastian.

Zaire stands, offering his hand. "Are we clear on the terms?" He studies my face. "Humor me," he adds as I give a single shake of his hand.

I spread my hands away from my body, enjoying the slide of my linen suit, which is tailored perfectly to never impede my movement, as though I'm wearing a second skin.

I lift my shoulder. "You wish for me to recount the particulars?"

"Hell, yeah, Paco. You're a particular kind of guy."

True. I smile and Zaire grins.

"I will have three months for this fantasy to come to fruition. I have three days from the time of this signing to submit the twenty-page questionnaire about the things that make me—uniquely me."

Zaire's eyebrows pop to his hairline.

"It will be an honest disclosure," I say.

"Nice. I like how my telepathy always works well between us."

Zaire's rough-around-the-edges manner is a *fachada*, a clever front for the smart-as-a-whip man who swims beneath the surface. He twirls his fingers, encouraging my continuation.

"I have agreed to a no-liability clause against you, even in the case of my death, pursuant to the… *activities,* which might or might not present themselves."

"And?" Zaire runs his fingers down the brim of his hat, where the evidence of the habit is in the curvature of the rim.

"I will tell no one. I understand and have agreed to the non-disclosure."

Zaire makes the universal symbol for money, moving his thumb against his four fingers.

"I shall pay half in the moment listed therein, and the remainder at the end of the three month term, regardless of the outcome."

Zaire slaps his palms together. "Hot damn!" His eyes glitter at me like captured stars. "I look forward to putting you through the paces, Paco. I ain't gonna lie—I've been wanting to get you like a fox in a trap since the beginning."

I stroke my chin, my fingers finding the cleft at the end and squeezing it together. "I am aware, Zaire."

"Yet you still agreed."

I nod.

"Why? You've signed, now I *have* to ask. Why would you take this kind of chance? Because I'll be straight with you. I don't care about your money." He pauses, his eyes moving to the ceiling. "Yeah, I do. What I mean, buddy, is you have *so much* to lose."

I shake my head. "When a man has every need met, and ones he did not think he had are satisfied, then he is left with a void." I cock my head, moving my hands to the pockets of my slacks. "You act as though you would talk me out of our arrangement."

Zaire shakes his head. "No. You said, and I quote, 'Your heart beats, but it does not live.'"

"Yes. I am familiar with contentment, but I am not on intimate terms with contentment's distant cousin, joy."

A slow smile spreads across Zaire's face as a flutter of emotion skates across the deepest part of me. Unease.

I embrace the uncommon feeling. For too long, I have felt nothing besides the slow, rolling river of time's passage. I welcome any emotion that causes my soul to surface through the murky waters of my complacent mediocrity.

Zaire shakes his head, and a low chuckle breaks the seam of his lips. "You're going to make a fun subject." He gazes around the room before his eyes land on the wide expanse of glass that flanks the entire wall. From this vantage point, seventy stories aboveground inside the Columbia Center, the clouds appear touchable. The gray Puget Sound churns like angry boulders of water beneath us.

I walk over to stand beside Zaire. Our heights are similar, though our heritage is different. "Why do you do this?"

Without turning, Zaire places a forearm on the glass. He gazes over the city, at the raging sea beyond. "I know what it is to be rich. To be so rich you could park an incinerator in the house and burn money twenty-four hours a day."

I say nothing, waiting for the point. Zaire Sebastian will have one.

He rolls his head on his forearm, facing me. "This isn't a game, Paco. Once we start, with the exception of the one-month markers, it's your new life. I have people everywhere. They can get to you anywhere in the world."

I nod. *I'm counting on it*. I travel extensively to oversee the manufacture of my beans. I can be in Costa Rica one day and Brazil the next.

He straightens from his slouch against the window. "Your preliminary physical came back as outstanding, by the way." His lips quirk. "My techs were making bets on how much time you spend on that build."

"Oh?" My eyebrow hikes.

"Yeah," Zaire turns and throws a punch toward me. I stiffen my gut and arch backwards, capturing his wrist and twisting as I dance into him.

"Shee-it!"

"And?" I ask. He struggles and I nestle his fist between his shoulder blades, cupping my opposite hand on his elbow.

I apply pressure.

Zaire taps my leg.

I drop his limb and step back, out of arm's reach.

We stare at each other.

"They said two hours—every day." He's breathing hard.

I'm not at all. "They would be wrong."

"How long, Paco? How much time do you devote to physical perfection?"

I cast my eyes down. *Too much.*

When I look up, he's massaging his arm. A wicked grin slashes the solemnness of his face.

"I don't worship my body; I use it. I have trained it to be used. There is a difference between doing one thousand sit-ups and forcing the body's compliance."

"Have you forced it?" Zaire asks.

"Absolutely."

Zaire snorts. "You realize I have you as a level-five risk on the form?"

For the first time since our meeting began, I get a thrill like an electrical current. Singing tension winds through me, causing my toes and fingers to tingle with anticipation of the unknown. "Yes."

"That means you're rating at the highest level for hand-to-hand combat, knife play—"

My lips twitch. "There is no such thing as *playing* with knives."

He stares at me for a moment before going on, "Stylized weaponry and a variety of martial arts background."

"Yes."

"Is that accurate?"

A beat of silence presses between us like a bomb before detonation.

"Yes."

"I will personally oversee your submission and handpick the girl."

I open my mouth then close it.

Zaire's wide grin angers me.

"Cat got your tongue?"

I'm unfamiliar with the idiom, though I speak several languages.

"You have utterly no say in this fantasy, Paco. This is what you're paying the big bucks for. This is a match-making enterprise of the highest order. We will find your love match."

I believe love to be an impossibility for me. However, I remain silent about my skepticism. "You trivialize it," I say and hear the sullen tone in my own voice. I can't shake it.

"It's not about what you can *get*, Paco. You could have a bevy of the finest tail on the earth. Hell, chicks smell money a mile away, they'd swarm you like bees to honey. That's not what's at stake here."

Zaire strides to the door, and I stroll after him.

He turns and gestures sweepingly, using the arm I didn't leverage behind him. "This is about a wealthy man—or woman—knowing the one who says *I do* really wants them for *who* they are, not *what* they have. This fantasy is engineered to pull out every stop to prove their worth. No one can pretend through the circumstances I provide at Club Alpha."

He meets my silence with his own.

"Three days, Paco. You have three days for dissolution. If I don't hear back, you can assume I've gone through your questionnaire, found it to be sound and withstanding further legalities, your fantasy will begin."

"And your failure rate?" I ask, though I know.

"Zero."

Neither one of us mentions some of the candidates have sustained injuries during their unique fantasy trials.

I've interviewed each one personally. Their answers are the same: they would do it again.

"I would never guess you were a lawyer in charge of fantasy matchmaking for the wealthy, Zaire."

He gives me a hard look. "And I would never guess you were an exotic coffee mogul with a ninth-dan black belt."

I wink at him. "I went… how do you say it? Ah yes, *easy on you.*"

The look we share is between two men wondering how it would be to give it a go.

"What art do you practice?" I ask.

"Jujitsu," Zaire replies.

We bow at each other, eyes locked—as it should be. Never take your eyes off your opponent.

"Now," Zaire says, straightening, "if you don't have any questions…"

"I have many questions."

Zaire's eyebrow lifts, and the corners of his lips twitch. "Ones I can answer?"

"No."

He opens the door, and I pass through. "Then we're through."

I turn as he shuts the door. I halt the swing of the solid Douglas fir with the slap of my hand.

"I'll see you on Halloween."

"Trick or treat."

Zaire closes the door. It latches softly behind me.

In three more days, the games begin.

CHAPTER TWO

Greta

I look up at Gia in disbelief. "Are you freaking kidding me?" I gaze back down at the—I don't know—*novel* in my hands. I grasp the edge of the paper and let the pages contained between the folder slip through my fingers.

Gia smirks. With golden eyes like deep whiskey, rimmed with smoky-kohl eyeliner, she blinks at me like a satisfied feline. "You want thorough, don't you?"

I shake my head, and my hair, fresh from the blowout Gia insisted on paying for, slides over my shoulders.

I nervously smooth my hands over the tight crimson pencil skirt and look at question number one million:

Have you ever partaken in illegal drug use?

I swallow hard. "I don't give a hot damn about thoroughness. I—hell in a handbasket—I don't even *know* about this." I tap the papers.

Gia saunters to where I sit at my desk at Roffe Enterprises. She puts one sculpted butt cheek on the corner of all that antique oak. "Listen here, Greta."

Oh Jesus, wonderful. "I feel an epic rant coming on, Gia."

Her full lips twist. "You better believe it. I've gone through every angle, point by point. My logic is irrefutable."

"That's just it—it's *your* logic."

Her lips flatten, and a nail tip taps her chin. "*Your* logic is working to death, having no life—hell, you have to make an appointment to poo."

I roll my eyes, not because she takes practicality to a new level, but because she's right. I almost schedule bathroom time. Everything in my life is a squeezeathon—from the bathroom, to sleep, to the gym. I factor breathing in there somewhere, too.

I do make time to sigh in frustration at Gia. I love her, but she's such a pushy broad.

"I know that look," she says, eyes narrowed at me.

"What look?" I ask innocently.

"The look where you're going to back out. I'm paying—I'm *sponsoring* you, Greta. There's no excuses. You've got—what? A billion vacation days built up."

I scrunch my nose. She may be overstating things.

Or not.

I scan the paperwork for Club Alpha on my lap. I find what I'm searching for. "It says here my work can continue, that the fantasy incorporates itself."

"It's organic in nature," Gia inserts.

"Like a disease?" I ask.

She pouts.

"Okay!" I shove the papers away. "You know I'm grateful. I understand this is like—I don't know—an intervention."

Her face becomes solemn.

"God, I'm not *that* bad!" I say, folding my arms.

Gia goes uncharacteristically silent.

"Am I?"

She nods. "You're twenty-four years old, for shit's sake." Her probing eyes capture mine in a gaze I've held countless times on the psych bench.

I grip the folder full of the stats of my life. Greta Dahlem, exposed. "But *why* do we have to go to this extreme? I can find a guy the old-fashioned way."

Gia stands and walks away from the desk to pace in front of the bank of windows overlooking the Space Needle grounds.

I admire her sharp figure, not with envy but a sense of pride. Gia is her own thing. And I'm *more* because of our friendship, *and* what she has done for me.

I blow strands of my pale-blond hair out of my face.

She whirls, pointing a pen at me. "You—*no*. You couldn't find a man the old-fashioned way if your life depended on it."

Probably right. I sulk, spinning in my chair.

My phone buzzes through. "Miss Dahlem."

Gia meets my eyes. Her expression says, "See?*"

I depress the button, giving Gia an eye roll. "Yes, Ashley?"

"Mr. Aros, line one."

"Thank you, Ashley."

I hold up a finger to Gia and she gives me the middle one in return. I suppress a giggle over her spontaneous lewdness.

"*Hallo*," I say.

"English is fine, Ms. Dahlem," Aros says.

"*Fint, ja*," I reply and switch to English from my native Norwegian.

Gia waits through my upcoming travel plans. They revolve around the latest swatches of material for wind, water and temperature repellent outerwear for the extreme skier. Another foreign client would be *so* good for my resume, and maybe Mr. Aros will be he. We briefly confer about our upcoming meeting. The conversation winds to a succinct close.

"Thank you, Mr. Aros," I say.

"*Farvel*," he says and the humming international connection abruptly ceases.

"Are you done playing Swedish twinkle toes with clients?"

I snort. "It's so insulting for you to mistake me for a Swede. Really? I am Norwegian—there's a difference, you know."

Gia shrugs. "It's all just broad for me, baby. Scandinavian. All you blond, blue-eyed perfect folk. Skinny. Tall. Whatever. It's simple to lump you all together."

I remember when that was a bad thing.

Gia's face falls. "No, I'm sorry, Greta. I wasn't thinking."

I say nothing, holding my chin to stop the quivering. I don't stop my other hand from stroking the scar at my wrist. Plastic surgery, another gift from Greta, made it a fine line instead of the twisted mess it was.

"It's okay. I've moved on." My eyes meet hers to push truth into the lie. My jaw tightens. "I *will* move on," I repeat decisively.

A Mona Lisa smile ghosts Gia's lips, and we leave the past behind us for the moment. "Say yes, Greta. Don't let what's happened rule you, overwork you. It's like—" She pauses, and I watch the uncertainty cloud her normally Zen features. "It's like you run from introspection. This might help your healing, Greta."

Nothing will. My work is safe, but exploring the boundaries of my fragile psyche? *Not so much.*

I stare at all those intimidating words on the form for Club Alpha, so they can make my life an atom among the spinning chaos of a new reality.

"I've already filled it out," I admit softly, trailing my finger over flat words that say so much, and so little, about me.

Gia squeals, clapping her hands. Her eyebrows arch. "Then it's only the physical left?"

I nod.

"Excellent," she grabs her handbag and shoulders it before jerking a thumb at the door. "Tell Ashley to cover for you."

I roll my lip into my mouth, mauling the tender flesh with my teeth. I do it so much that I'm surprised I have any lip left. "You're so bossy," I finally grumble, hitting the intercom with a finger.

"And you need it," she quips.

Maybe.

I tell Ashley then let Gia drag me to Club Alpha.

I find it very difficult to let this man, whom I don't know at all, circle me like a cow on the auction block.

I stifle the urge to moo.

"I have a copy of your questionnaire, Ms. Dahlem."

He butchers the pronunciation.

"It's Dahl-em. Like *doll* then *em*."

Rich hazel eyes scrutinize me, and I curse under my breath as my fair complexion springs to life in a blush I don't have to see to know that bright pink color has flooded my cheeks.

"You betcha, darlin'," Zaire Sebastian replies in a droll voice.

"Cut the cute, Zaire. I told you Greta's a little shy."

Zaire winks at her, tipping his huge cowboy hat, which hides curls of moppy dark-blond hair. His gaze moves back to me, appraising me. "Not *that* shy. I'd say detail-oriented is more Greta's style."

I kick my chin up a little at his assessment. "Have you seen my paperwork?"

His eyes are shadowed as they meet mine. "I've skimmed it. But soon I'll practically know it by heart." He crosses his fingers over his muscular chest and puts two fingers up, mimicking a Boy Scout pledge. "Promise."

Zaire's eyebrows plunge, his expression instantly morphing to seriousness. He looks at an image of me as I was when I first arrived. I was wearing a silk shell blouse in a soft pearl so lustrous and light it resembled a cup of cream instead of white, a deep red pencil skirt, and four-inch heels in nude, which matched my stockings to perfection. I buy only Italian-made hosiery. They have the sizes someone of my height needs for a true fit.

I'm a sweaty mess now, though. Yoga pants and a sheer T-shirt cling to every crevice of me. I swipe a strand of hair out of my face. The tight dutch braid that sinks into a low knot at my nape never quite holds all of it.

"What did you say you do for conditioning?"

His eyes boldly rove my body. I feel the blush swim back to healthy life.

Damn.

Gia grins.

I scowl back.

"I ski during the colder months…"

His eyebrows jerk up. "You're…" He appears to think about it, then says, "Twenty-four?"

I nod, puzzling over his bewilderment.

"It's not typical for someone your age to be a skier; snowboarding's more like it."

I shrug. "I'm Norwegian. They toss us out the front door as toddlers with skis instead of shoes."

"Yes," he says with a thoughtful small smile, "I read that in your nationality breakdown." He gives me steady eyes. "Pure, yes?"

My heart thuds, and fresh sweat dampens my palms. I feel Gia at my back.

I push images of fair flesh on hands, pale eyes in shades of blues and greens far away. My attackers are Caucasian.

I lick my lips. "Yes, one hundred percent."

Zaire turns toward his desk and picks something up. "That's a rare thing in America nowadays. Melting pot and all."

I nod. I know. *I so know.*

"Dual citizen?" he asks, turning with a tape measure in his hand.

I shake my head. "No, orphan."

Zaire says nothing while taking the measurements of my waist, hips, and bust.

I blush again when he tightens the tape around my breasts.

"Don't breathe," he says, winking. "You're five-ten?" His eyes rise to mine.

I nod.

He writes nothing down.

"A few things off the bat we should straighten out before y'all get started down this path." He looks at me expectantly.

"Okay," I say, cupping my elbows and retreating a step.

"There are a few candidates who have a very narrow idea of what they find attractive."

Gia makes a disbelieving noise in the background. "She's so perfect it's sick, Zaire—you know this."

I think I'm going up in flames at this point.

Zaire raises his palm while I study my feet. *God, Gia.*

"She is a wonderful specimen of the female form, yes. A regular Eve. However…" He pauses, and my head snaps up from admiring the lush carpet of his office. "She is tall, very blond, and thin. Not every man wants to be with an Amazon who looks like a Nordic goddess."

I suddenly feel as inept as I did when Gia first coerced me into trying Club Alpha. Of course, the fee of fifty million dollars made participation unlikely for me to ever be a part of it.

But Gia is old money. That's nothing for her. She makes Paris Hilton look like a pauper.

"Hey, girl, quit that face," Zaire says, placing a gentle finger underneath my chin.

I stare into his face. Zaire's eyes are kind, and he says nothing about the sheen he must see in mine.

"Some of us gents think a filly with legs longer than ours is primo." He pushes the blond tendrils of hair still loose from my unraveling bun behind an ear. "Some of us love a girl so fair, she's skin and ice in the flesh. With eyes like glacial seas." He clears his throat, clearly somewhat embarrassed by his verbal poetry.

"I forget the golden tongue you have," Gia comments wryly.

Zaire grins. "Helps in court."

"Though you make so much money now you don't bother with law much anymore, do you?"

"No, I'm cupid for the rich." Zaire mimes nocking an invisible arrow in a bow. I can almost hear the whisper as he lets go for his imagined target.

I shake my head. "That's not really true. There's— there is *stuff* in here about dismemberment, injuries… things."

Zaire sets his jean clad butt up against his desk, his eyes at half-mast. He crosses his feet at the ankles, regarding me. "True. I'll try to keep you out of the true danger but these fantasies have a way of progressing in a natural way. Exponentially." He spreads his arms away from his body, and I notice how big his hands are. A trigger niggles, and I quickly look away.

"That line I gave you about your looks?"

My face swings back in his direction.

"Well, there are a lot of clients where you're not within the standards of attraction."

I deflate, air sliding out of my tight chest.

"Then there are a few where you fall in like a round peg in a perfect circular hole."

I open my mouth then close it.

Gia steps forward. "So there are a few possible matches for Greta?"

Zaire grins. "I think we can give it the old college try."

He sees us to the door. Having been weighed, cataloged, and measured, I feel as though Zaire knows me better than he should. Once he reads through the questionnaire, he'll know me better than anyone alive.

Zaire opens the door. He touches my shoulder as I pass, and I flinch.

His eyes tighten imperceptibly at my reaction. "One question?"

"Okay."

"You're not racist are ya, darlin'?"

I laugh. *Hell no.* "No."

"Good."

His eyes meet Gia behind my shoulder. "Three days."

"My accountant will square up with you, Zaire."

"Always a pleasure, Ms. Township," he says. His gaze moves to me.

"So long, Ms. Dahlem."

He says my name perfectly as he takes my hand. Instead of shaking it, he squeezes my hand softly and lets it drop.

I turn away and don't look back.

Three more days of my old life.

Available everywhere e and paperback books are sold!

Acknowledgments

I published both *The Druid and Death Series*, in 2011 with the encouragement of my husband, and continued because of you, my Reader. Your faithfulness through comments, suggestions, spreading the word and ultimately purchasing my work with your hard-earned money gave me the incentive, means and inspiration to continue.

There are no words that are sufficiently adequate to express my thankfulness for your support.

I truly feel connected to my readers. It is obvious to me, but I'll say the words anyway for clarity: a written work is just words on pages if they are not read by my readers. As I write this I get a lump in my throat; your enjoyment of my work affects me that deeply.

You guys are the greatest, each and every one of ya~

Tamara

xoxo

Special Thanks:

You, my reader.

My husband, who is my biggest fan.

Cameren, without who, there would be no books.

Works by Tamara Rose Blodgett and Marata Eros:

Tamara Rose Blodgett:

The BLOOD Series

The DEATH Series

Shifter ALPHA CLAIM

The REFLECTION Series

The SAVAGE Series

Vampire ALPHA CLAIM

&

Marata Eros:

A Terrible Love (**New York Times** Best Seller)

A Brutal Tenderness

The Darkest Joy

Club Alpha

The DARA NICHOLS Series

The DEMON Series

The DRUID Series

Road Kill MC Serial

Shifter ALPHA CLAIM

The SIREN Series

The TOKEN Serial

Vampire ALPHA CLAIM

The ZOE SCOTT Series

Never miss a new release! **Subscribe:**

Marata Eros NEWS *And/or* TRB News

Win FREE stuff—*subscribe* **to my** YouTube channel

About the Author

www.TamaraRoseBlodgett.com

Tamara Rose Blodgett: happily married mother of four sons. Dark fiction writer. Reader. Dreamer. Home restoration slave. Tie dye zealot. Coffee addict. Digs music.

She is also the *New York Times* Bestselling author of *A Terrible Love,* written under the pen name, **Marata Eros**, and over ninety-five other titles, to include the #1 international bestselling erotic Interracial/African-American **TOKEN** serial and her #1 bestselling Amazon Dark Fantasy novel, *Death Whispers.* Tamara writes a variety of dark fiction in the genres of erotica, fantasy, horror, romance, sci-fi and suspense. She lives in the midwest with her family and three, disrespectful dogs.

Connect with Tamara:

TRB News:

https://tinyurl.com/Subscribe2TRB

Marata Eros News:

https://tinyurl.com/Subscribe2MarataEros

Instagram:

https://tinyurl.com/FollowTRBonINSTAGRAM

BLOG:

www.tamararoseblodgett.com

FaceBook:

https://tinyurl.com/LikeTRB-MEonFACEBOOK

Twitter:

https://tinyurl.com/FollowTRBonTWITTER

https://tinyurl.com/FollowMarataErosonTWITTER

Subscribe to my **YouTube** Channel:

https://tinyurl.com/Subscribe2TRB-MEonYouTube

Exclusive Excerpts!

Comedic Quips

Win **FREE** stuff!

Marata Eros

Made in the USA
Columbia, SC
12 September 2018